CATCH

SARAH BRILL

CATCH

First published by Allen & Unwin in 2025

Copyright © Sarah Brill, 2025

All rights reserved. No part of this book may be reproduced or transmitted in any form or by any means, electronic or mechanical, including photocopying, recording or by any information storage and retrieval system, without prior permission in writing from the publisher. The Australian *Copyright Act 1968* (the Act) allows a maximum of one chapter or ten per cent of this book, whichever is the greater, to be photocopied by any educational institution for its educational purposes provided that the educational institution (or body that administers it) has given a remuneration notice to the Copyright Agency (Australia) under the Act.

Allen & Unwin
Cammeraygal Country
83 Alexander Street Crows Nest NSW 2065
Australia
Phone: (61 2) 8425 0100
Email: info@allenandunwin.com
Web: www.allenandunwin.com

Allen & Unwin acknowledges the Traditional Owners of the Country on which we live and work. We pay our respects to all Aboriginal and Torres Strait Islander Elders, past and present.

EU Authorised Representative: Easy Access System Europe, Mustamäe tee 50, 10621 Tallinn, Estonia, gpsr.requests@easproject.com

A catalogue record for this book is available from the National Library of Australia

ISBN 978 1 76118 203 7

For teaching resources, explore allenandunwin.com/learn

Cover design by Debra Billson
Cover art by Shutterstock: CooiCo (girl), Grynold (man on roof), Md Al Ekram (bike), Anna Kutakova (streetscape), Srgr (colour swirl overlay)
Text design by Hana Kinoshita Thomson
Set in 12/19 pt Minion Pro Display by Midland Typesetters, Australia
Printed and bound in Australia by the Opus Group

10 9 8 7 6 5 4 3 2 1

The paper in this book is FSC® certified. FSC® promotes environmentally responsible, socially beneficial and economically viable management of the world's forests.

For those of us afraid of falling

ONE

SOMETIMES life suddenly changes. For me, everything changed on a Friday.

I was walking home with two shopping bags stuffed full of everything Mum needed for dinner when I had a sudden urge to throw up. It was so sudden, so strong, I stopped walking. I put the bags down, looked up and there he was. Falling towards me. He'd been painting a sign above the bookshop and fallen from a long ladder.

I stretched out my arms and he fell into them.

Everyone around us kept walking like nothing had happened. Like it was normal for a sixteen-year-old to be standing on the footpath holding a man in her arms.

He looked only a little older than me. Solid and unshaven. Blue eyes and strawberry-blond hair. I could feel the muscles in his back and legs as

I held him. I would have blushed if I wasn't so surprised. He was wearing overalls covered in dried paint of various colours and he held a paintbrush in his hand.

He cleared his throat like he was trying to interrupt my thoughts and said, in a strong Irish accent, 'Would you mind putting me down now?'

I reluctantly let him go. I liked holding him. I liked that large, solid body in my arms. He didn't feel heavy to me. He felt like comfort. I helped him get steady on his feet.

He looked at me, and then he looked at the paintbrush, covered in light blue paint, in his hand.

'Thank you.'

It was weirdly formal.

'No problem.'

We stared at each other for a bit longer.

'Well . . .' he said, as a kind of goodbye.

'Okay,' I said, like I was giving him permission to leave.

He tried to smile. I think he was in shock. I might have been too. He looked up to the sign he'd only half finished, and shook his head a little, like he'd decided to never go up a ladder again. The sign read *More Boo* in light blue script. The rest of the sign was the clean, bright white of the background. He walked away in the opposite direction from me, the paintbrush still in his hand.

The bookshop was one of the few low-rise buildings left on the street. Buildings were being knocked down now to make room for taller apartment buildings with shops below. The bookshop owner was going to be a bit surprised by the half-finished sign and the ladder still in place.

I picked up the shopping bags and kept walking.

At home Mum was frantic. She'd left work later than she wanted to and was trying to clean the house and prepare dinner at the same time. It wasn't good. The house was getting messier and the dishes for dinner were all only half made. Some of them were waiting for the ingredients I'd just bought, others had been put aside because she'd become distracted by cleaning.

Mum's hair, which was short and curly and often out of place, looked as chaotic as the house. My sister Meg had invited her boyfriend Rik and his parents over. Mum was freaking out because she didn't know what to cook or how to behave.

'I just want everything to be right, you know, Beth? For Meg.'

I put the yoghurt, pomegranate and basil on the bench along with everything else I'd bought and took the broom from Mum's hand. I had grown over the summer, in a sudden and surprising burst, after being the smallest one in the family for so long. I was still trying to get used to my bigger feet, my bigger frame. But mostly, I was still trying to get used to looking down at the top of Mum's head.

'I'm sure it will be fine, Mum.'

I swept the floor. It wasn't really dirty, but I wanted to look busy so Mum didn't ask me to get the seeds out of the pomegranate. Mum was hunting through the cupboards looking for salad bowls and starting to fire out her questions. Mum was a social worker. Conversations with her were often more like interviews. I kept my head down. Mum's questions didn't always need answers. Sometimes she just needed to ask the questions.

Today they were things like:

'Why do you think Meg wants us to meet them now?'

'Why here rather than a restaurant?'

'Are you sure your new uniform is long enough?'

'How are you feeling about starting Year Eleven?'

'Do you think your father will get home in time?'

'Is it going to rain?'

Dad got home from his bike shop in time to shower, change and finish off a few of the dishes Mum had started. I assured Mum that my uniform was long enough and Year Eleven was most likely going to be just like Year Ten. It was probably the wrong thing to say, but it was the best I could come up with at the time. I managed to avoid answering any questions about Meg by going to set the table. I knew what the evening was about. I'd known for a few weeks, but it wasn't my news to tell.

When Rik and his parents arrived there was a lot of polite hand-shaking. Mum and Dad had been debating whether they should do a traditional Japanese bow to greet them, but Rik's parents put out their right hands straight away and introduced themselves as Mariko and Tadashi. They asked us to call them Mari and Tad. Everyone seemed happy with that and moved inside to have a drink.

Meg waited until we were all sitting down at the table and the dishes had been passed around before she just came out with it. By that point Mum was probably thinking it was going pretty well. Everyone had food, Rik's parents seemed to be enjoying themselves. Mum must have thought she'd passed the hardest hurdle of the night.

Then Meg spoke.

'Rik and I are having a baby. It's due in June, which is pretty good timing school-wise. We aren't going to get married or live together, but Rik will be here a lot to help with the baby while I'm studying for my exams. At the end of the year we'll work out whether we move in together, but for now the baby and I will be here and Rik will be at his home. No one will be giving up their study or plans.'

Meg looked around the table. Everyone had stopped eating. She said in a quieter voice, 'We're really excited about this, and we want you to be too.'

Meg waited, but when no else spoke up she started to eat again. Everyone sat watching her. Mum looked at Dad, then at Rik's parents. Dad looked from Mum to Meg, but then somehow his gaze got stuck on Rik. Rik's mum, Mari, couldn't look at anyone but Rik. Rik's dad, Tad, was looking around at anything, anything that wasn't a person.

I sat looking at my hands. There was light blue paint on them I hadn't noticed until this moment. I knew Meg would want me to say something to break the tension. I thought back to the Irishman in my arms and considered telling the story to the table. I tried to imagine their reactions, and all I could see was them staring at me for telling such a ridiculous story at a time like this.

Mari stood up. She said, 'Riku,' in a tone that made Rik stand up too. They walked out into the backyard, shutting the door behind them. Then she started. We could hear everything, and even though she was speaking in Japanese the message was pretty clear. Rik hung his head for a bit, then tried to talk to her, but she cut him off and spoke some more.

At the table Meg kept eating. I scratched at the paint on my hands and wondered what the painter was doing now, whether he'd ever climb a ladder again or even keep working as a painter. Tad tried to continue to eat the salad on his plate. He smiled at us and complimented Mum on the meal. After a few more minutes of trying to be polite, he excused himself and went to retrieve his wife and son.

Tad came back into the house with his family behind him and announced that they would be leaving now. Mari wouldn't look at anyone.

Rik kissed Meg quickly. 'I'll call you later.'

Meg nodded into her food and kept eating.

Mum followed them out. 'It was lovely to meet you both.'

Tad herded Mari and Rik into the car.

Mum kept trying. 'We should do this again soon.'

He closed the car doors, trapping his family, and came back to Mum. He took her hands. 'It will be okay. She just needs some time.'

Mum nodded. She needed some time too.

TWO

NOTHING really happened after Rik and his parents left. Dad questioned Meg on why she thought announcing a pregnancy that way was a good idea. Meg rolled her eyes and took herself to bed, and I slunk after her to my room. Mum was too stunned by Meg's announcement to insist we stay and do the dishes.

The next day, though, was a big talking day in our house.

In the morning, I came down the stairs first. Mum was mad that I'd known what was going on with Meg and hadn't told her.

'How long have you known about this, Beth?'

She had me cornered in the kitchen.

'Not long. But you know, we share a bathroom and Meg's been a bit sick the last few weeks, so—'

'Meg's been sick? Why didn't you tell me?'

'It wasn't my news to tell, Mum.'

Mum accepted this, at least. She's always been so proud of what good sisters Meg and I are. Our closeness. How nice we are to each other. Even if it did mean she often felt left out.

The conversation reminded me of the nausea I'd felt on the street just before the painter fell into my arms. I'd been feeling sick for a few weeks. Not strongly like yesterday, but a little bit. I thought it was because I'd been listening to Meg cough into the toilet every morning. I thought the sound of her vomiting was making me feel sick too. But ever since I'd caught the painter that sickness had gone away.

Meg came into the kitchen. Mum stopped questioning me and moved on to her.

'How could you tell us like that? In front of Rik's parents when we'd never met before? Why didn't you tell me sooner?'

Meg shrugged. The pregnancy made her slow in the mornings, but because it was school holidays Mum hadn't noticed. She'd been leaving the house for work before Meg got up.

Meg went into the lounge room and crawled onto the couch to lie down. Dad was in there taking off his shoes after an early-morning ride.

'I thought it would be nice. Memorable. It could have been if Rik's mum didn't ruin it like she did.'

Mum couldn't speak for a bit after that. She let Dad come in with some questions about how Meg was feeling and whether she'd seen a doctor.

I could see how hard it was for Mum. She'd thought she was the kind of parent her kids could talk to. She wanted her children to come to her with their problems. To confide in her. But what kid ever really tells their parents everything?

When Mum was ready to talk again, she repeated her questions to Meg about why she didn't tell them sooner.

'I needed time. I had to think about what I wanted, and then what Rik wanted. Then we had to work out how we were going to manage. I wanted to have all that straight between us before we brought parents into it.'

I thought again about telling them the story of the painter. I could have shown them the few small spots of paint I'd left on my hand as a reminder that it really happened. Instead, I sat quietly while Mum, Dad and Meg talked through what she wanted to do and how she thought she could juggle her final year of school and a baby.

The conversation kept going around and around with Mum and Dad questioning everything Meg was saying. I went upstairs to my room and rang my best friend Lin. I'd been wanting to call her since I caught the painter, but with everything else going on I hadn't had a chance. I started by telling her about Meg's announcement and how Rik's mum had reacted. Lin had known the announcement was coming too, but I'd sworn her to secrecy.

I had just said, 'But listen, something else happened. Something really weird,' when there was a whole bunch of shouting in the background. Lin's parents were chaos. Nice people, both well-respected doctors, but loud and disorganised. Their house was full of half-finished projects, and things like phones and keys often got lost. Lin was the opposite. She loved order and finished everything she started. With me, she was calm. But when she was at home, her family's chaos got to her. Lin shouted that she hadn't seen the car key before she came back to me.

'I'm really sorry, I've got to go.'

I tried to say, 'No, wait, just a minute,' but Lin was already gone.

I walked back down the stairs to see how the conversation there was progressing. Mum had moved into planning mode, saying she might need to take time off work. Meg didn't want Mum changing anything for her. She was convinced that she and Rik would be able to manage the baby and keep up with schoolwork. That wasn't the point for Mum.

'You know, bringing a baby into this house is going to change things. Not just for you, but for all of us. Surely you understand that, Meg. This isn't just about you.'

Rik arrived. It had been about a year since he and Meg met at a university open day. Rik was a first-year, and her guide. They went from chatting about uni options to dating in about three months. Mum and Dad had been cautious at first, but they liked him and he was generally a welcome visitor.

Today was a little different. Mum greeted him at the door and led him through to the lounge, where everyone was sitting. Rik sat next to Meg and held her hand.

'Mum's not happy.'

'I think we all got that last night.' Meg took her hand from Rik's. She was getting tired.

'I mean really not happy. Mum was brought up to think that having a baby when you aren't married is not something good people do.'

'She'll calm down.' Mum said it like a statement, but it was more of a question.

Rik shrugged. 'Maybe. But at the moment she's pretty insistent that we get married.'

Meg stood up and stretched her arms above her head. 'I'm going to go lie down. You should get home and let your mum know that's not part of the plan.'

THREE

ON the first day of school I let Meg have the bathroom before me so she could get her morning vomit over with. The nausea I'd been feeling had returned in a vague sort of way, but it couldn't compete with Meg's. I splashed my face with water and dressed in my larger, longer school uniform.

They all watched me from the kitchen as I came down the stairs, and I could see my parents preparing nice things to say about the day and the way I looked. Dad started with, 'Here's our Beth,' and Mum quickly followed with, 'I like the way you've done your hair.'

As Mum moved in for a closer inspection I ducked out of the way. I took a few things from the fridge to put my lunch together. Meg was making a sandwich and eating her breakfast at the same time. The morning sickness didn't seem to do anything to dull her appetite – she'd crowded the bench with bread and cheese, milk and yoghurt.

As she tried to make space for me, Meg pushed some bowls to the side. The bowls pushed the milk to the edge of the bench. I watched it wobble there. I watched it fall. I reached out quickly and grabbed it mid-flight, my now-long arms easily making the catch.

I looked around. Dad had his head in his bike pannier making sure he had everything he needed. Mum was at the sink rinsing out her teacup. Meg was scrolling on her phone.

No one had even noticed. I put the milk back in the fridge.

Meg and I left the house soon after Dad rode off. I had what I thought was that usual first-day knot in my stomach, but Meg was bright and happy and ready to go. She wasn't at all fazed by having to tell the principal she was pregnant and would need some special study provisions later in the year. She'd always been more comfortable talking to teachers than I was. She took my hand as we left and gave it a squeeze. 'It's just school, Beth. It's going to be okay.'

We'd walked about two steps out of the house when Meg let out a little scream and dropped my hand. I looked up and saw Etienne walking towards us.

Etienne and Meg had been friends ever since his parents bought the house across from ours about four years ago. I considered him my friend too, and they often included me in whatever it was they chose to do. There had even been a time when Etienne and I were obsessed with a car racing game he'd brought back from a holiday that Meg had no interest in. The two of us had played that for hours while Meg sat nearby reading a book. But even then, it was clear that he was Meg's friend and I was there as her little sister.

Etienne was the boy at school everyone wanted to know or date. He was stupidly good-looking. Even when he was thirteen. He was also kind and fair. He was polite and respectful. It made him different to most of the other guys at school. The girls in my year were always asking me about him. They were absolutely convinced there was something more than friendship going on between him and Meg, no matter how many times I told them there wasn't.

I'd actually expected he and Meg would end up together too. Maybe even Meg did, though she never said it. But then she met Rik. I remember watching Etienne at the time. Watching him around Meg and Rik to see if there was any jealousy or sadness. But there didn't seem to be. He never looked upset or lonely when they went out together and left him behind.

Meg ran to Etienne. She wrapped her arms around him and held him tight. He laughed and hugged her back, and looked over her head towards me. I was hanging back, feeling even shyer than I normally felt. Etienne kept one arm around Meg and raised his other to give me his usual high five, but something about me made him stop. I put my hands to my hair – maybe my ponytail looked weird.

Etienne let his hand drop, but he smiled at me and said, 'Hi,' in a way that made me think my hair might be all right. I smiled back, and Meg looked between us as we stood, locked in place, smiling at each other. She pushed Etienne towards the footpath, saying, 'Yes, yes, Beth grew tall and beautiful over the break,' which made me blush and Etienne laugh.

We started walking to school.

'So remind me, where were you this time?'

Meg had forgotten the details but I hadn't.

'Hong Kong, Aspen, Manhattan. How was Manhattan?' I tried to look at him as I asked my question.

Etienne smiled at me again. 'Noisy. Cold. The snow at Aspen was okay.'

Etienne and his parents went away most summer holidays. His parents always managed to have business to attend to in beautiful or interesting places. For years I'd thought it was all about theme parks and ice-cream and his parents introducing him to the world. Later I'd found out it was mostly Etienne in a hotel room on his own while his parents held meetings in the restaurant downstairs.

'When did you get back?'

'Last night. Pretty late.'

He answered me the way he'd always answered my questions, but he looked at me differently, like he wasn't sure who I was anymore.

I would have spent longer thinking about Etienne and the way he looked at me. I would have spent longer worrying about how other kids at school were going to look at me now that I was taller than most of them. But I couldn't.

I'd started to feel sicker, a slow, creeping nausea that started at the knot in my stomach and was working its way up to my throat. The closer we got to school, the sicker I felt. I tried telling myself it was nerves, that it was my normal first-day-of-school weirdness, but the nausea just got stronger.

I lost focus on Meg and Etienne's conversation, which had moved to Friday night's dinner. Underneath my nausea was a feeling, a pull towards the school; it absorbed all my attention. Etienne and Meg didn't notice my silence. It's not unusual for me to be silent. Especially in their conversations.

By the time we got to the school gates the nausea was so bad I felt as if I was going to throw up. Meg and Etienne were still talking. I could barely take in what they were saying. I think they tried to include me at some point by turning and asking me a question, but I couldn't hear the words.

As we walked into school, something inside of me took off and I felt like I had to run. I couldn't, though. I couldn't just run like that. No matter how I felt. It would be too weird. I mumbled something like, 'Goodbye, have a good day, see you later,' and tried to head as quickly as I could away from the main entrance.

Meg called after me. She knew I was meant to be meeting Lin at our usual spot. She was probably thinking I was in such a dream state I didn't know what I was doing. But I wasn't feeling dreamy, I was feeling desperate. I needed to get away from everyone.

So I waved my hand at her like I knew exactly what I was doing, and made my way to the back of the school. The area behind the school, at that time of day, was out of bounds to students. I knew kids weren't meant to be here before the school bell rang, but I wasn't thinking about rules at this point. I had no idea what I would do or say if a teacher caught me. I was just walking as fast as I could. This part of the school was the right place to be.

I walked towards one of the classroom blocks. The building was older than the rest, with red brick and white wooden windows. I looked up and saw Peter, the school's general assistant, trying to open one of the windows from the second floor.

Peter was well known to all the students at school. He was the one who got the balls off the roof and fixed the leaking taps. We all liked him because he wasn't a teacher and because he was pretty friendly, in a dry, sarcastic way.

The sight of Peter through the window made me stop. I watched him as he pushed against the window to force it open. I kept watching as he leant out to scrape at the paintwork. He was trying to get it smooth so the window would easily open. The painters had been in over the school holidays and painted these windows shut.

I positioned myself below the window Peter was working on. I could feel his frustration, his annoyance that the painters had done such a bad job. I could almost hear the speech he was preparing to deliver to the principal about it.

I had a vague thought that I should move away and go find Lin, and another that recognised the nausea was easing but I couldn't move. I felt completely calm. I felt like I was exactly where I was meant to be. I didn't want to lose this feeling.

Peter hadn't seen me. He was focused on the window with his lips pursed and his brow furrowed. He was putting everything he had into fixing that window. I couldn't tell you what else was happening around me. I couldn't tell you if the school bell had rung or if there was an angry teacher behind me. All I could do, all I could focus on, was Peter.

And then it happened.

For me, it happened in slow motion. As I watched, it was like I knew. Like I'd always known.

Peter leant out of the window to do one final scrape. He used all his weight against the paintwork, as if he was mad at it for not giving way more easily. He pushed against the wood and stretched just that bit further.

And then he fell.

He tried to stop himself by grabbing onto the window sill but the force of that last big push had thrown him too quickly off balance. His head dragged him towards the ground. Towards me. At some point he realised he was falling and tried to turn himself around.

I took a moment to shift my position a little. I had plenty of time. I watched him with the patience of a loving parent. When Peter saw me standing there his eyes locked onto mine. He waved his arms wildly. He wanted me to move out of the way.

I stood my ground. I stood where I was because it felt right. Because I felt calm. Because I could see everything happening in precise detail and knew, just knew, I could do this. It wasn't like catching the painter on the street. It wasn't a surprise or any kind of mystery.

I judged the distance he had left. I held out my arms. I heard him shout, 'Move!' I heard the panic in his voice. I stayed where I was. I flexed my knees a little, and I waited until Peter fell into my arms.

When he was safe, I held him to me.

Everything around us went back to normal speed. We were back in real time. Back in life's fast motion. Peter was looking at me, our noses practically touching. Neither of us had anything to say. So we just stood there, me holding him like he was my overgrown baby.

The school bell rang and jolted Peter out of wherever he was. He looked at the ground. I didn't want to let him go. I wasn't ready. I thought, *If I let him go I'll lose this feeling of calm I have right now*, but Peter looked up to the window he'd been working on. I guess he still had jobs to do.

'You'd better put me down now.'

I put him carefully back on his feet.

'Thanks.'

'That's okay.'

'You should get to class. Don't want to be late on the first day.'

Suddenly all the calm I was feeling disappeared. Peter was right. I didn't want to be late on the first day.

FOUR

I slipped into my rollcall class just in time. I could see the back of Lin's head at the front of the room. We hadn't been in rollcall together since Year Seven when we first met. Our rollcall teacher was Ms Bhat – my Maths teacher from last year, and not a favourite.

Ms Bhat eyed the class, particularly me as the last kid in, and went through her rules. No talking in rollcall. No moving around in rollcall. We were all expected to sit quietly while she read through daily notices. Lin turned and spotted me. She stared at me hard, and I knew she was asking me why I hadn't met her this morning. She was asking me where I'd been.

I shrugged an answer and mouthed, 'Lunch,' because I wouldn't get a chance to say everything I needed to say until then. Lin nodded and frowned so I'd know she was annoyed that I hadn't been where I'd said I would be.

I wasn't worried about Lin being annoyed with me. Lin and I had been best friends from the moment we met and I was confident me being late wasn't going to change that.

Rollcall was the one and only class Lin and I could hope to be in together. Lin had chosen all the hard subjects for Years Eleven and Twelve. All the science and maths that I'd never even contemplate. I chose anything I thought would be easy. Anything I thought I had a small chance of passing.

Meg and Lin, they both loved school. They enjoyed learning and books and even tests. Etienne also seemed to get along with teachers and find some enthusiasm in studying for his subjects. But I never did. Maybe for moments here and there, maybe there were patches of getting it, but mostly I'd sit down to read a book or do a worksheet and my thoughts would have me drifting off the page and floating out the window. They never seemed to stay in one place.

I took the book Mum bought me for Christmas from my bag, feeling pleased I'd listened to Meg's advice to bring it. I didn't read it. I opened it in front of me and thought about catching Peter. I tried to work out how I'd known to be in the right place at the right time. What the nausea meant, and that weird pull, whether it guided me to the right spot to catch Peter or whether I was just there by chance, like the first time after I'd been shopping. I wondered how I could have had the strength to catch a grown man, twice now.

I remembered standing with time slowing around me and thinking at my normal speed. I remembered how I'd felt that first time, holding the painter in the street, and how I felt with Peter in my arms. How I felt so right and calm. How I'd never really felt like that before.

The bell rang to let us know it was the end of rollcall. Lin and I exchanged a final look. Hers was a question. Mine was still a shrug of an answer. Then we were thrown into the chaos of the school hallways.

My first class was Food Tech. I had no interest in cooking or food production, but Mum had convinced me it would be a good subject to do and other kids had said it was easy.

I was one of the first to arrive. I chose a workstation in the middle of the classroom where I thought I'd stand out the least. As the class started to fill up, the spot next to me stayed empty until the last moment, when a boy I'd never seen before slipped into it. He was just a bit shorter than me, with dark floppy hair that hid his face.

When Mr Wong called the roll, the boy next to me answered to the name Rohan. Mr Wong pointed out to us that Rohan was new and then made his welcome-to-the-school speech. The speech ended with Mr Wong telling us to be nice. Mr Wong was somewhere in his sixties. He'd been at the school forever. Telling us to be nice was his thing.

Rohan kept his head down during Mr Wong's welcome. He let his hair hide his face and then he looked at me out the side of his fringe and rolled his eyes. I smiled. Rohan smiled back.

Our first Food Tech class didn't involve much work. Mainly it involved Mr Wong telling us about all the work we would be doing, and his hope that we didn't pick this subject because we thought it would be easy.

Meg had warned me the day would be like this. She said it was the job of the teachers in the first week of Year Eleven to scare the kids into thinking it was going to be really tough. She said they would all be telling us how hard we needed to study.

'But once you get started you realise it's not that bad.'

It was such an easy thing for Meg to say. I was pretty convinced it would be bad.

At the end of the class Rohan shouldered his bag and said, 'See you.' I was surprised he seemed so confident after one hour at a new school. I'd been here for years and wasn't feeling that confidence.

As I stepped out into the corridor I noticed people looking at me. Some didn't seem to recognise me, so it was as if they were staring to work out who I was. Others were commenting on my sudden height change to their friends.

I hated the idea of people talking about me.

I made my way to my next class, Personal Development, Health and Physical Education. I'd had to spell it out for Mum, because it wasn't a class Meg had ever expressed interest in or that even existed when Mum went to school. But it was the one subject I actually wanted to do, because I thought it would be a good mix of moving and book work.

The teacher was Ms Tan. She was young and small and strong and fit. She greeted us all as we came into the gym, and even though I saw her clock my growth she didn't say anything about it. Ms Tan gave us the same talk as Mr Wong had about how Year Eleven was hard work and this subject would be no different. Then she said she'd take it easy on us today because it was the first day, and looking around the class I thought we were all pretty grateful for that.

We played a few different games on the basketball court. I had always been okay with a ball, but today I was better, maybe one of the best in the class. My throws were strong though not always accurate, and I felt fast and confident on my feet. I caught anything that came my way. I didn't think about it. Etienne walked past with some of his classmates. It distracted me for a moment, but I didn't let it stop me. I kept playing and had a good time.

At the end of the class Ms Tan pulled me aside. 'You did good today, Beth. What sport are you playing?'

I shook my head. I'd never played any sport at school or outside of school. It wasn't something our family did.

'You should be doing something. You're good. And you seem to like it. Have a think about it.'

'Okay. Thanks.'

I smiled at her, but I didn't seriously think about what she said. I just kept moving through the day, counting down until I could talk to Lin.

At lunchtime I found Lin at our usual table outside. As I sat down I saw Rohan, sitting on his own on one of the benches off to the side and out of the way of the main student traffic.

I pointed him out to Lin. 'New kid. I sat next to him in Food Tech. He seems nice.'

'Should we invite him over? He's on his own.'

'There's something I really need to tell you first.'

Lin nodded and settled herself ready to listen to my story, but before I could say anything else Meg and Etienne joined us. I looked around – their usual table, and all of the other tables, were filled. Their friends followed them to us, and our table became crowded and noisy. There was going to be no way of talking to Lin about anything.

Lin didn't seem to notice the interruption. She was smiling at Etienne and asking about his holiday. The talk moved from holidays to teachers and schoolwork. I faded out of the conversations around me. There were too many going on and I was starting to feel sick again.

I wanted to work out what the feeling was, whether it was linked to catching or fear. I considered going to check if Peter was working on any upstairs windows again, but it wasn't the same as this morning. This was a faint feeling, like the one I'd woken up with, not a strong need to throw up, and there wasn't the pulling feeling that seemed to guide me to Peter. In this lighter form it felt familiar. Like something I knew. I sat without hearing any of the talk around me and tried to understand what I was feeling. There was something in me that had felt this way before. There was something telling me this had always been here. I'd just never paid it any attention.

Etienne's voice saying my name cut through the chatter and brought me back to the table.

'Hey Beth, I saw you on the basketball court today.'

Meg gave him a gentle push. 'That's a bit creepy.'

Etienne didn't let Meg distract him from what he wanted to say. He gave her a look and then turned his attention back to me.

'You were good. Why don't you try out for the team?'

Etienne was captain of the basketball team. He loved it and was always trying to get people to join.

We laughed. Not just Meg and me, but also Lin and most of the others. Everyone at that table knew Meg and I didn't do sport. Most of our friends knew about Dad and his cycling past, his medals and trophies. But they also knew us. They knew sport wasn't Meg's thing and assumed it wasn't mine either.

When the laughing died down Etienne was still looking serious. Meg gave him a small punch on the arm. 'Beth and I don't do sport. You know that.'

But Etienne shook his head. He turned to Maye and Tommy, who were also on the basketball team. 'I'm telling you, I know what I saw. She's got skills.'

Meg, Lin and I tried to laugh again, but the rest of the table had stopped. Tommy and Maye were looking at me, noting the change in my height and sizing me up for the team.

Etienne was looking at me too, waiting for an answer. I shook my head. 'I don't know . . . I don't think so, it's not our thing. Thanks, though.'

I had to keep talking because Etienne wasn't letting up with the attention he'd turned on me. I looked to Lin for help, but she was just glancing between Etienne and me, trying to work out what was going on. The bell ringing saved me and we all got up to go to our next classes.

On our way I leant down to Lin.

'My place, after school.'

'Definitely.'

When the final bell of the day rang I rushed to the gate to wait for Lin. Meg and Etienne passed me on their way out and invited me to join them on the walk home. Etienne was still looking at me differently. I could see him, like some of the other boys, trying not to stare at my suddenly long legs, but I was too focused on wanting to speak to Lin to think about Etienne. I shook my head to their offer and told them I was waiting for her.

Lin turned up after most of the school had left. She turned up after teachers had walked past me with questioning looks, or actual questions about whether I was all right and what I was doing there. She turned up with her arms full of books, smiling at me like she was carrying puppies. When I asked her where she'd been, even though it was pretty obvious she'd been in the library, she looked at me with surprise. It had never occurred to her that everyone else wouldn't be running to the library after the first day of school.

We started walking towards my house. Lin struggled with the volume of the books she was trying to carry as she talked about her day and how great her classes were. I reached over and took the books from her. I couldn't stand to see her trying to manage their weight and size any longer. The books fitted easily into my arms and the weight didn't bother me. Lin stretched out her arms. 'Thanks.'

Without the books Lin started to focus on me. She went back to the half-started conversation we'd had at lunch.

'So, what's going on?'

I had waited so long to tell her that I couldn't find the words. Everything I'd practised in my head sounded too weird.

'Let's wait until we get to my place.'

Maybe when I was in my own room I'd be able to find the words. Maybe if I shut the door, if I shut out my family and school and the rest of the world, I'd be able to tell Lin what had happened.

FIVE

AT my house Lin went to speak to Meg and Etienne in the lounge room while I grabbed some food from the kitchen. They were talking about Rik and his mum, but when I walked in everyone looked up expectantly. They waited for me to speak, like it had been decided I was going to make an announcement.

'Lin and I have some stuff to go over in my room.'

Lin stood quickly and headed for the door.

Up in my room, she took her usual position on my bed and I started pacing. Lin chose not to speak first and I still wasn't ready so I started eating the sliced apple. Lin didn't eat, she just kept watching me. I ate everything on the plate while I tried to work out where to start. How to start.

I started with Peter.

'I caught Peter today.'

'Peter?'

It wasn't the conversation Lin had been expecting.

'The school assistant. He fell out of a window and I caught him. It was really weird, Lin. Something pulled me there, and when he fell, I caught him.'

I didn't tell her how calm I'd felt with him in my arms. How I'd held him like a baby.

'And before that, I caught someone else. A painter. He fell off a ladder. I just stopped on the street and he fell into my arms.'

There was more I could have said, but it felt like enough to start with. I watched Lin try to understand what I was saying. She was nodding at me like I was still talking. Like everything I had just said was still rolling around in her brain and she was trying to make sense of it.

'Okay.' Lin kept nodding. 'You caught Peter.'

I didn't know if it was a statement or a question. 'Yes.'

'And another random guy.'

'A painter.'

'A painter? Like an artist?'

'No, like someone who paints signs.'

'On the street?'

'Yes.'

'Why?'

'Why what?'

'Why did you catch them?'

'They were falling. I stopped them hurting themselves.'

'Why didn't you get out of the way?'

'I think I knew I could catch them.'

'You thought you could catch grown men who were falling?'

I nodded. 'Yes.'

'Why?'

'I don't know. I just did.'

Lin got up off the bed. She was still kind of nodding. 'But how did you catch them?'

'I think . . . it's like I'm strong now. I mean, I carried all your books no problem. I caught those men.'

'And it didn't hurt?'

'Not really.'

'Okay. Has anything unusual happened? I mean, apart from catching grown men. Is your mum giving you any new weird vitamins?'

I took Lin's place on the bed and lay down. 'No. Nothing unusual has happened. You'd know if it had.'

'Maybe you knocked your head and forgot about it?'

'I didn't knock my head.'

'You grew.'

'What do you mean?'

'At the end of last year you were the same height as me. You've grown. Really fast.'

'I guess. But Dad's tall. And he said he grew late too.'

'Yeah.' Lin didn't sound convinced.

'Maybe growing so fast released some weird hormones.'

Lin came onto the bed and stretched out next to me. We used to lie together on my bed a lot. Countless sleepovers where we'd sleep top and tail until Lin got sick of me kicking her and opted for the floor. It was nice lying next to her. I started to feel calm again.

'I don't think anything's happened. I think it's just in me. I think it's always been in me. Maybe growing gave me the strength to do it, but it's always been there. I can feel it.'

Lin got up and started pacing again. She'd stopped nodding. I'd remembered a few other weird things.

'Remember the time we went for yum cha and that dumpling flew off the table?'

I tried to work out how many years ago it was, but Lin nodded. She remembered. 'Meg was trying to get it with her chopsticks and ended up flipping it in the air.'

We were silent for a moment.

'Remember how I caught it?'

We'd all laughed at the time at what a lucky catch I made. I'd thrown it back to Meg and we'd laughed some more until we were reminded that we were in a restaurant and none of the people at other tables thought it was funny to be throwing dumplings. Come to think of it, neither did Lin's parents.

Lin sat.

'And remember that day in Year Eight? When we all had to play softball? Remember the catch I took in the outer field?'

Lin shook her head. 'Remember all the ones you missed?'

'I wasn't trying for those ones.'

Lin shrugged. 'I guess.'

I thought about that day. How the ball had felt in my hands after I caught it. How I'd known where to stand, where to place my feet. I looked at Lin sitting up on my bed.

'I really wanted to get Karen Langfield out.'

Lin laughed – back in Year Eight we hated Karen Langfield.

She leapt off my bed and looked out my window, then turned back to me.

'Do you think you could catch me? If I jumped out the window?'

I stood up and joined her at the window to look down to the ground. It felt high, even though we were lower than Peter was when he fell. I moved away.

'I don't know. Let's not take the risk.'

Lin nodded and got back onto the bed. I lay down next to her.

She turned to me. 'Tell me again about how you think it's always been in you.'

'Before each catch I felt sick. Like I was going to throw up. I've been feeling a bit like that anyway, but I thought it was just some kind of sympathy morning sickness because of Meg. And then at lunch today I felt sick again, and it was familiar. I've felt it before. Lots of times. I'd just never really thought about it. It was only catching Peter that made me realise it might mean something. Be something.'

Lin checked the time on her phone. 'I need to go, but I think we should try to find out what this is.'

'I don't know if I want to.'

'Of course you do.'

She told me I needed to write down anything I could think of that was relevant. Anything at all. I nodded my agreement.

'I don't think we should tell anyone about this until we've worked it out a bit more,' I added.

Lin looked to me as she put her schoolbag back on her shoulders. 'Not even your parents?'

'Not yet. Think how Mum'd react. And maybe it will never happen again.'

'Meg?'

I shook my head. 'Meg's got enough going on right now.'

I walked Lin to the front door. Meg and Etienne were in the driveway playing basketball. Well, Etienne was shooting hoops while Meg stood nearby chatting and looking at her phone. Etienne stopped when we appeared. He stood bouncing the ball in a casual way without even looking at where it was landing.

I looked. I looked at his hand and at the ball as it hit the ground and floated back up to him. I looked at his arm, up past his elbow where his bicep flexed each time he pushed against the ball. Etienne had grown over the holidays too. Maybe not much taller, but his arms and chest had broadened. He'd somehow picked up a tan from his holiday on the snowfields and he looked just a bit shiny from shooting baskets in the heat of the afternoon.

The hoop attached to our garage had been there since Meg started high school. Dad put it up for her to learn how to play. He'd hoped she would be inspired once she realised how big basketball was at our school. But Meg was never interested in balls and sport. She liked boys and study in equal measure. The hoop only started to be used when she became friends with Etienne.

Watching him with the basketball reminded me that I'd forgotten to talk to Lin about how he'd looked at me. I thought about grabbing her and dragging her back inside, but she was already heading down the driveway.

I waved goodbye as she shouted back at me, 'I'll call you tonight.'

Meg's phone buzzed and she started to head after Lin.

'Where are you going?' I called out to her.

She waved back at me. 'Driving test.'

Rik pulled up in his car and jumped out so that Meg could get into the driver's seat. He waved to Etienne and me as he put the L-plates on.

'Good luck!'

Getting her licence was part of Meg's plan to manage having a baby and school. She was so determined to follow that plan she didn't really need luck, but I said it anyway as a way of saying goodbye.

As the car drove away Etienne bounced the basketball towards me, forcing me to catch it. 'Come on, show me what you can do.'

I smiled as I bounced the ball a bit and tried to get around him. Etienne took it from me easily and threw it towards the hoop. He bumped into me a little as the ball went through, laughing, teasing me. I started to try to play properly then. Like I'd played at school earlier in the day. I grabbed the ball as it came towards us and bounced it down the driveway. Then I wove around him, purposely pushing at him a little with my hip as I passed to shoot. I missed the hoop, but at least I managed to get the ball past him.

We continued to tussle up and down the driveway. My play improved each time and I got a few balls away from Etienne and through the hoop. Etienne got more, of course, but I felt fast and strong and did well enough not to consider myself a complete disgrace.

Etienne was laughing and serious in equal measure as he focused on the ball. This was new for us. We'd never played or even really spent much time together without Meg around. He seemed different. Like a different Etienne. I tried to stop thinking so much and enjoy the moment.

Etienne had the ball. He was teasing me with it, encouraging me to get closer to him. I stood in front of him and reached up. He held the ball higher and behind his head. I was almost eye level with him now. It didn't feel as weird as it did this morning. At least my height was starting to feel normal.

I stopped reaching for the ball. Etienne was looking at me in a way that no one ever had before. I put my hands to his chest and felt his heart, his warmth. He threw the ball over his head, towards the hoop. It bounced off the house, nowhere near the hoop, and came back towards us at a weird angle.

Neither of us looked to see where the ball was going. We were only looking at each other. But I knew where the ball was. Even though I couldn't take my eyes from Etienne, I knew the ball was coming. I took my hands from his chest and reached up to catch it.

Etienne tore his eyes from mine and stared at the ball in my hands.

I realised my mistake. I shouldn't have been able to catch that ball. Not when I was looking at him. It was impossible. I'd just made an impossible catch.

I took a step away from Etienne and dropped the ball. It was a stupid thing to do, but it's what I did. The ball rolled down the driveway and into the gutter. Neither of us made a move to go and get it.

Etienne looked like he was about to speak, but it was too much for me. I had ruined everything with my weird catch. I moved towards the front door.

'I should . . .'

I didn't know what the end of that sentence was. I didn't know what I should do. I just knew I needed to get away from him. That I couldn't keep standing there with him looking at me like that. I didn't know what to do with it all.

My words jolted him out of wherever he was.

'Okay, me too. I should be going too,' he responded as if I had finished my sentence.

I turned towards the door. I wanted to run. I wanted to run into the house and slam the door. I also wanted to wind back time to when we were having fun. To before it got so intense. To before I took that impossible catch.

I tried to move slowly. I tried to look like I wasn't running. When I'd managed to get my hands on the door Etienne spoke.

'Beth?'

Hearing him say my name stopped me moving. I didn't recall him saying my name before, ever. I knew he must have, but in that moment, I couldn't remember. It felt like the first time I'd heard my name from his lips. It made my heart stand still.

Etienne said it again. 'Beth, you really should try out for the team.'

I shrugged, nodded a little and tried to speak in my most normal voice. 'Maybe.'

I took a deep breath, turned and looked at him. He was smiling at me now. Smiling kindly, like he was worried about me. I gave him a small wave, like everything was fine. Then I walked into the house and closed the door.

SIX

I went to school early for the rest of the week – so I could meet Lin in the library and avoid walking to school with Meg and Etienne. Meg didn't even ask me why I wasn't walking with them. She was probably too busy teasing Etienne about how she passed her driving test first time, while he was about to make his third attempt. Or catching him up on the latest arguments between Rik and his mum. The library time was to give Lin and me a chance to talk about what was going on with me.

Lin showed me the schedule she'd made for herself. It had her week set out in bright block colours. Lin had always had a schedule. In Years Seven and Eight she'd made them for me too, but by Year Nine she'd worked out that I wasn't, I said couldn't, following them, so she gave up. Lin pointed to the yellow on her schedule. *Beth time.*

On Wednesday after school, while we were working at Dad's bike shop, Lin ran me through the breathing exercises she'd been researching. She thought these exercises might give me clarity, and if nothing else, would possibly take away that sick feeling I still had a lot.

I tried to take it seriously. I could see from her schedule how much time she was devoting to me, and I could see from the stack of papers she waved at me how much she believed in the breathing idea, so I really did try. But it felt ridiculous. I ended up in fits, with Lin torn between being cross and joining me in the laughter.

By Friday Lin decided the reason the breathing wasn't working was something to do with her teaching methods, and she took me to a meditation specialist. I wasn't convinced a specialist would be any better, but Lin told me this kind of meditation was easy. Something anyone could do. I didn't take offence given my behaviour in the breathing exercises.

We caught the bus straight after school.

'I want you to take this seriously, Beth. Don't laugh or make fun of the teacher.'

I felt like I had been trying with Lin, but maybe she was right. Maybe there was a part of me not taking it seriously because it was Lin. I agreed to try.

The meditation teacher worked out of a white, bright apartment near the beach. Lin waited in the kitchen with her schoolbooks while the teacher took me to her meditation room which was also her lounge room. She was smaller than me, with jangling bracelets on her wrists and her long hair loosely tied at the back of her head. She wasn't wearing shoes and she looked young, maybe not much older than us.

I had pictured someone ancient and wise, but perhaps wisdom doesn't come with age. Perhaps it comes with other things, with breath and experience. She looked me in the eyes like she was trying to read the inside of my head. I tried to copy her stare without fear, but I felt worried about what she was seeing in there.

The meditation teacher told me there was nothing to be frightened of. She told me that meditation could heal my mind and body. It could form the connections and the release I needed. I nodded, wondering what Lin had told her and why they thought my mind needed healing.

She told me to sit anywhere I felt comfortable. I looked around the room as if it was a test. The right place to sit was probably the floor, but the couch looked far more comfortable. The teacher repeated her instruction to me. *Anywhere that seems comfortable.* So I took the couch, feeling like I was managing meditation class about as well as I managed all my other classes.

She instructed me to close my eyes and then gave me my mantra. She explained it as a secret. A word that was only for me. She asked me to repeat the word to her. To repeat it out loud over and over again until it felt like mine. She told me to quieten the word. To draw it into my body. To hold it in my mind. I tried to pull the word into me. I tried to picture it as letters being sucked in through my mouth, but I couldn't picture it. I didn't even know how to spell it.

Then we just sat. She said it was twenty minutes. It felt like hours and then nothing at all. I don't know what she did during that time. I had my eyes closed. She could have been meditating with me or scrolling on her phone.

At the end of the twenty minutes the teacher touched me lightly and guided me out of the meditation. She asked me how I felt and how many thoughts I had. I had to admit that I'd had many. So many. She told me that was normal.

Before we went back to the kitchen to join Lin, the teacher took my hands again and looked into my eyes. I looked back into hers, wondering if there was more I should be doing. More I should be feeling in that moment. Whatever it was she saw, she seemed satisfied.

As we walked into the kitchen Lin looked to the teacher to see if I'd been a good student and the teacher nodded to her as if they'd had a discussion. Her assessment of me as a student of meditation was passed in that nod, and Lin looked pleased.

Lin and I headed down to the beach to buy ice-cream. We sat and watched the surfers and wished we'd thought to bring towels and something to swim in. We took our shoes off and waded into the water up to our knees, then dried off to start the bus journey home.

On the bus I thanked Lin for arranging the meditation session. I told her I was going to try to do it twice a day, like the teacher had suggested. Then I told her I felt lighter, better somehow, and that was enough for Lin.

On Monday morning I was racing out the front door just as Etienne arrived. I barged straight into him and knocked him off balance. As he fell backwards I reached out to grab him at the same time as he reached out for me. I think it all happened so quickly he didn't notice it was me who pulled him back to his feet.

We stood like this for a while, holding each other's elbows. His skin was warm and I felt a glow from touching him that moved up my arms and into my face. He looked at me with a question I found hard to believe.

It didn't feel possible that Etienne was standing here looking at me like that.

I looked down at the ground and let my hands fall from their hold on him. He held me a little longer and then dropped his hands too.

We didn't say all the normal *Hello, how are you?* things we used to say. All those automatic, polite phrases we'd been saying to each other through the years he'd been friends with Meg. The knock, the arm-holding, it seemed to have taken care of all that.

'I noticed you haven't put your name down for basketball trials yet.'

I stopped staring at the ground and looked at him again.

'No, not yet.'

'So you are thinking about it?'

'I guess.'

We were still standing weirdly close together – he hadn't stepped back from me.

'That's good, because I put your name down for you.'

He smiled, gently testing me, teasing like he used to. Except that he was standing so close. He never used to stand so close.

Etienne must have seen doubt on my face. 'Don't worry about it. You'll be great. The team needs someone like you.'

'Yeah, sure.'

I wasn't at all convinced they weren't going to laugh me out of the gym.

Meg appeared behind me. 'Hey Etienne, what's going on?'

'I signed Beth up for basketball trials.'

He took a step back like he had finally become aware we were standing too close together. Meg frowned a little as she looked at the two of us from the doorway.

I moved past Etienne and towards the street. 'I've got to get to school. See you.'

'Can't you wait? I'll only be five minutes.' Meg called to me.

I shook my head. 'I've got that project with Lin I need to do.'

Meg probably had questions about that, given she knew I didn't share any classes with Lin, but she shrugged and let me go. As I walked away I heard Etienne shout after me.

'Trials next week. We should have another practice session on the weekend.'

I turned and called back, 'Sure.'

I felt braver away from him than when we were standing close, and there was nothing I wanted more than to spend time with him.

As I headed for school, I heard Meg say, 'What's going on between you and my sister?' I was too far away to hear his answer. I imagined him saying, *Nothing, we need more players on the team*, but I hoped he was saying something about how I'd changed, how I wasn't a little kid anymore. How he couldn't stop thinking about me.

I thought about asking Meg later. I could ask her what she thought was going on, how he had answered her question. But I also knew that when the time came to ask her I wouldn't. I would be too afraid of the answer, of the pity on her face as she worked out how to let me down gently.

In Food Tech Rohan came to sit next to me again. I thought he'd make new friends and move away, but he stayed and we talked a little as we did the practical work. I learnt to follow his lead because there was nothing in this subject that interested me. Rohan seemed to have a good grasp of what to do, and he didn't mind if I copied him. He seemed weirdly enthusiastic about the whole subject and happy to share.

I meditated at the school library in the mornings with Lin while she did schoolwork, then again after school by myself. When Lin and I were alone working at Dad's bike shop I sat in a corner of the workshop with my legs crossed and my eyes closed. Sometimes Lin would put the *Back in 20 minutes* sign on the door and sit with me. She'd read meditation was more powerful in groups. I liked having her there. I didn't think it was more powerful or even that the meditation was useful for me trying to make sense of everything that was going on, but I wasn't ready to tell her that and it was nice to have her company.

SEVEN

I was home alone when I felt it.

It arrived as an urgent need to throw up. I didn't know what to do. I knew I didn't really need to be sick. I sat for a while with the feeling. I tried Lin's breathing exercises to see if I could make it go away. It didn't. It grew until I couldn't sit still anymore.

I ran out of the house and down the road.

I didn't know which direction to run in. I didn't know what I was doing. I needed to stop. To find stillness. I stood and did the breathing again. Then I let the pull of the nausea take me where I needed to go. It worked and got me running towards what felt like the right direction.

Then it was like playing Hot and Cold. I ran past a house and the feeling got stronger. I kept running and it faded. I ran up and down in front of a few houses until I was sure I'd found the one.

The one was a house with a big wall and a locked gate. I couldn't see how to get in – there was nothing to climb on and no way of opening the gate. I went into the neighbour's property instead.

I didn't stop to think about what I was doing. About whether it was legal, which Lin asked me later, or whether I was getting myself into trouble. I was too focused on getting there. Too focused on finding out if what I was feeling was real. There didn't seem to be any other option. Any other way to act.

The wooden fence between the two properties was high, but there were some bins nearby. I stood on them and used the wooden crosspieces on the fence to climb over. The drop into the other house's front yard was further than I would normally want to risk, but the grass looked soft. I scrambled over as best as I could and let myself fall.

I checked around the house, but that didn't feel like the right place to be. It was the tree. The large tree in the yard. I stood under it and was looking up through the leaves, hoping I hadn't just climbed the fence and broken into this property to catch a baby bird, when a kid fell into my arms.

His face was serious, his eyes wide and unnerving. His focus wasn't on my face, it was more on my shoulder or past my ear. I turned to see if there was anyone behind me and then I stared back at him. Where had he come from and why didn't I see him fall? I couldn't tell his age – he could have been a big five or a small eight. He was lighter in my arms than the men I'd caught, but I felt that same feeling of comfort and calm. I tried to hold the kid close to me to let him know that he was safe, but he started screaming and hitting at me. I put him on the ground. He added kicking to the hitting and the screaming.

I left through the front gate and shut it behind me with the kid still screaming on the other side.

On the footpath I listened to the noise he was making and tried to regain some sense of the calm I'd felt when I first caught him. It wasn't possible. I couldn't control my breathing, and I felt completely confused. I heard the front door to the house open and a woman's voice call out, 'Jake?'

I walked away. I tried to walk in a way that looked like I'd done nothing wrong, but I felt like I'd done something wrong. Like I was guilty. Like if anyone saw me on the street right then they'd know I'd done something terrible and they'd call the police.

When I got home I called Lin. I told her about the catch. I told her about following the pull of the nausea. I told her about climbing the wall and the kid coming out of the tree. I told her about how he wouldn't look at me and about the screaming and hitting and kicking. I told her how guilty I felt, how awful the walk home was.

I heard Lin on the other end of the phone making notes, recording everything I was saying. I knew she was trying to help me and I wanted her help, but I was thinking, *Please don't let her mum find these notes.* Lin's mum had been known to search her room now and then when she'd lost something important and I didn't want to know what she'd make of them.

I walked into the kitchen to find Mum staring into the fridge.

'Honestly, I can't keep up with you girls. Either no one is eating and things start to go off, or I shop and the next day it's all gone.'

I put the blame on Meg. It wasn't a nice thing to do, but I couldn't tell Mum that some days I felt too sick to eat and others I ate almost everything in the fridge. I think Mum guessed it wasn't Meg. Eating disorders were high on her list of illnesses to watch out for with us, but I also knew she didn't like to harp on about it too much. I think she was worried she might actually plant the idea instead of warn us away.

She changed tack and started in on me with a question.

'Is trying out for the basketball team something you really want to do?'

I thought about Etienne's hand pushing down on the basketball. His bicep in the sun.

'It's okay to say no to Etienne if it's not.'

I didn't know how to respond. I wasn't sure I wanted to try out. I just wanted to spend more time with Etienne away from Meg, but I couldn't say that to Mum.

'It's surprising, you know, Beth. I mean, you've never shown any interest in sport before.'

I still didn't say anything. I didn't need to, because Mum started to have a conversation with herself, slowly working through her thoughts out loud. I tried not to listen.

'I guess you did inherit your father's height, so it makes sense you might want to be involved in something with other tall people. Maybe basketball is where you'll find a boyfriend who's the right height.'

She looked at me when she said that.

'I know you've never been that interested in boys, but you will be soon, and you'll want one at least as tall as you.'

Then she backtracked, because Mum is always striving to be politically correct. 'Of course, height doesn't really matter. Neither does gender. It's really all about finding the right person for you when you're ready.'

I don't know what she said after that. I was too busy thinking about how Etienne was that bit taller than me. About how, height-wise at least, we'd look right together.

Meg walked in. 'I'm starving. What's for dinner?' She looked from one of us to the other. 'What's going on?'

'We were just talking about whether Beth might find a partner of suitable height in the basketball team and whether height really matters.'

Meg raised her eyebrows at me and frowned a little. 'I didn't realise Beth was looking for a partner.'

'Well, maybe not now, but one day.'

Meg frowned at me some more. I tried to keep my head down and ignore the conversation. I didn't know how to make it stop.

Meg probably knew I liked Etienne. She'd probably always known. But she was looking as if she didn't approve. Maybe because Etienne was her friend or because she knew something I didn't. Or maybe, like Mum seemed to be saying, she still saw me as too young and not ready.

EIGHT

I spent Saturday at the bike shop with Dad. I knew there was an expectation in our family that I would take over the shop when Dad retired. No one ever said it outright, but it was there underneath all the conversations around the shop.

I didn't want the shop to become my life like it was his. I didn't mind working with Lin, and I did enjoy the time I spent there with Dad. I liked fixing the bikes with him. I liked listening to his cycling stories as we worked. I liked the joy and beauty he found in each individual part as we broke them down, cleaned them up, and put them back together again. I preferred it to school, but not enough to want to make it my life.

I didn't work in the front part of the shop where the bikes were sold. That was Dad's job. Or Lin's when she was working. Sometimes Mum's on weekends. Never Meg's. I couldn't remember the last time she set foot in the place. Like team sports, the bike shop wasn't her thing.

My place was in the workshop. I started working properly soon after I started high school, but I'd always been in the workshop. Always watching over Dad's shoulder or passing him tools. I started by greasing chains and pumping up tyres while Dad fixed bikes that came in for repair. Now I knew enough to help him with those repairs. In our quiet moments we rebuilt vintage bikes and then sold them.

We were just about to start working on a 1980s racing bike. Road racing was Dad's first love, though he didn't do it anymore. He still rode every day if he could, all day if Mum would let him, but he didn't race.

When I first became friends with Lin, when she first came to our house, I showed her the drawers that held Dad's medals. We took them out and held them to each other's necks, giggling and posing. Lin grew to like the bike shop almost as much as I did, but for different reasons. She liked the order of the shop, the accounts and the booking system for repairs. Her parents weren't that keen on her working. They would rather she spent the time developing hobbies, but they liked my parents, and they wanted Lin to be happy, so they let her work there with me.

As Dad checked the frame we were going to use for any cracks or dents he talked about one of his last races. Dad's stories often came out like this, at unexpected, quiet moments. He talked about how he'd lost focus. How he hadn't been thinking about the race. His mind was at home, with Mum and us girls. We were only little at the time.

That was the race where he came off his bike. Where they scraped him off the road and into an ambulance. The race that didn't completely stop the racing, but made Dad pick and choose carefully the ones he would do and the ones he would miss.

'When things like children come into your life, other things have to go. That's how it works. That's how it should work.'

I knew he was thinking about Meg. He was worrying she wouldn't be able to do everything she had planned and have a baby. Normally I would tell Meg the stories Dad told me at work. I would come home and share them with her because Dad didn't talk like this at home. But this one I kept to myself. Meg didn't need to hear people's doubts about her ability to juggle a baby and schoolwork.

On Sunday I was in my room attempting to read *Romeo and Juliet* for English when Meg came in.

'Etienne's here to practise for the basketball trials with you.'

I hid my face in my book to hide the excited expression I knew I had.

Meg stood there watching me. 'I can tell him you're busy if you want. You don't have to do this, you know.'

I got up quickly and tried to keep my voice normal. 'No, that's okay. I'll be down in a minute. I just need to change.'

As soon as she was out of the room I rushed around choosing something to wear and trying to make my hair look decent without looking like I'd tried too hard.

When I got downstairs Etienne was in the driveway with Meg. He was wearing shorts and a singlet, passing the basketball from one hand to the other before casually stretching up to put it through the hoop. Meg was stepping through her latest plan to talk Rik's mum around to her way of thinking. Mari was proving to be about as stubborn as Meg, so it wasn't an easy fight. Etienne nodded along as she spoke, retrieving the ball and throwing it again.

Meg had set herself up in a camping chair beside the driveway, clearly showing her intention to stay for the whole practice session. She had a book on her lap, but she didn't look like she planned to read it. I frowned at her as I walked out of the house – *I don't need a chaperone.* She smiled back at me.

Etienne smiled too when he saw me. A spontaneous smile, as if he was really pleased to see me. I couldn't help but smile back. He said, 'Ready?' and bounced the ball towards me.

I tried to think of him as just Etienne. As the boy who was always hanging out with Meg. The boy I'd known since I was twelve. But it was hard to do when he was standing in front of me, an almost-eighteen-year-old, smiling at me like he was pleased to see me for me, not just because I was Meg's little sister.

Etienne had planned out the drills he wanted me to learn, but he started with the basic rules of the game. I'd seen the school teams play, but I'd never paid close attention to the rules. Etienne said I'd pick up the rest when we started playing actual games. I found it hard to imagine myself on a court playing in front of other people, but I liked that Etienne didn't.

The drills Etienne had planned were fun. He had me zigzagging from side to side down the driveway and swapping my dribbling hands at each turn. He also made me practise shooting hoops from both hands, and at the end he stood in front of me with his arms outstretched, encouraging me to try to get past him.

At first I was aware of Meg at the side, sighing and rolling her eyes at us whenever Etienne told me I'd made a good pass or in those moments when we both stopped to catch our breath and smile at each other. Etienne wasn't paying her any attention; his focus was on me and the ball, and after a while I was drawn into what he was showing me and forgot Meg was even there.

Etienne kept up instructions the whole time. He was constantly talking me through what to do, how to move my feet or my arms, how to control the ball. Each time I did the drills I got better. Etienne seemed to know when enough was enough, and would move me to the next drill and then back again if I looked like I was starting to level out.

By the end of the practice session Etienne and I were both sweaty but still smiling. Meg had fallen into a doze in her chair. The pregnancy sometimes made her do that. Etienne suggested a friendly game and I was happy to try using what I'd learnt against him.

The game started slow but got competitive quickly. We knocked into one another as we fought over the ball and I looked for opportunities, any opportunity, to push my body against his. Etienne seemed to be holding back a little, letting me have control of the ball but trying to stop me if I ever got close to the hoop. I got the ball through a few times and Etienne started to get more competitive. We began to fight over the ball in earnest, each pushing at the other, both of us reaching and twisting, until our legs became tangled together and we fell on to the grass alongside the driveway.

We lay there, hot from playing, high from the exercise, our legs still entwined. We were laughing and looking at each other. Etienne started to move closer. Just a little bit.

As I watched him consider his move I saw he had changed. As much as I had changed over the summer, he had too. He wasn't Meg's Etienne anymore. I felt it, I saw it in his eyes, and I knew he wanted to kiss me. He got close, really close.

Then Meg started to loudly pack up her chair. 'You finished then?'

We quickly moved apart, untangling our legs. Meg didn't ask why we were on the ground. She just picked up her chair and moved towards the house. 'Beth, we should probably start dinner.'

Our parents were both at the bike shop until late to do a stocktake, and Mum expected dinner on the table when they got home.

Etienne got to his feet and offered me his hand, which was large and warm and difficult to let go of.

'You did good, Beth. I think you'll do great in the trials.'

'Thanks.'

I looked him straight in the eyes and kept hold of his hand. For the first time since Etienne suggested it, I actually wanted to go to the trials. I wanted to get into the mixed team – and not just for Etienne. I wanted to do it for me. Maybe it was something I could be good at.

Meg was standing at the door. She made a signal to hurry me inside. I let go of Etienne's hand and started to walk reluctantly towards her. Etienne called goodbye to us as he picked up the basketball to shoot one last hoop before heading towards his own house.

I would have liked to have had a shower. I would have liked to stand under cool running water and think about Etienne, our legs twisted together on the grass, his face moving closer to mine, but when I looked at Meg I could see that wasn't an option. I washed my face and hands quickly and went to the kitchen to help her with dinner.

As we prepped that night's curry, Meg told me not to get my hopes up.

'You know, a lot of people try out for the basketball team. I don't want you to feel bad if you don't make it.'

I knew Meg. I knew her better than I knew anyone else. I knew she wasn't just telling me to not get my hopes up about basketball. She was talking about Etienne. I nodded and shrugged like it didn't matter to me either way.

Meg's words stayed with me while I chopped the vegetables. They took away some of the pleasure I'd felt with Etienne and they made me worry I wasn't good enough. They soured my night and made me want to get away from Meg and the rest of the family.

I tried to focus on other things. I tried to bring my mind back to catching the kid. To whether I could find other people to catch. But every time I closed my eyes, I saw Etienne on the grass, his body close to mine, and Meg, standing nearby shaking her head at me.

It was a slow, nervous week waiting for the basketball trials.

After school I practised alone on the driveway, running through the drills Etienne had shown me and trying to get the ball through the hoop. Before work on Wednesday afternoon I stood with Lin in front of the hoop with my eyes closed. I threw the ball towards the hoop and then tried to catch it on the rebound. I managed to catch it about half the time. The other times I had to open my eyes and chase the ball as it headed down the driveway and towards the road. Lin watched me and made notes.

On the day of the trials Etienne made a point of coming to sit with Lin and me at lunchtime. He checked to make sure I was okay. That I felt ready. I told him I was fine, but I didn't feel fine.

'You're a natural, Beth. I'm sure you'll do well. Want me to meet you outside the gym after school so we can walk in together?'

I nodded, relieved to have his support.

After school I stood outside the gym waiting for Etienne. Kids poured in. Some were trying out, others were just there to watch. I had no idea the trials were such a big deal, something people would want to go to as spectators.

Etienne arrived and guided me into the gym, his hand lightly touching my back. I liked the feel of his hand, but I also had a strong urge to turn and run the other way. Instead I walked in, wrote my name down where Etienne pointed and started stretching. I looked around to see if I knew anyone else who was trying out.

The basketball coach was not my PDHPE teacher, but I knew him. He was the head sports teacher, known only as Coach, close to retirement but with seemingly boundless energy for school team sports. Etienne went to talk to him like they were old friends. Coach was not tall and Etienne almost had to bend to be heard. Coach nodded and smiled as Etienne laughed at something he'd said. I didn't have much time to wonder what they were talking about, because Coach blew the whistle and had us lining up and running.

At first I was just jogging through the exercise. The noise of the gym, the pounding of feet on the floor, the Coach's whistle, it was all a bit much. I looked at Etienne sitting at the side and saw him lean forward, focusing on me. I picked up my pace, matching it to the faster kids in the group.

When we got our hands on the ball I started to feel more confident, though I still struggled to get it through the hoop. Thanks to Etienne, the drills were familiar and I could manage them with an appearance of ease.

When it came to playing a game I was shy about grabbing the ball from others. Coach kept blowing his whistle for fouls, and most of the time I had no idea why. At one point the ball came to me, almost falling into my hands, and as I looked around the court trying to work out what to do with it, I felt an urge to throw up.

I tried to ignore it. I told myself it was nerves, but I recognised it as something more. I stopped to try to work out what to do, where I might need to go.

Another player took the opportunity to grab the ball from my hands. I struggled for a moment to remember where I was, what I was doing. I looked towards Etienne, who was watching me with a confused expression, and felt lost.

I put my hands on my hips and my head down like I was trying to catch my breath so I had space to work out what I was feeling, but as soon as I did that the nausea was gone. In its place was nothing. An emptiness. I stayed down and breathed through the nothing like it was a loss. Then I straightened up and looked for the ball so I could rejoin the game.

At the end of the trial Coach told us the teams would be announced next week and a list would be placed on the school noticeboard. He thanked us all for coming in a way that suggested we had disappointed him. I looked around for my things, wondering if I'd blown my chances by freezing mid-game like that. Etienne found me through the crowd of kids gathering their bags and friends who had watched, and we headed for my house.

We walked across the school grounds without speaking. It felt like my performance in the gym had let him down. Once we were out of the school gates Etienne spoke.

'I think you did well enough to get a spot in the team if you want it.' He looked at me then, hard. 'Do you want it?'

He was asking about more than basketball.

I took a deep breath. 'Yes, of course. Why would you think I wouldn't?'

Etienne smiled, like I had said exactly the right thing.

After that our conversation became more natural. We talked about the trial, about the different kids there. Etienne explained how the teams worked, who was on the team from last year, and which new kids he expected to make it through the trials.

When we arrived at my house we paused. Neither of us knew what to say, but we weren't yet ready to leave each other. Etienne started to move towards his own house, but then he stopped like he'd just remembered something and turned back to me.

'Hey, do you want to go to a movie with me sometime?'

'Sure.'

I answered in as calm a voice as I could manage, but my heart was racing, my head was racing. I wanted to ask, *Just me? Just you and me, or will there be others? Is this a date, or are you just lonely because Meg is pregnant and spending more time with Rik?*

I didn't say any of those things. I smiled and waved goodbye as I walked towards the house. I wanted to run and skip and scream, but I walked and tried not to look back at Etienne. When I got through the door I did turn. I saw the shape of him at his own front door and then I saw him turn to see me watching. He waved again. I waved back, my mind crowded with thoughts.

What am I going to wear? How am I going to sleep? When are we going to go?

NINE

THAT night I called Lin and told her about how I'd felt in the middle of the trial game. I told her about how I'd had to stop and how I lost the feeling that would have told me where to go. I wanted Lin to tell me I did the right thing by not leaving the trials, but she didn't. She just asked me a whole lot of questions about how I felt and why I thought the feeling went away.

'Did you meditate before the trials? Where you worried about them? Maybe you ate something off at lunch or after school?'

'This isn't anything to do with the trials or what I ate, Lin.'

'Did it feel like the other times, or was it different?'

'I have no idea. I didn't have a chance to work it out.'

Lin could tell I was annoyed, but me being annoyed didn't stop her from saying what she thought.

'You asked me to help, and this is me helping.'

I thought back to that day in my room. Did I ask Lin for help? I guess I did.

'I think you should step up the meditation. And really try to remember what you are doing and feeling before you start to want to throw up.'

I thought about how I felt before I caught Peter. Before I caught that little boy. I couldn't remember anything before feeling sick that linked the two together. And the meditating had slipped as the basketball practice picked up. I hadn't told Lin that.

'You don't have to work it out now. You just need to think about it.'

There was silence while I considered what might have happened to the person I didn't catch. I tried to tell myself they probably just broke their arm.

'All you can do is try, Beth.'

The next morning I walked to school with Etienne and Meg like I always had. We talked and joked around the same as before, only this time it was a bit more me and Etienne and a bit less Meg. She'd struggled to get out of bed and was walking with her head down as if each step was hard. When we asked her if she was okay she said she was fine and that she'd probably pick up later. Etienne didn't mention the movies again on this walk, but he looked at me, really looked at me, when he said goodbye – and he touched me lightly on my shoulder as we parted.

That spot on my shoulder felt like it was burning as I stood watching Meg and Etienne walk away. It stayed warm through rollcall and my first class of the day. I tried to concentrate on schoolwork. Really I did.

But my mind wandered constantly to Etienne or to my conversation last night with Lin. I spent a lot of time searching through what I was feeling.

After school it was just Meg and me at home. I could tell as soon as she left her homework and came into my room she had something on her mind, and I didn't have to wait long. Meg stood at my window for a bit, then flicked through the schoolbooks I had scattered around the room. But she didn't ask me about school or whether I needed any help.

'What's going on with you and Etienne?'

I felt my face get a little hot and my heart beat faster. This was going to be the conversation where she told me everything I wanted to hear or didn't want to hear. I shrugged. 'I'm not sure.'

Meg sighed and lay back on my bed. 'That's what he says.'

I felt a bit disappointed by that. I wanted a great declaration of love or passion, from him through her. Some kind of secret, burning desire to be revealed.

'He asked me to the movies.'

Meg didn't offer a response.

'I don't know if it's a date.'

Meg sat up. She looked at me closely. 'Do you want it to be a date?'

I had to nod. If I didn't, she'd know I was lying.

She got up off my bed and I could see the slight bulge of her belly as she stood in my doorway.

'Well, just be careful.'

'Of what?' I still couldn't work out what she was worried about.

'Of getting your hopes up, of him. I don't know.'

'But it's Etienne.'

'Yeah.'

'So what do I need to be careful of? What do you think he'll do?'

'Beth, you haven't really . . . I mean, you don't really . . .'

She was saying I had no experience. That I was just a kid, despite my new height. I couldn't argue, because suddenly I wasn't thinking about Meg or Etienne – there was something else going on.

'I have to go.'

I tried to say it calmly as I pushed past Meg in the doorway and ran down the stairs.

I rushed out of the house and ran down the road. At least this time I knew where I was going. I went to the neighbour's house, straight to the bins and climbed over the fence much faster this time. I peered carefully into the tree trying to spot the boy, but I still couldn't see him among the leaves and branches. I knew this was the spot. This was where I needed to be. So I waited. I studied the plants in the garden and waited until he fell into my arms.

Then I held him tight, close to my body. I was so pleased I had got here at the right time. I looked at him and I looked into the tree. I tried to work out how far he'd fallen.

The boy was silent at first. I hoped he felt the same sense of calm I did, but when I looked into his eyes I saw that stare where he seemed to be looking past me rather than at me. Then he started screaming and hitting at me again. I placed him on the ground, but he kept up with the hitting and kicking.

I didn't think too much about what I did next. I didn't want to keep coming to that yard, particularly if the kid was going to keep kicking me.

I went to knock on the front door. The boy followed me, still kicking the backs of my legs and screaming. A woman came to the door. She looked at me and at the kid kicking me.

'Jake? It's all right, Jake. Everything's all right.'

She spoke to him in a calm, loving voice, but she didn't bend down to him, she didn't hug him or try to comfort him in any other way. I found it weird. He was obviously distressed.

'How did you get in here?'

I chose not to answer her question. 'He fell from the tree. I caught him. It's the second time I've come over and caught him. He's climbing too high. You need to watch him.'

I waited for her to speak. For her to thank me. But she was just staring at me, trying to work out who I was, and then at her son who was still kicking at me. She appeared completely confused.

'He never thanks me, you know. He just kicks and screams at me.'

I was hoping pointing out that he didn't thank me might prompt some manners from her.

'He doesn't speak. Ever. Never has. And he doesn't like being touched. But he does love to climb trees.'

I looked at the boy, still kicking at me but with less force and regularity. His screaming had died down too. 'Okay, but he's still climbing too high. He needs watching.'

The woman gave a small nod. I watched her face moving between emotions. I started to feel bad for her. She was looking upset.

'I don't mind catching him. It's just that I've got school and work and other stuff going on. I don't know if I can always get here in time.'

'I didn't think being a parent would be like this. Some days I don't know what to do so I let him out into the yard, into the tree. It makes him happy.'

She actually did start to cry then. I turned to the boy and got down on my knees to look at him. He didn't try to hit me. I took it as a good sign.

'Hey, Jake.'

He became still. I don't know if it was me trying to talk to him or if he'd just run out of steam. I tried some more.

'You like climbing trees, Jake?'

Jake looked towards his mother and into the house behind her.

'Maybe just don't go so high. One day you might fall and I might not be here to catch you.'

Jake ran past his mother and into the house. Jake's mum was looking at me. She'd stopped crying and I could see the questions starting to form.

She was about to ask me how I'd known he was going to fall. Not once, but twice. She was about to ask me how I'd known to get here in time. How I got into the garden. I started to head for the front gate. I didn't want to answer those questions. I didn't know if I could answer those questions.

'I have to go now,' I called over my shoulder.

I thought about my family, who would be sitting down to dinner and wondering where I was. I opened the gate from the inside and closed it firmly behind me. Then I ran.

At home dinner was already on the table. Everyone watched me walk in and sit down. Mum and Meg looked disappointed in me. I could only assume Meg had told Mum about our Etienne conversation and they had analysed my reaction to run away as childish.

Dinner was quiet. I couldn't think of anything to say, and Mum and Meg kept exchanging glances like they were having a silent, private conversation about me. Dad was tired from his early morning ride and day at the shop, so he was pretty much just eating dinner and looking ready for bed. Mum started up a conversation with Meg about her first pregnancy appointment and then about some fantastic pram she'd seen in her lunchbreak.

'It's too soon for prams, Mum.'

Meg told Mum it was too soon for baby things most nights, but I knew, and Meg probably did too, that Mum was already buying stuff. Outfits and little blankets. She was hiding them in the back of her wardrobe where she'd hidden our birthday and Christmas presents since we were little.

I wondered if Rik's mum was also buying outfits and blankets, but from what Meg had told me it sounded like she was still looking for a wedding venue and a celebrant.

Dad and I did the after-dinner clean-up. Normally we'd just talk about bikes, about auctions he'd gone to or a vintage frame he'd seen online. But tonight he had a go at asking me about school. I assumed Mum had suggested it. It was not comfortable ground for Dad. But he tried.

'How's Year Eleven going then?'

'It's all right.'

Dad paused, as if there was more he was meant to ask me but for some reason had decided not to. He nodded like that was all the information he needed and we both worked silently for a while.

I was happy to have the silence. To have a chance to go back over catching Jake. I wasn't thinking about Jake or his mum, I was trying to remember how I knew to go, how I'd felt beforehand. Whether there was something I was missing that would help me to get to others further away.

Before Dad and I left the kitchen he motioned towards his backpack sitting in the corner. He pulled out a rear derailleur. New in the box, but old. It was exactly what he'd been searching for. The piece that would mean the bike we'd been working on could be completed.

I took it carefully out of the box to admire it. I told Dad it was too good to use and he nodded his agreement, though I knew he would. He'd want to finish the bike so he could sell it and put the money aside for Meg and the baby. He took the piece from me, replaced it in the box and put it back in his backpack, hidden from Mum. I was pretty sure Mum knew what we did in our spare time at the bike shop, but she probably had no idea how much Dad spent on antique bits and pieces and how many he had in the storeroom, just waiting for the right bike.

I gave Dad a goodnight kiss on the cheek and headed up to my room to work out some of the catching thoughts I'd had. I decided to try meditating. I heard Meg come in during my twenty minutes and sit on my bed. She didn't know meditating was a thing for me. Between her pregnancy and everything that was going on with me, our relationship had shifted – telling each other everything wasn't something we did anymore.

It must have been pretty obvious that I was meditating – I was sitting straight-backed in a corner of my room with my legs crossed and my open palms face-up on my knees. She didn't speak, so I decided to finish my session. I kept my focus. I held my mantra and my stillness and my breath and I sat out the full twenty minutes in the hope it would lead me to some kind of understanding about how I knew Jake was going to fall.

I had planned to write as soon as I finished. To write down everything I had remembered or was feeling up to the point where I knew I had to start running. But with Meg sitting there I couldn't. I opened my eyes and waited for her to speak.

'How long have you been meditating? Why are you meditating?'

'Lin suggested it. She thinks it will help me focus.'

It wasn't a lie. Meg probably assumed I meant to focus on schoolwork, but it still wasn't an outright lie.

'Okay. And why did you run off today like that? Was it because of what I said about Etienne?'

I shook my head. 'I just really had to go. I didn't think it would take so long, but I didn't have any other choice.'

'That doesn't make any sense, Beth.'

Meg didn't understand why I wasn't telling her more.

'There's something going on, that's all. Something I'm not ready to talk about yet. It doesn't have anything to do with Etienne. Or school.'

'So tell me.'

I shook my head again. 'I will. Just not yet.'

She sighed when I said that, like she didn't really believe anything I was saying. 'Are you okay?'

'Yeah, I'm okay.'

'I'm worried about you.'

I could have told her then. I could have talked through what I was trying to work out on my own. Maybe it would have helped. But I knew I wasn't ready. That like her waiting to tell Mum and Dad about her pregnancy, I needed to figure this out for myself a bit more.

'I'm fine.'

Meg didn't show any signs of preparing to leave my room. There was obviously more she wanted to say. I got up from my position on the floor and moved to my desk. I took out paper and a pen in the hope this would be a hint for her to leave, but Meg wasn't taking hints and she wasn't going to leave.

Meg started to talk about Etienne. About all the girls who'd liked him in the past. I was very aware of the girls who had liked Etienne. I'd heard the two of them talking about it after school for years. I'd heard Meg teasing Etienne. I'd heard girls talking about him at school. I knew how attractive girls found Etienne.

'In all the time I've known him, Etienne has never shown any interest in those girls. He's never shown any interest in any girls.'

'I always assumed he'd end up with you.'

Even though Meg shrugged off my words, I could tell by her face she knew people still assumed that.

'We've only ever been friends. We'll only ever be friends. I wouldn't be good for him. He needs someone quieter and calmer than me.'

She was probably trying to describe me, to make me feel better, but I wasn't sure that quiet or calm were good words to describe me now.

Meg got up to leave, but paused to ask if I wanted her to talk to Etienne. She could find out what he was thinking. I shook my head and then, unsure if that was enough, said, 'No, that's okay.'

I didn't want Meg to be involved in anything to do with Etienne and me. I wanted to keep it for myself.

Meg lingered at the door. 'I think Rik's going to ask me to marry him.'

She didn't sound happy.

'Do you want to marry him?'

'We agreed we wouldn't. We made a plan, and marriage wasn't part of it. He'll say it's because he really wants to but it's only because he wants to stop his mother nagging him about it.'

Then she sighed and left the room.

I felt sad watching her go. Meg had always been there, right beside me or in front. Shielding me from the things she knew I wasn't comfortable with. Now there was space between us. Parts of each other we couldn't share. Her pregnancy and my catching were pulling us apart.

I turned to my blank piece of paper and tried to think back over catching Jake and everything that happened before I started running. I wrote it all down. Anything I could think of. Not all of it was full sentences or even made sense, but I wrote it down as best I could.

I went to bed thinking I'd show what I'd written to Lin the next day and maybe she'd be able to make sense of it. Then I went to sleep and dreamt about Etienne falling out of a big tree in a locked yard as I stood there, waiting, wondering if I'd be able to catch him while Jake kicked me and hit me and his mum stood at the doorway crying a little and Meg and Mum called all the way from our house, 'Get back here for dinner,' and Dad rode past on his bike as fast as a blur, and Lin sat with her back against the trunk of the tree asking, 'But what are you feeling?'

TEN

WHEN the basketball teams were announced I didn't need to go look at the board. Kids started congratulating me as soon as I walked through the school gates. Kids I knew, kids I only kind of knew. A couple of kids I didn't know at all. I guess I was pleased. It was nice to have been picked, nice to have people come up and shake my hand or pat my shoulder. I went to look for myself just to see my name up on the mixed team list with Etienne's. I was listed in the girls' team too.

I checked the practice times, game times and the first meeting date, and wondered how I was going to manage both teams and schoolwork and working at the bike shop on top of the occasional catch.

I felt Etienne standing beside me before he spoke. I felt his warmth, the solidity of his body close to mine. He put his arm around my shoulders and squeezed a little. Like a side hug. He told me he knew I could do it, and I smiled at him. I told him I wouldn't have done it without his help, and maybe without him in Coach's ear. Etienne shook his head, denying he had anything to do with it.

I loved standing there with him in the school corridor with his arm around me, but I felt self-conscious too. We didn't normally talk much at school and we definitely didn't touch like this. I was embarrassed by the attention. By people looking at us as they walked past.

The bell rang for rollcall and I picked up my bag to head off. Etienne stopped me from leaving by grabbing my hand.

'Hey, how about we go see that new action movie this weekend? To celebrate?'

I saw the principal coming down the corridor towards us. I freed my hand by trying to make it look like I needed to adjust my bag.

'Great, sure, yeah.'

Etienne looked a bit confused by me pulling away.

'I'll come by your place on Saturday afternoon to get you?'

'I'm working at the shop. How about we meet at the cinema?'

He smiled at me then in a way that made my stomach flip and my feet sink a little into the floor. It was a smile that made it really hard to leave and get to class.

During rollcall I grabbed Lin. 'I'm going to need to leave the shop early on Saturday afternoon. Can you cover for me?'

Lin nodded. 'Fine, but you know I don't do any of that greasy stuff.'

I smiled at her gratefully. 'I wouldn't let you anyway.'

For everything that Lin is, a bike mechanic she is not.

I spent the rest of rollcall figuring out how I could avoid telling my family about the movie, and whether I could just pretend I was going to Lin's after work. I wanted to see how the date went before I suffered through Mum's questions and Dad's raised eyebrows.

The rest of the school week dragged by with the first basketball meeting as the only highlight. We didn't pick up a ball, but we did sit with Coach so he could run through how the teams and the season would work. I looked around at the people who were about to become my teammates.

Kids sat in their year groups. Not because Coach had asked us to, just because it was high school and that's what you did. Etienne was sitting with the Year Twelve boys and a couple of the Year Twelve girls I knew through Meg. I sat with the other Year Elevens. And then there were a few Year Tens who must be really good to make it into the senior team, but who looked even more out of place than I felt.

I stopped looking at the faces around me and tried to focus on what Coach was saying. Most of it was about making sure we made it to training or we'd jeopardise our places on the team. Coach went on to explain the structure of the season, but by then I was focused on Etienne – he looked so comfortable and happy to be with his friends. He saw me looking and smiled, like he was happy I was there too.

On Saturday the bike shop was quiet, so I showed Lin the bits and pieces I had written down about what I'd felt before I caught Jake last time. Reading my notes got Lin talking about her latest research.

She'd been reading about people who claimed to perform religious miracles or to be psychics or to have extra-sensory perception. She went through some of the stories where people, children sometimes, believed God had spoken to them and asked them to heal strangers. Other people insisted the dead could speak through them or that they could see into the future.

'I don't see anything. It's just a feeling about a place I need to go.'

'Extra-sensory perception also doesn't explain your strength or your ability to physically catch,' Lin pointed out.

Thinking about why I could catch, how that was possible, led me down a long, dark tunnel of confusion. I changed the subject.

'I've been thinking about telling Meg. I've never kept a secret from her for so long before.'

Lin nodded. 'What do you think she'd say?'

'No idea, but she knows something's going on.'

'Do you think she'd tell your mum?'

'Maybe.'

'And you're ready for that?'

'You don't think I should tell her?'

Lin shrugged. 'Maybe just give it a bit more time. Maybe it will go away as suddenly as it started.'

I agreed to give it more time. To see what would happen. It was a relief, really. I wasn't ready and I couldn't imagine the reaction of any of my family being anything but bad.

When it was time for me to leave, Lin hugged me because she could tell I was really nervous – and it made it worse. Bigger somehow.

Etienne had messaged me the details of when and where to meet him at the cinema, and I read them again to make sure I was going to the right place at the right time. Lin and I had talked through whether it would be just us or whether he'd invited friends along. We'd decided that it would most likely be just the two of us, but as I walked to the cinema I became unsure. Etienne's friends were Meg's friends, so I knew them, but it would be weird to go to a movie with them and Etienne. Especially without Meg.

Just before I reached the cinema I texted Meg and told her where I was going. I figured she could tell Mum if she wanted to, and then I could manage their questions after the movie was over.

At the cinema I couldn't see Etienne anywhere, and was starting to feel a little sick. I told myself it was just nerves or fear that this was all some kind of joke.

When I saw Etienne walking towards me with two tickets in his hand, on his own, beaming and saying, 'My treat,' I started to feel better. But that feeling of nausea didn't go away. It just moved a little to the background.

Etienne gently took my hand and led me towards the snack bar. He made it seem so natural and normal, but we'd never held hands like that. I tried to act as if it was no big deal, but it was. It was such a big deal. I looked at him and there he was. That new Etienne. The one who could be mine.

Etienne asked me if I wanted popcorn, but I shook my head and told him I'd go to the toilet before the movie started.

Etienne gave me my ticket. 'I'll go find us some seats.'

In the bathroom I splashed water on my face and tried to shake myself out of the sickness. I wet the back of my neck. I looked in the mirror, and tried to breathe through the way I was feeling. Telling myself it was nothing, just nerves.

When I found Etienne in the cinema, he smiled up at me from his seat. I felt so sorry I couldn't fully enjoy that moment. I tried. I really did. I pushed the nausea back down as far as I could. When I sat down and he took my hand again, I hoped the pleasure of being so close to him would take the sickness away.

Etienne looked down at our clasped hands, then into my eyes.

'Is this okay?'

I wondered if he could see the nausea on my face. 'Yep, yes.' I tried to speak in a natural voice.

Etienne moved towards me in a way that made me think he might be about to kiss me, but the movie started and we both settled back to watch, our hands still entwined.

I felt Etienne relax beside me and I tried to do the same, but I couldn't. As the lights dimmed I got more tense. The sickness grew and changed and became something more urgent. I tried to concentrate on the movie, to relax into the chair, to enjoy the warmth of Etienne's hand in mine, until I just knew I had to leave.

I took my hand from Etienne's. He turned to look at me as I got up quickly. I whispered, 'I'm sorry, I'm really sorry. I've just got to . . .' and then I ran.

I ran out of the cinema and down the street. I ran faster than I'd ever run in my life. I had no idea where I was going, I just trusted my feet and that urgent feeling of being pulled. I ended up running down a lane, then stopped suddenly in front of a large apartment block. I felt grateful that the running had stopped. That it wasn't too far from the cinema. I settled my feet into the ground and rolled my shoulders back.

I looked up to see what was coming my way and braced myself for the weight about to hit my arms. At the last moment, I closed my eyes. I had seen the person falling. I knew who it was before they reached my arms. I didn't ever think of leaving, of walking away from the catch. It wasn't like that. But I thought, *This is going to make school more complicated* as Rohan fell into my arms.

Rohan was so shocked to see me, and so amazed. He couldn't stop talking, and even though I knew everything he was telling me, I let him tell me anyway. It gave me time to catch my breath and think about how I was going to explain myself to him.

He told me that he had jumped. That he hadn't thought he would, but then he did, and he knew beforehand it was a stupid thing to do but he did it anyway, and when it was too late to change his mind he knew, really knew, he'd made a big mistake.

I placed him firmly on the footpath and he looked at his feet like he couldn't believe they were his, safe on the ground. Then he hugged me, really hugged me. I hugged him back because I felt so sad that he'd jumped and so pleased I was there to catch him when he did.

As we hugged I looked around over his shoulder. I had become conscious there could be people who had seen us. But no one had stopped to stare. No one, that is, except Etienne, who was standing at the end of the lane watching me hug Rohan.

I wondered how long he had been standing there. How much had he seen?

Etienne's eyes locked with mine and I saw something I couldn't read. I tried to escape Rohan's grasp to go to him. I didn't know what I was going to say. I wasn't ready to tell Etienne about catching. If he hadn't seen me catch and had just arrived in time to see me hugging Rohan, I didn't know how I was going to explain that either.

Rohan started crying and holding me tighter. It made it impossible to leave him, and I guess I didn't try that hard to go to Etienne because I was scared of what he might say when I got there. Of what he might be thinking. Of what I would have to tell him.

Etienne turned and disappeared around the corner. I hugged Rohan back once Etienne was gone because I needed a bit of holding too. When Rohan had finished crying, he invited me up to his apartment. He pleaded with me when it looked like I was going to say no.

'I'm not ready to be alone, and my mum won't be home for a while.'

Rohan's apartment was small, but even with its limited size it still looked empty. It wouldn't have taken much to fill it, but they had even less than that. Rohan made me a cup of tea and found a packet of biscuits that he opened and put on the bench between us.

I felt it was better I didn't know too much about Rohan. I thought school was already going to be weird enough, but Rohan said he needed to explain why he jumped.

I shook my head. 'No, you don't need to explain anything, I'm just glad you're okay.'

'We ran away from my dad. Mum and I. In the middle of the night. We had to.'

Rohan turned the biscuit in his hands.

'Last night, Mum said we would have to move again. She thinks he's found us, but I don't want to move again. And I'm sick of being scared. It just made sense there for a minute that if I wasn't around it would be easier for Mum to keep running. Or maybe if I wasn't around Dad would think that was punishment enough and stop trying to find her. Then Mum could get a proper job and live a proper life.'

Rohan was still staring at his biscuit. He looked up at me. I was shoving another biscuit in my mouth. I'd already eaten half the packet.

'I know it was a stupid thing to do. It just all got too much.'

I nodded with my mouth full. Everyone knows what too much feels like sometimes.

I walked home slowly. At first I was thinking about Rohan and his mum. About how hard it had been for them and how Rohan seemed so confident in Food Tech. You couldn't tell what was going on for people by the way they acted on the surface.

Then I started thinking about Etienne. It was pretty hard for me to think about Etienne. It hurt. I remembered how he'd held my hand. How it felt to have his hand in mine. How good that moment would have been if I hadn't felt so sick. Almost perfect.

Then I worried. I worried that he might have seen me catch Rohan, that he would tell people. I worried he was never going to speak to me again because I was some kind of weird freak.

I worried about Rohan, too. About whether he was going to be okay. About whether he was going to tell people at school I'd caught him. We hadn't got around to discussing that.

Meg and Mum were waiting for me at home. They looked at me expectantly, wanting to hear how the movie was. I walked straight through the lounge room where they were sitting, snacks ready, eyes trained on my face looking for traces of I don't know what. Kissing, probably. I said, 'I don't want to talk about it,' as I walked past them. I went straight up to my room and lay face-down on my bed.

I knew it wouldn't work. Even as I was walking through the lounge room I knew it wouldn't work, but I was thankful only Meg knocked on my door. At least I had halved the interrogation team. I didn't lift my head to look at her. I just repeated what I'd said downstairs.

'I don't want to talk about it.'

Meg rubbed my back a little. 'That bad?'

I nodded into my pillow. 'It really was.'

Meg wanted to know why, what Etienne had done, but I shook my head. I told her he didn't do anything. That it was just bad, and that I wanted to be left alone.

She walked quietly out of the room and shut the door. She'd probably call Etienne to ask him what happened. There was nothing I could do about that. I imagined Etienne telling Meg what he'd seen, what I'd done, and then her storming back into the room and demanding to know what was going on with me.

She didn't. No one else bothered me for the rest of the night. I ended up lying on my bed, fully clothed, moving between moments of sleep and being fully awake until morning when I crawled into my pyjamas and spent the entire day in bed, eating just enough to stop Mum from having a panic attack.

I had no idea how I was going to face school on Monday.

ELEVEN

I left the house early on Monday morning to avoid having to walk to school with Meg and Etienne. Lin had been messaging all Sunday, but I'd only managed to give her a brief rundown. *Disaster. Had to leave to catch. I think he SAW! Can't talk.* I knew she would be desperate for details, but I couldn't bring myself to say any of it aloud right then. It was like if I said it, then it had really happened, which was stupid because obviously it had really happened.

When I walked into Food Tech and took my usual seat, Rohan wasn't there. I thought about sitting somewhere else, but that would bring on a whole thing about taking someone else's seat. We were about halfway through term and the seats in classes were all pretty set.

Rohan slipped in beside me just as Mr Wong started talking. At first it was really hard. We were both sneaking looks at each other. Each of us trying to look without looking like we were looking. Each of us catching the other and then looking away. Eventually Rohan leant in towards me and whispered, 'I have a million questions, but I promise I won't tell if you don't.'

I nodded in agreement. 'Deal.'

Then we smiled at each other and I felt relieved to have one less thing to worry about.

In class we were all tested on our knife skills. I'd never been an expert in the kitchen, but I knew how to use a knife thanks to Mum making Meg and me cook dinner on a regular basis. Rohan, on the other hand, was some kind of kitchen genius. I watched him chop a carrot into perfect discs, the blade flashing in front of the teacher. It made Mr Wong nervous, but Rohan was confident and precise. The rest of the class stopped what they were doing to watch. Rohan shrugged it off like it was no big deal.

He told me later he watched a lot of cooking shows with his mum. That they'd always found cooking together a relaxing thing to do. I told him he was on cutting duty for the rest of the year and he smiled at me as if I'd given him a present.

At the end of the class I asked Rohan to come and find me at lunchtime. I told him my friend Lin wanted to meet him. I didn't mention I'd noticed him eating lunch alone each day. How I'd watched him and thought about inviting him over but had never actually got around to it. I tried to ask him as if it had just occurred to me it would be a good idea.

At lunch I turned up to find Rohan and Lin already in deep conversation as though they'd been friends for years. Lin was getting Rohan to run through his list of teachers for her. I watched Rohan answering Lin's questions and I wondered if he was thinking he might not be at the school long so it didn't matter, but if that's what he was thinking he wasn't showing it. Instead, he was listening intently to her, nodding as she told him what she knew about his teachers.

I looked over and saw Etienne sitting by himself at a table. It was a rare opportunity to speak to him alone. I quickly got up and walked over before I could change my mind. He was in his school uniform like everyone else, but Etienne no longer looked like a schoolkid. His broad shoulders filled his school shirt, making the material stretch tight across his back when he moved. I could have stood there and looked at him all day. Even just at the back of his head.

When I got close enough I said, 'Etienne?'

He looked up and then quickly away.

I tried again. 'I'm not sure what you saw or what you think . . .'

He looked at me briefly and then over to where I had come from.

'I saw you run out of the cinema and when I followed you to make sure you were all right I found you hugging someone in a lane.' He nodded his head at Lin and Rohan. 'Hugging that guy.'

I opened my mouth, but I hadn't thought it through and didn't know what to say. I was relieved he didn't see me catch, but amazed he could think I'd choose Rohan over him. That he would even worry about that. Before I could say anything else, Etienne said, 'It's fine, Beth, don't worry about it.'

I wanted to say, *I'm sorry*. I wanted to say, *I wish I could tell you why I left, I wish I could explain it to you, but I just can't right now.*

I tried again. 'Etienne—'

'Can you please just go?' he said quietly, almost under his breath.

I looked up and saw that Meg and a couple of their other friends were sliding into the seats around him. Meg looked from Etienne to me. I glanced at her face, then quickly back at Etienne, then left. If Meg got a proper look at me she'd see I was about to cry – and I couldn't cry at school. Not here, not out in the open.

I walked back to Lin and Rohan, who had finished talking about teachers and moved on to what they wanted to do after they left school.

'Okay?' Lin said with concern in her voice.

I nodded. 'Yeah sure, fine.'

They went back to their conversation. Rohan was telling Lin that his mother worked in finance as a contractor, that they often had to move because of her work. He looked at me, checking to see if I was going to call out his lie. I pulled my lunch out of my bag and focused on the contents of my sandwich. Not only because I didn't want my face to give Rohan's lie away, but also because I was still trying not to cry.

Rohan asked Lin what subjects she was doing, and when she listed them all he joked that she was studying to be a doctor.

'I do want to be a doctor.'

'Oh. Sorry.' Rohan looked embarrassed.

'It's fine. I mean, I know it's a cliché that the Asian girl with doctor parents wants to be a doctor, but it's what I want to do. What I've always wanted to do. My parents are happy, of course, but they didn't pressure me. They wouldn't really care what I did.'

'What sort of medicine are you interested in?'

'I always thought some kind of surgeon, but lately I've been thinking about psychiatry.'

I'd been keeping my head down, half-listening to their conversation, half-trying to breathe back the tears, fully trying to get Etienne's face and voice out of my head as he asked me to leave him alone. Trying to take small bites of my sandwich and then trying to swallow them. But when Lin brought up psychiatry I looked at her. She'd never mentioned that to me before.

She caught my eye and shrugged a little. 'Just something I've been thinking about.'

I'd been confident Lin was on my side. That she believed me and was working with me. I'd never questioned her. She acted like she believed me. Right from the start, she'd acted like everything I said was true. I started to wonder what she really thought and why she was asking me to write down everything I felt.

Lin caught my look and shook her head at me, as if she knew what I was thinking and was telling me silently it wasn't true. She turned back to Rohan and explained further to him, but I understood that this bit was for me.

'I've started to get really interested in how the mind works, in what it might be capable of.'

It was meant to be a statement of support. She was trying to tell me she believed me. That she believed in me. But I could read Lin too, just the way she could read me, and I wasn't convinced.

'You think there's something wrong with me. You think it's all in my head.'

'Beth.'

'That's why you don't want me to tell anyone.'

'Beth . . .'

Lin was pointing at Rohan. She didn't want me to reveal my secret in front of him.

'I caught Rohan. Tell her, Rohan. Tell her I caught you. That I'm not her first psychiatric patient.'

I was standing up now. Ready to walk away.

Rohan beat me to it. He gathered his things and quickly left without looking at either of us.

Lin looked at me. 'Beth.'

I don't know if she said anything after that. I'd walked away too.

I struggled through the rest of the day, sometimes thinking about Rohan and Lin and at other times Etienne. I felt bad about telling Lin I'd caught Rohan when I'd said I wouldn't. I felt angry at Lin and convinced myself that she didn't believe me. That she thought everything I'd told her was a delusion I'd created for myself. And then Etienne. I had no idea what he was thinking or how I could make that situation better.

At home I went straight to my room and lay on my bed. I refused dinner. Refused conversation. I knew they were worried by the way they were leaving me alone and Mum wasn't asking any questions, but there was nothing I could do about that. I lay in my room as the day darkened to night and let my misery wash over me in unrelenting waves. I lay there fully dressed. Too miserable to change. I ended up half sleeping, half dreaming.

It took a while to realise I wasn't thinking about myself anymore. That the waves of feeling coming over me were not waves of my own embarrassment or misery. These waves were other people's pain. Maybe just one other person's pain. I felt it over and over. It was pain and fear and misery, deep, deep misery, far deeper than my own. I started to feel the sickness strengthen in me. I wanted to run.

When I left my bed, when I was out on the street, I had no idea which way to go. I couldn't make a decision. There was an urgency telling me to run, but nothing to tell me the direction. I started spinning in a circle, like a dog trying to pick up a scent who ends up chasing its own tail. I could feel everything. Pain and fear and desperation. It was coming at me, and I knew in those feelings there was someone I could catch. I just didn't know how to sift through. I didn't know how to find that one thread to follow in the tangled ball of pain.

I started to run. Not because I'd figured out a direction but just so I was doing something. I ran towards Jake's house even though I knew it was ridiculous, wrong. It wasn't the boy. I turned down random streets, streets I didn't know. Streets that maybe would be familiar in the daytime but now seemed foreign and strange.

Every now and then I stopped running to catch my breath and try to make sense of what I was feeling. I tried to close my eyes and feel which way to go, but eyes open or closed didn't make a difference. Only breathing helped. Somehow breathing deeply gave the pain and nausea a direction. I focused on my breath. Then I ran. That was the pattern. Run. Stop. Breathe. Run.

I ended up on the outskirts of the city at a tall apartment building. I knew I'd arrived, but I was scared. It was late. The streets were dark and empty. The building I was standing in front of was tall. Really tall. I'd never caught someone from so high. I'd never been in the city on my own at night, either.

I looked around. The only movement I could hear was a few cars on a nearby road. I looked up. I sank my feet into the ground, making my legs feel solid beneath me. Then I focused on breathing.

It took some time for her to reach me. Maybe not for her, but for me it took some time. I saw her falling. I saw how high she'd come from and I watched her as she slowly came towards me. It wasn't as easy as the others. She gasped as she landed. Gasped and struggled. When I put her on her feet, as carefully as I could given the way she was struggling, she stumbled before straightening up and looking me in the eye. Then she slapped me across the face.

To be honest I felt a bit like slapping her back. I didn't though, because after she slapped me she burst into tears. I put my arms around her. She didn't hug me back the way Rohan had. She let me hold her a little, then pushed me away and ran back towards the building.

I dashed after her and reached out to grab her arm. To stop her.

'You can't go back up there.'

She stared at me. I readied myself for another slap.

'He pushed you, he wanted to kill you. You can't go back up there.'

I didn't know where these words were coming from, but I knew I was right. I knew by the way she looked at me. By the way she nodded.

'Do you have somewhere else to go?' I asked.

She nodded again. I let go of her arm and watched her walk away. I didn't know if I should follow her. If I should take her to the police or the hospital. If I should take her home with me. So I just stood and watched her walk away.

I stood there until I couldn't see the woman anymore. Until it was just me, alone, on a dark street in the city.

I stood for longer than I should have. When I turned to start walking back towards home, I noticed the nausea returning in waves, bringing the pain and misery I'd been feeling earlier with it. They had stopped while I was focused on catching, but now they were back. Weaker than before, but back. I tried to breathe through the mess again. I tried to work out if she had gone back up. If she was going to fall again.

And then I started running, because I'd found something else and it wasn't her. It wasn't there. I ran and stopped and took a breath and tried to work out where it was coming from. I made my way towards home in a roundabout way, searching through the sickness that kept hitting me, surrounding me, fading and then returning. I couldn't find where to go. Even when I stopped to focus, to breathe, I couldn't find a solid direction.

It was getting light by the time I was close enough to home to give up. I let myself into the house and crept up to bed.

I didn't sleep. I lay there trying to focus on my breath, trying to calm my mind and sort out everything that had happened and everything I was still feeling.

TWELVE

I didn't go to school the next morning. I told Mum I hadn't slept and that I felt sick. She gave in pretty quickly, so I guess I looked as bad as I felt.

I turned my face away when Meg came in to check on me before she left. I knew she would assume it was all about Etienne, and I couldn't tell her about my night. About running through the dark streets. About the nausea that was starting to feel strong and constant. It seemed easier to let Meg think it was Etienne than to try to explain everything else.

I spent the day in bed, searching for feelings that weren't my own. I tried to breathe through them when I found something. I tried to make sense of it.

Lin came over after school. She said she was checking to see if I was alright, that she was worried about me. I looked up at my bedroom ceiling as if what I needed to tell her was written there.

I hadn't forgotten our lunchtime conversation. I wanted to ask Lin more. I wanted to know whether she really believed me or thought there really was something wrong with me. I wanted to know if Rohan was okay.

Instead, I told her about my night.

'I opened something.'

I looked at her to see her reaction. She leaned forward, maybe to study me, or maybe because I was speaking quietly. I raised my voice a little.

'I don't know what it is or how I opened it, but I feel sick all the time now. Waves of sickness that isn't mine. It's like a pain. Other people's pain. At least I'm not thinking about Etienne anymore – well, I am, but it's not so bad. Not compared to other people's pain.'

I sat up on my bed so I could look at her, wanting to see her reaction. 'I don't know what I'm meant to do with it.'

Lin didn't really react. She just watched me closely. I lay back and closed my eyes, but now that I'd started talking I didn't want to stop.

'Can you see it? Can you see people's pain swirling around me?'

Lin sat near me on the bed. She reached out to hold my hand and put her other hand on my shoulder like she was trying to make sure I understood she was really there with me. But I had lost sight of her now. I was focused on the pain. Even though it was faint, I could see it swirling in front of me.

I closed my eyes. 'Who are they, Lin? Why are they in so much pain?'

When I opened my eyes again I saw Lin was crying. There were tears rolling down her cheeks.

I guess she thinks I've really lost it now.

I stayed home for the rest of the week. Everyone else in my family went to work or school, but I lay on my bed or sat at my window.

From the window I could see Etienne leave his house in the mornings and come to ours. I watched as he and Meg walked down the street, towards our school, and I wondered what they were talking about. If Etienne ever asked Meg about me.

In the afternoons I watched him come home. The time he arrived changed every day depending on whether he had study or basketball training that kept him at school later. I worried it was friends, girls, who were making him arrive home late. At night I watched the light in his room. I imagined him sitting at a desk with books around him, his pen in his hand, his laptop in front of him.

Lin called or texted me every day. I didn't answer the calls, but I read the texts. At first they were questions about me. *How are you feeling? Do you feel any better? Are you okay?*

I drafted long texts about everything I was feeling. Every thought that was running through my head. Then I deleted them and replied with a word or two that let her know I was okay but still not really okay.

As the week went on Lin changed tack and started to ask different questions. She was trying to draw me away from wherever I was. She told me about her shift at work, about the bikes that had come in. She asked me questions about where things were in the shop. The last message she sent me was a picture of a bike in disarray. I knew she was hoping to annoy me into coming to work, but I felt stuck in a place I couldn't leave.

When I lay on my bed everything I had started to feel became stronger. My head spun with the nausea, but I wanted to feel it. I wanted to understand it. I wanted to find the people within it. I lay there searching through my sickness for someone, something to run for.

At night I took to running through the streets anyway. I would wait until everyone was asleep and then I'd creep out. It was frightening being on the dark streets on my own, but it was better than lying in my bed searching through other people's pain.

One night I ran back to where I'd caught the woman who slapped me. I stood alone on the dark street, fighting my fear. I looked up at the balcony she had fallen from, wondering if she'd gone back to him. If she was safe.

I would come home in the early hours of the morning without catching anyone. Creep back up the stairs hoping the running had tired me out and I'd be able to sleep.

By Saturday morning Mum started to talk about taking me to the doctor if I didn't get out of bed and go back to school on Monday. I didn't want to sit in a doctor's surgery explaining everything I could feel and how those feelings weren't mine. They'd probably send me straight to a psychiatric ward. I decided I was going to act as if the nausea wasn't there. Like Meg had in those first few weeks before she told anyone she was pregnant.

I went to work in the bike shop as I normally would. I didn't update Lin about what I was feeling. Mostly because Dad was in the shop with us, but also because it was part of my act-normal plan. I could see Lin looking at me strangely now and then. Like she had a question she was just about to ask.

When I sat with my family for dinner I forced myself to eat in spite of the sickness I felt. I tried to go to bed at a normal time. By then I was so tired I even managed to fall asleep for a bit. I still crept out just after midnight, but I put a time limit on it. I gave myself a couple of hours to search.

The time limit did more than keep me from getting too tired. It allowed me to find a thread, something to follow. I didn't know if it was the pressure of not having much time or if I was just getting better at it after a week of trying, but I managed to find a thread. A single thread of someone else's pain that I followed in the hope of finding a person at the other end.

It didn't work. I didn't get to the end. I didn't find a catch. It was hard to stop at the time limit, but I'd run out of thread anyway and had started to feel confused. Lost.

I tried again on Sunday night, still with a time limit. But even though I found a thread again I didn't find anyone to catch within the two hours I'd set myself.

On Monday I went back to school and tried to focus on my classes. I tried to block out any other feeling. I searched out Rohan and apologised for spilling his secret to Lin.

Rohan nodded. 'Well, you did save my life.'

'It's all been so weird.'

'For you and me both.'

'Maybe I just need some more time. I'm sorry though.'

'At least it was only Lin, right?'

I managed to stay in class and block out everything else until lunchtime, when I didn't want to resist any longer. I wanted to feel those things. I wanted to see what I could find in them. By the time the bell rang for the end of lunch I felt like I had found a thread worth following. I walked out of the school gates, then broke into a run.

I caught a girl from another nearby school. She jumped from the tallest building she could find because she didn't think she was good enough, because she would never be good enough, and she was sure this was the only way out. She cried in my arms for so long I started to feel embarrassed. I saw her on the street a few days later, in her school uniform, with her friends. She caught my eye and looked away.

I left school the next day to catch Jake, the wordless boy who kept falling from the tree in his front yard. This time the gate was ajar. I didn't know if it was just a coincidence or if Jake or his mother was unlocking the gate for me now. If I had become a game to him or a safety net for his mother. When Jake fell I couldn't read him like I could the others. I didn't know if he felt fear as he was falling or relief when I was there to catch him.

Basketball training became the best and hardest part of my week. I had missed the first week of training, but once I got back to school I tried really hard to be there for practice. At basketball training Etienne couldn't ignore me. When we crossed paths on our street or in the school corridors I saw him look the other way. He'd change direction to avoid walking near me. It hurt every time.

In basketball he had to see me. He had to throw the ball to me if I was his best option. It was all I had come up with so far to try to repair the damage I'd caused between us.

Basketball was easier for me to concentrate on than Biology or English. I still didn't fully understand the rules of the game and the drills we did were constantly changing so I often felt lost in training, but I wanted to be good at it. I wanted Etienne to see me as an important part of the team.

I started to feel as if I was getting everything under control. I was improving at basketball, I was managing to get to a couple of catches during the day or in my night-time time limit, and my school absences seemed to be going unnoticed. Then in training one day I felt so sick I had to stop halfway through a drill with the ball in my hands. I dropped the ball, shouted to Coach that I had to go, and ran.

I saw Etienne note my departure. I saw his disappointment in me, but I couldn't not go. I couldn't not try.

Even though I ran in circles without finding anyone to catch until the nausea went away, I couldn't bear to think of the consequences if I could have found someone and had chosen not to go.

THIRTEEN

I was in Food Tech watching Rohan cook when I had to leave so fast I didn't have time to say anything to anyone. I ran out of the school gates and down the road. I didn't need to go far, but I knew I had to hurry.

When I got there I saw an old woman falling from a ladder. I only just made it. The woman laughed, but I had felt what was about to happen and I couldn't laugh with her. When I put her on her feet, she patted me on the arm. I could tell she was about to go back up that ladder as soon as I turned away, so I went up the ladder for her. She told me she wanted to clear her gutters before the winter rain set in. I looked up at the clear blue sky and thought about my schoolbag sitting in Food Tech, obvious without me. I cleared her gutters as quickly as I could.

The old woman offered me tea and cake when I finished. I took the cake but refused the tea. I thought about it. I thought about sitting with her and telling her about running through streets at night or sitting at my window and watching Etienne's light turn off at ten-thirty. About how one night it had stayed on until midnight and how I thought about that all the time.

As I walked back into the school I was spotted by Ms Bhat, my rollcall teacher, who questioned where I'd been. Peter, the general assistant, was nearby. He came up to us.

'Beth was out doing something for me.'

Ms Bhat looked confused, unsure – it was weird for a student to be doing anything for Peter. She accepted it or at least decided not to make a big deal out of it. As she walked away I looked to thank Peter, but he brushed off my thanks.

'I don't want to know where you've been or what you've been doing – just try not to get caught leaving school again.'

After school I had basketball practice. Our first game was still weeks away but Coach was putting pressure on us. Winning was personal for him, not just a job like it probably was for some of the other teachers.

I hated being so close to Etienne and not be able to talk to him like I used to. I turned my focus to the ball, to what Coach was saying. If I did well in basketball, maybe Etienne would forget about the disastrous movie date. Maybe we could go back and start again.

I focused on the ball, the drills and the people around me. I pushed myself to be the one out in front. To be the fastest in the team. I could do that when I tried. It was almost easy. I didn't know if it was part of my ability to catch or if it was because of all the night running I'd been doing.

Coach kept us moving through drills where we worked together in small groups, passing the ball to one another or shooting hoops. Sometimes Etienne ended up in the group I was in, but more often than not he was on the other side of the court, nodding and encouraging teammates but not smiling like they were.

Towards the end of training Coach split us into two teams and we played a short game against each other. Coach positioned me in the centre of the court. He explained that my role in the game was to get the ball towards our end, to other players who would shoot. Etienne was in the other team and took his position near their end without being told.

The game was fast and competitive. Different to our training sessions. I lost track of the score, but it seemed fairly even and each team was getting more and more competitive as Coach egged us on, telling us that time was running out. I was feeling focused and strong when the ball came my way. I grabbed it and tried to dribble it down to our end of the court as Tommy moved quickly towards me.

I wasn't really sure about Tommy. He still treated me like a junior player. Someone not worth passing the ball to in drills. This time he was on the opposite team. I didn't have to wait for him to pass the ball my way. I just had to get away from him.

Tommy took the ball from me anyway, with a roughness that made me fall hard to the ground. Coach blew the whistle, so I guessed he didn't do it legally.

I caught my breath and looked across the court. Etienne was watching me from his position. He took a step towards me and then stopped. A hand reached down to help me up and I grabbed it gratefully, only to stand up and realise that it was Tommy's hand. That I was standing face to face with the person who had knocked me down.

'Sorry about that, Beth. Thought those big feet of yours would keep you more steady.'

He was smiling, teasing me. Coach declared the ball to be mine, and instead of throwing the ball over Tommy to get away from him I decided to run at him. I dribbled the ball a couple of times and knocked him with my shoulder as I passed. Running the ball to our end of the court before Tommy had a chance to catch up to me, I passed quickly to Maye who shot for goal. It went through and my team rushed to congratulate us.

I looked over their heads and saw Etienne smiling at me. I smiled back. Then he must have remembered he hated me, because he turned quickly away.

At home I walked straight to my room and lay on my bed, thinking about the schoolwork I had to get through. I knew it was there, that there were things I needed to get done, but I always told myself I was too tired, that I would do it another day when I'd had more sleep or when I wasn't so exhausted from training. It was starting to pile up.

Meg came into my room. I had been thinking about how and when to tell her about catching. Mum and Dad as well, but mostly Meg. I'd never kept anything this big from her for this long before. It felt bad.

I could see that she missed Etienne being over all the time, too. They still met in the street to walk to school, but he didn't come in after school like he used to, and when I saw them together it was different. Some of the jokiness, that closeness they'd always had seemed to have disappeared. I felt bad about that too.

And then there was her pregnancy. Her belly was noticeable now. She rubbed it all the time without even realising she was doing it. I saw it as her letting the world know that she had bigger things on her mind these days. Rik had told her that his mother had given up on the idea of them getting married. Now Mari was just pretending the baby wasn't happening at all.

Meg sat in my chair and I waited for her to speak.

'Etienne says you've been leaving school and skipping basketball practice in the middle of training.'

I didn't say anything. I was torn between feeling pleased that Etienne might be worried about me and feeling annoyed that Etienne had told Meg I'd run out on training.

'What's going on, Beth?'

I still wasn't ready to tell her. I didn't want her to tell Mum and Dad. I didn't want to be dragged to doctors and told I there was something wrong with me. 'How are you feeling? Are you still tired? I haven't heard you being sick in the mornings lately.'

'It's not so bad now. Are you going to tell me what's going on?'

'Not yet.'

'When?'

'Soon.'

'Are you in some kind of trouble?'

'No. I don't think so. It's just . . .'

'What, Beth? Why can't you tell me?'

'I will, I promise. Just not now. Not tonight. I'm too tired.'

This was true, but it was also unlikely that I'd sleep. Meg let my silence sit between us a bit longer and then left me alone.

I waited until the house was quiet, until I was sure everyone was asleep, and then I sifted through what I was feeling to see if there was anyone I could catch.

At first I found nothing. There was no urgency that had me rushing down the stairs and sneaking out the front door. I drifted in and out of sleep as I waited, occasionally waking with a start, but when I sifted through again I still couldn't find anything to run for.

It was about two in the morning when I felt it. It was so strong it made me leap from my bed and pound down the stairs before I remembered to be quiet. My pockets were already packed with everything I needed. Keys, phone, a bit of money and a whistle. The whistle was Lin's idea. Something she thought would make it safer for me on the dark streets. She'd also suggested a hat or a mask, but that wasn't something I felt I needed.

I still wasn't used to running through empty streets at night. Sometimes it was okay, and I could forget my fear and enjoy the quiet and the coolness of the night air, but most of the time I was just running, frightened of what might be around the corner and trying to focus on getting to where I thought I needed to be. Most of the time there was something in the back of my mind telling me I shouldn't be out there and that I was likely to get into trouble at any moment.

I ran as hard as I could. My legs still felt tired from training, but I knew they could carry me to where I needed to go. I stopped to catch my breath and get my bearings, shaking my legs out and stretching my quads. Stopping was more frightening than running, but I needed to breathe and I needed to work out which direction to go in.

I started running again, a little slower now. Going slower helped with finding my direction. I thought it was all right. I thought I had time. Then I started to feel uneasy. I thought I was imagining it when I heard the steps behind me. I'd been worried about it for so long it was hard to believe it was really happening. I glanced behind me and picked up my speed.

And then he was there. Running along beside me.

I looked at him and he caught my look. He gave me a big smile. I tried to act like it was no big deal and ran even faster.

'What's the big hurry? How about we stop and talk for a while?'

His voice was calm, but there was a hardness beneath it. I didn't like the way he was trying to sound all friendly and nice. I didn't like his face. I was taller than him, but he looked solid. I didn't want to test my strength against his.

He put a hand on my arm and gripped it. I shook him off and turned down a different street. It wasn't the right way, but I thought there was a chance of more people around. A car at least. It would only add a block or two.

He kept pace with me and grabbed at me again. 'What's the problem? I don't bite.'

I shoved him away from me, and he fell towards the gutter and lost his footing. I didn't look back. I heard him shout after me.

'Bitch!'

I kept running. My feet pounding, my heart pounding.

I tried to shake off the fear, because I was close now. I put everything I had into getting there. I pushed and I pushed. I had just got to the corner. I thought I was there, that I'd made it.

I heard the thump on the ground. I heard the weight of the impact. I heard breaking.

The pain, the sound, it made me sink to my knees. I was too late. I couldn't approach the shape on the ground. I couldn't get close. I knew she was gone.

I pulled out my phone and called triple zero. They asked me questions I couldn't answer. I said, 'Just come,' and they told me an ambulance was on the way. They asked me to confirm my location and I had to look around for street signs. They asked me to approach the body, to check if there was life, and I whispered into the phone, 'No, please, please don't make me do that.'

I wanted to leave. I wanted to go home. I wanted to lie down between my sheets and feel the safety, the familiarity of my room and my life in that house. But I couldn't. I couldn't leave her alone.

I stayed on the ground at the corner of the building, just on the other side where I wasn't able to see her but was still near. I went over her last moments. Moments I knew, but had been too busy running, too busy fighting that stupid man, to really understand. I knew her despair, her feelings of hopelessness and fear. Her absolute resolve and her immediate regret. I apologised to her. Over and over in my head, I apologised for not being fast enough.

The ambulance arrived with a police car right behind it. The lights were flashing, but the sirens were off. I rose when I saw them and moved towards the road to direct them to her body. The ambulance officers ran to check her. One of the police went with them.

The other stayed with me. He looked quite young for a police officer and was shorter than me. It was still strange to meet adults who were shorter than me. I guessed he was there to make sure I didn't run. It occurred to me then that I could be in trouble. That it was suspicious for a teenager to be out at this time of night.

The second police officer joined us. I saw the young one in front of me look to her, asking a silent question she answered with a small shake of her head. She was older. His height. Solid. She looked like someone who could hurt you or hug you depending on the situation.

I tried not to look too scared. Too guilty.

She started to ask me questions. 'Did you know her? What are you doing here? What did you see? Did you see anyone else?'

'I was out jogging. I was running past and I saw her fall, heard it. I didn't know her.'

She looked a little confused, but not suspicious. I guessed police had to deal with weird teenager stuff all the time.

'Where do you live?'

I told her my address.

'Okay. Get in the car. We'll get you home.'

In the car they acted like I wasn't there. She guided me into the back seat and then got into the front passenger seat while he drove. They listened to the police radio and called in to the station. Then they just talked about their dogs and plans for the weekend. I listened without really hearing. The back of the police car felt surprisingly comfortable and safe.

When we got to my house they suggested I didn't make a habit of late-night jogging anymore, and they gave me the number to a free counselling service helpline in case I needed it. I nodded and thanked them for the ride. They watched me walk into the house and waited until I had closed the door behind me. Then they drove away.

FOURTEEN

I woke in the morning feeling like I hadn't slept. After the police dropped me home, I crept back upstairs and lay on my bed. I kept hearing her fall, as if she was calling my name. I could feel others, too. Their stories blending with the sound of her fall. Each time I fell asleep I'd jerk back awake again. Like I was still there on the street. Still late. And like she had just hit the ground.

Meg was in the kitchen when I walked in. She looked at me with horror.

'Jesus, Beth. You need to get off to school early before Mum has a chance to see you.'

She'd been making her lunch, but she shoved it at me instead and held my arm.

'We're talking tonight. You need to tell me what's going on.'

I nodded. She was right. It was time to tell her.

At school I sat by myself in a quiet part of the grounds. I leant my head on the wall behind me and waited for the school day to start. It was hard to keep my eyes open, but I was scared shutting them would be worse.

With my eyes open, the sounds in my head slipped into the background of my mind. I tried to stay awake. I tried until my eyelids felt like they were the weight of bricks and I just had to let them fall.

Lin found me sitting up, fast asleep. I was having a nightmare, but it wasn't about missing the catch. It was the man chasing me. I kept running but I couldn't lose him. He was always right behind me. When I opened my eyes to see Lin, I wanted to tell her everything even though I was still worried she thought something was seriously wrong with me.

'I missed, I was too slow.' It was all the detail I could manage.

I started crying. I tried to hide my face in Lin's shoulder, which was hard because she was so much smaller than me now. I felt like I was squashing her. She wrapped her arms around me and let me cry. Behind us I heard Rohan walk up and felt Lin wave him away.

Lin led me into the toilets and I washed my face.

'Maybe it's time to stop, Beth.'

I shook my head. 'I can't do that. I have to get better, faster.'

I wondered again if Lin really believed me or if she thought it was all in my head. I couldn't tell.

'I can't let them fall like that, Lin. I just can't. Not when I know I can catch them.'

After school I got home before Meg. I waited nervously for her in the kitchen. As soon as she walked in the door I blurted it out.

'I've been catching people.'

Meg sat down. 'Okay . . .'

She said it in a way that was more of a question than a comment, so I started to tell her everything.

I told her how sometimes I just knew when people were falling, and how I'd been working at trying to find them. I told her about not being able to sleep, and how I felt sick almost all the time. How the sickness was part of knowing there was someone to catch. I went back to the beginning and told her about that first catch on the street, the Irish painter, and catching Peter on the first day of school. I told her about leaving the movie date to catch someone from school and how I couldn't tell Etienne why I left.

I could see Meg wanted to say something at that point, but I hadn't finished.

I told her about last night. About the creepy man on the road trying to grab me and about how I got there too late. I didn't go into details about missing. I didn't tell her about crouching by the building or getting a lift home in the police car. I just told her I needed her help. I needed someone to drive me so I could get there faster. So I didn't miss again. So I was safe.

Meg looked at me doubtfully. 'At night? Every night?'

'Sometimes, some nights.'

'What about during school?'

I shrugged. I didn't know if I could ask her that.

She shook her head. 'I don't know if I can, Beth.' Then she looked at me and could probably see I was about to burst into tears. 'I'll try, though. Let's see if I can.'

Meg has never been able to cope with me crying. She studied my face carefully.

'Can you feel anyone who needs catching now?'

'No.'

I couldn't, but I was also trying to block feeling anything so I could get some sleep.

'Good. I've got a ton of schoolwork to do.'

I think I loved my sister in that moment more than I'd ever loved her before. I loved that she didn't question me. I wasn't sure she believed anything I'd said, but she didn't question me. I looked at her belly with a bit of sadness. I knew her baby would be fantastic when it arrived, that I would love it, but I also knew I'd lose Meg a little more than I already had.

I went upstairs to lie on my bed and sleep. I slept a beautiful, deep sleep for the rest of the afternoon and all night. I didn't dream, I didn't feel, I just slept.

In the morning I woke up hungry. I ate last night's dinner and my usual breakfast all at once.

Mum walked in, saw what I was eating, and looked at me with worry in her eyes. She didn't say anything.

After telling Meg about my catching and sleeping for so long I started to feel better. At basketball training that week I had more energy and focus than I'd had all term. I trained well, and when we played our practice game I started to get the hang of the plays Coach had been going on about. I thought I'd done okay, but when I looked to Etienne to see if I might get another smile he was looking the other way.

After training I went straight to Lin's house. She was sitting at her desk, and next to her on the floor she had spread out a large map of where we lived. She'd made the map herself, printing out the pages she wanted and then carefully sticking them together. The map extended to the ocean on one side and the edge of the city on the other. It included suburban areas like my street of single or double storey houses, and then other areas with block after block of low-rise apartments or the new high-rise buildings that had started to go up along the busier roads. On the map she'd drawn a thick red line – a boundary, Lin said.

She explained her calculations and her logic. Why she drew the line on this street; how long she estimated it would take me to run or drive to different locations within the red line. She showed me where the tall buildings were and pointed out landmarks I knew.

I looked at the map while Lin explained what she wanted me to do. I was to study the map. To learn the different streets and laneways. I wasn't to hear or feel or think of anything outside of the red line.

It sounded weird. Impossible, really, but I was willing to try. It kind of made sense to see if I could limit what I was feeling.

Studying the map properly turned out to be hard work. It was big, and difficult to negotiate. Lin suggested I meditate, so I sat on the map and closed my eyes. I focused on my breath. I tried to picture the map. To follow the streets in my mind.

That night, in my room, I spread the map across my desk and traced the boundary with my finger. I closed my eyes and let my mind follow my finger. I tried to follow the red line through the streets, but had to keep opening my eyes to check when I lost track or my finger went astray.

I tried to imagine a wall on the line. A tall brick wall I could build, brick by brick. A wall so high it closed off most of the world and left me with just a small manageable section to focus on.

That night, maybe because of the map and or maybe because of Meg's offer to help, I didn't feel as sick as I had been. I hadn't got the wall right yet, but the idea of it, the start I'd made, was working. I still felt that tangled ball of nausea mixed with other people's pain and misery, but it was receding to the background of my mind.

I sat at the table with my family and ate a normal meal. I didn't run through the streets searching. I slept like a normal person.

The end of term was approaching, and teachers started to demand assignments and worksheets and projects I hadn't done. That I hadn't even started. I sat down to tackle them, but the volume of work quickly overwhelmed me. The wall on the map I'd been trying to imagine collapsed and I was left on the floor of my room feeling waves of nausea.

I decided the wall was more important than schoolwork, so I spread out Lin's map over the top of my assignment pile. I traced the boundary line with my finger and tried to rebuild the wall in my mind.

The first time I needed Meg to drive me to a catch was midweek. Rik was over. He'd been coming over a bit more often. Probably so Meg didn't go there and show her growing belly to his mum, who was still in denial.

We were sitting down to eat dinner. I was still feeling stressed about schoolwork and trying to think of a way to complete my pile of assignments without destroying my imaginary wall. The wall was starting to take shape and hold firm. I didn't want to mess with that.

Rik continued to tell us about his mother, trying to explain her behaviour to us so that Meg would be a little more understanding towards her. Meg was happy Mari had calmed down, but she wasn't ready to be understanding.

The conversation inevitably turned to planning for the baby. Most of the conversations in our house seemed to eventually come back to discussing these plans. Mum couldn't help herself. If she wasn't hounding me about how much or little I was eating, she was talking about the baby. There were questions about how Meg was feeling and what appointments she had next. There were discussions about what needed to be bought, and where the money was coming from.

I stayed out of the conversation and focused on finishing the food on my plate. Then I felt sick. It started small and built quickly. I put my fork down and looked at Meg to try to catch her eye, but she was focused on Mum.

'I'm not going to get sucked into buying a whole bunch of stuff I don't need just because I'm having a baby.'

'I think you'll find they need more—'

I stood up and said, 'Meg!'

Everyone stopped talking and stared at me in confusion. I looked straight at Meg, ignoring Mum, Dad and Rik.

'I've got to go. You need to drive me.'

'What do you mean, you've got to go? We're in the middle of dinner.'

Mum wanted to know where I was going, but I was almost at the front door in the hope that Meg was following me.

I was at the car door by the time Meg rushed out of the house. She unlocked the car as she moved towards it and I got into the passenger seat. Meg was a little out of breath when she got in.

'Where are we going? Is it a catch?'

'I don't have an address – you just have to drive and I'll direct you.'

'Do you know who . . .'

'I can't chat, Meg. I have to focus.'

We drove towards the city. When we were close enough and had been stopped by a traffic light, I got out to start running. I pointed to the building I was heading to and told Meg to find a parking spot. Then I weaved my way through the traffic and hit the footpath running.

I could feel him by now. He'd been drinking. He'd been boasting and bragging and having a good time. He was showing off a new office space that was still under construction, and he was becoming aware that the people around him weren't as impressed as he thought they would be. But it was too late to stop. So he kept going. Then he stepped away from everyone else and ducked under some tape to have a look at the view. When he looked back at the people he was with, he saw the horror in their eyes and realised his mistake. He looked down at the planks of wood he'd walked onto. He saw that wood fall away beneath him, and then he fell after it.

When I got to the place I needed to, a few other people were standing nearby. 'Something's falling, get away from here,' I shouted at them. Maybe it was my tone or the wild look in my eyes, but for whatever reason they all moved away.

I turned and saw Meg standing at the corner. I put my hand out to her, shouting, 'Stay there.' I wasn't looking at her anymore, so I didn't know if she was going to listen, or even if she heard me. I was focused on the two pieces of wood that were coming towards me. And on the man who was coming behind them.

I needed to be out of the way for the wood and in position for the man. I didn't want to misjudge the catch and get hit by the wood. I didn't think I could catch them first. They were too large, too heavy. I didn't want to try.

I moved a little to the left as the first piece hit a car to my right and then forward as the second fell behind me on the road. I took my place near that second piece to be ready for the man.

He was in a suit and tie. I could see the tie blowing in the wind. I felt his fear. He wanted to throw up. So did I.

When I caught him, the first thing I smelt was alcohol mixed with his aftershave. It wasn't a bad smell. Or maybe it didn't seem bad because I was just happy I'd caught him. Happy the wood had fallen so that no one was hurt.

He stared at me in absolute amazement, and I wondered how drunk he was. I held him for a while and he didn't complain. He didn't try to move away from my arms.

His phone started to ring in his pocket. He tried to reach for it while still in my arms, like he didn't want to leave the safety of my hold. He couldn't manage to get his fingers on it while I held him, so I put him carefully on the ground. He was still staring at me as he pulled out his phone. When he saw who it was he smiled at me apologetically, letting me know he had to take it. He made a *stop* motion with his hand, asking me not to go. I turned to look for Meg, who was slowly walking towards us.

The guy in the suit tucked his phone under his ear and started to search through his pockets. Meg came to stand next to me, struggling for something to say. I realised she hadn't believed me before this moment. I admired her ability to act like she had when of course she would have had so many doubts and questions. I wanted to go home. I wanted to get back in the car and let Meg drive while we decided on the story that we'd tell Mum and Dad.

The guy in the suit had found his wallet and was shoving money at me. Meg poked me, but I shook my head at him. He was still on his phone, reassuring whoever he was talking to that everything was in place. He waved the cash at me, and Meg poked me again. I took the money. I didn't want to, I just took it so we could go. He hadn't finished, though. He handed me his business card too, and moved his phone away from his mouth long enough to say, 'Call me,' before going back to his conversation.

Meg led the way to the car. I was feeling a bit leaden, happy I'd made the catch, but tired. At some point as we were walking away the guy remembered his manners and shouted after us, 'Thank you.' Meg and I looked at each other and laughed. She turned back to wave at him, but I couldn't. I wouldn't have been able to keep a straight face.

In the car Meg looked at me as she started the engine. 'That was amazing, Beth.'

I nodded, because it was.

'Is it like that every time?'

'It's always different. I've never had falling wood before. And never a guy in a suit.'

We laughed again at how ridiculous it was.

'How come no one's reported you?'

'What do you mean?'

'I mean, all those people on the ground watched you catch him. Why doesn't anyone say anything about it?'

'There aren't usually people around. I don't think anyone's ever really seen me before.'

'What about the people you catch? Why don't they say anything?'

'I guess those people don't want anyone to know what's happened any more than I do.'

When we got home Dad was still at the table. It wasn't that late, but Mum had taken herself to bed and Rik had apparently left soon after we did.

'You've upset your mother, girls. You can't leave like that without saying where you're going.'

Meg and I nodded and apologised, grateful Dad wasn't asking for an explanation. We'd been so busy talking about the catch on the drive home we'd forgotten to come up with an excuse.

When we were alone, I told Meg I was sorry about Etienne. I was sorry I'd made it weird for him to come over to our house. 'I know you must miss him.'

Meg shrugged it off. 'We still walk to school together, and things were bound to change anyway with the baby coming.' She sighed a bit. The baby was becoming pretty real. 'I better go call Rik.'

I hugged her before we went to bed. 'Thanks for driving me.'

She hugged me back. 'Thanks for letting me in on your secret.'

I felt her belly push against me. She wasn't as easy to hug anymore, but I kept hugging her anyway.

FIFTEEN

LIN and I worked a few extra days together in the bike shop over the school holidays. I had decided it was time for Lin to see me catch, so in that first week of holidays, when I suddenly felt like throwing up over the bike chain I was greasing, I grabbed her by the hand and dragged her towards the door. I shouted to Dad that we would be back soon, and then I urged Lin to run.

We didn't actually need to run, but I wanted Lin to see as much of the catch as possible. I wanted her to know what it felt like to race, heart pounding, to where I needed to be.

The catch was a few blocks away. A nice house, with a nice man on the roof. He wasn't thinking about what he was doing. He was thinking about his kids. About how he'd spoken to them earlier. He was thinking he'd been a bit harsh and that when he finished replacing the tile on the roof he was going to take them out to the playground. Maybe stop for a milkshake on the way home.

He wasn't thinking about where to place his feet, or the slope of the roof. He was making plans. Nice plans.

I left Lin at the entrance to the garden, where I knew she'd be able to see but where I didn't need to worry about her. The nice man didn't understand what was about to happen. He didn't think he was in any huge danger. When he slipped he thought he'd roll off the roof and into the bushes. He thought it would only hurt a little.

I caught him and held him to me. I didn't correct him. I didn't let him know what I knew. I just held him and turned to see Lin's expression. Her face was a mixture of delight and pride.

I put him on his feet and the nice man brushed himself off. We chatted a little about how you had to be careful where you put your feet on a roof, and I made sure that he wasn't going back up there again. The nice man said goodbye to us both and got on with his day. Lin and I walked back to the bike shop.

'So do you believe me now?'

Lin stopped walking and took my arm. She looked up at me. 'I wanted to believe you, Beth.'

'You thought it was all in my head.'

Lin shook her head, then changed her mind. 'Maybe I worried a little.'

'The map you made helps. I don't know if it's working like you thought it would, but I mostly know where to go now and how long I have to get there. And I'm mostly acting like a normal person again, though not enough to convince Mum. She's booked a therapy session for me.'

Mum had held off as long as she could, but it got to a point where she couldn't contain herself anymore, so she'd just booked it and told me she expected me to go. That if I didn't want to talk to her, I could talk to a therapist.

'I think I'm ready to add a few extra streets to the map.'

Lin was firm. 'No. Not yet. Remember how overwhelmed you felt? Remember what missing felt like? You said it's only just starting to work. Why would you want to mess with that?'

'I'm still missing catches. There are people falling outside of that red line. The map doesn't stop people falling. It just stops me getting to them.'

'If you try to go too big you might end up not being able to help anyone. Including yourself.'

It was good advice. But there were days when I was tired or stressed or distracted, and the wall I imagined on the map fell a little. When that happened I felt all the other people, the people outside of the red line. Those days made the advice hard to follow.

The conversation was put on hold for the rest of the day while we worked alongside Dad, who was putting the finishing touches on the bike we'd been fixing. He had a buyer coming that day and he was excited about selling it.

After work Lin and I were walking back to her house to look at some data she'd been working on. She was talking about research she'd been doing. Theories she was looking into. I put my hand on her arm.

'Hang on, wait here.'

I had walked us past Jake's house. He'd been up that tree for a while now and I figured it was about time for him to fall. I went through the gate and stood in the garden, under the tree, looking up into the branches. I thought about Lin's continued search for some kind of answer to the mystery of what had changed in me. About whether having an answer would make any difference, whether there was even an answer to find.

Jake fell into my arms and started his usual hitting at me. There was less screaming these days, but he still didn't want me to hold him. I put him quickly on the ground and walked back out of the garden to where Lin was waiting. She had been peering around the wall, watching the whole process.

I decided to change the subject and started talking about schoolwork.

'I didn't do any of the work I needed to do last term. I've missed all the due dates and I'm behind on everything. I don't even know if I'll be able to pass at this point.'

Lin shrugged. 'Maybe this is more important right now. There'll be time for school later.'

It was a weird thing to hear coming out of Lin's mouth.

In Lin's room we discussed the upcoming therapy session Mum had booked for me. Lin thought it was time to tell her what was going on.

'It will save your family money on therapy sessions.'

'If I tell Mum what's going on she'll want to spend even more on therapy.'

'Maybe. Maybe not.'

Lin showed me the data she was working on. She had been gathering all kinds of statistics from anywhere she could find them. Most of them were average rates of falls by area. Suicides, accidental deaths or injuries. She had dates and averages from places all over the world. To me it was a jumble of numbers, but to her it was a puzzle. Something she thought she could work out.

'What do you think these numbers will tell you, Lin?'

'I'm not sure yet. I just think maybe there's an answer in here if I keep looking.'

I looked again. It would have taken Lin hours to gather all this information. I hoped it would give her something, some answer she was looking for, but I was confident that any answer I wanted wasn't in those numbers.

When I got home from Lin's I did all the jobs Mum had written down for us to do, including Meg's. I felt bad about getting Meg out of bed last night to drive me to catch the woman who'd slapped me the first time I caught her. She'd slapped me again, but not as hard. I couldn't tell whether she was pushed or she jumped, but it was the same apartment building, so she'd gone back. Something had drawn her back to him.

Meg said the driving was fine and she wanted to do it. She didn't want me running around on my own at night. I was relieved because I didn't want to be running around on my own at night either, but I couldn't ignore what it cost her. This morning she'd slept late and lost study time. She swallowed the supplements Mum had left on the counter for her. The iron to counteract her tiredness, and the super pills that were going to make her and her baby the healthiest on the planet. Meg took them without complaint, saying she had the most expensive wee on the block.

We talked about the therapist appointment and how Lin thought I should tell our parents what was going on. We both fell silent for a bit, imagining how Mum would react to the news. Meg said quietly, 'Maybe they'd help with the driving,' and I realised that waking her up in the night to drive me places would soon be too much for her. It wasn't fair with everything else she had going on, no matter how often she told me it was okay.

I changed the topic of conversation to school and how holidays were nearly over, which meant the first basketball games were coming up. I told her how nervous I was about having to leave games to go and catch. I didn't say I was just as worried about disappointing Etienne as I was about missing catches, but I figured Meg realised that anyway.

'If you are going to the bother of telling Mum and Dad, you might as well tell him too,' Meg said, in her usual blunt way.

I shook my head.

Meg started to get out cutlery to set the table. 'I think he'd understand.'

'He won't even talk to me. He can barely look at me.' I reached for the plates.

'Yeah, that's weird.'

I wanted to know more about why Meg thought Etienne's behaviour towards me was weird, but Meg started to talk about Rik and his parents. 'I have been "invited" to dinner. More like summoned. She's given up on denial and is trying to move back into control. Apparently, she's worried about what her friends will think. I keep telling Rik I'm the one who has to do this. I'm the one who has to turn up to high school pregnant with everyone staring. I'm the one who has to push out a baby and then go do my exams. Why would I care what her friends think?'

I asked her what she planned to do, and she said she would go there and listen and then carry on doing it her way. She said at least Mari was starting to accept the idea of the baby, so that was progress. And Tad was nice to her, just the way he'd always been. She even thought he was starting to get excited about the baby. I looked at Meg to see if she was upset by having to deal with all of this, but she just smiled.

'It'll be fine. And if it's not, then Mari's the one who's going to lose, not me.'

⸻

After dinner Mum and I cleaned up the kitchen together. I knew I needed to tell her about catching people, but I couldn't find the words. So instead I answered her questions about school and Lin as best I could. I told her we'd made friends with Rohan, and we talked about him for a while, which was a good distraction from talking about me.

When I went to leave the kitchen, Mum stopped me by reminding me about the therapist appointment she'd made.

'I really don't need to go, Mum.'

'I know you think you don't, Beth, but something is going on with you and you need to talk to someone about it.'

'I don't need to speak to a therapist. It's too expensive.'

I tried to explain that I was just a bit nervous about the first basketball game coming up. How it was something I'd never done before and how uncomfortable I felt being out there on the court with people watching me. Loads of kids and parents would come to watch the mixed team.

'What if I mess up and let the team down? I'd kind of be letting the whole school down.'

Mum sighed. 'You mean letting Etienne down?'

I nodded. Maybe if I admitted to this I wouldn't have to admit to catching people, and it would get me out of the therapy session.

'Can we just wait and see how things are after the first game?'

Mum wasn't looking convinced, but she hugged me tight. 'I'm just worried about you, Beth. I'm worried about both of my girls.'

'I know, but I think I'll be better after the first game, and we both know Meg will be fine.'

Mum said she'd postpone the session until a week after the first game, but if she still felt worried I would have to go, no matter what. I nodded agreement, not because I agreed but because it bought me a bit more time to work out how to tell her about catching.

I went upstairs to look at the assignments sitting on my desk. I arranged the pile in order according to when they were due. They didn't look so bad when they were in a nice, neat stack.

SIXTEEN

MEG came back from her dinner at Rik's more determined than ever to show people she could do it all. Mum had bought her a couple of larger-size school shirts, and Meg buttoned them over her belly and went to school with her head held high, safe in the knowledge that she was ahead in almost every class.

I spent the first two weeks back at school on edge, the upcoming basketball games and late assignments constantly on my mind. At every lesson I waited for the teacher to call me up or call me out. Whenever I heard my name I jumped, convinced I'd done something wrong. But when the teachers did call me out and I had no answer or no completed assignment to offer, they sighed and moved on. Like they had already given up on expecting anything from me.

Coach was the opposite. He called me out at practice all the time. Shouting at me to move or to stop or to shoot. Half the time I understood what he wanted. When I didn't, I would end up frozen on the court trying to work it out until another player swooped in and took over.

Tommy took on the role of explaining the finer points of the game to me. I had the basics down and had made some progress on fouls. I didn't always know when I'd fouled or why, or when others fouled against me. But it was starting to make more sense. Tommy also patiently explained the strategies behind the plays Coach was teaching us. I don't know what changed Tommy's mind about me. Maybe that first practice game run-in, or maybe because when I got it right I stood out from the team. Whatever it was, I was grateful for the time he was willing to spend teaching me.

Sometimes when Tommy was talking me through a play I would look over and see Etienne shooting hoops or talking to Coach. Basketball would be a lot easier if it was Etienne explaining these things to me. If it was Etienne and me in my driveway, running plays and talking fouls.

At the end of the last training session before the first mixed game, Coach pulled me aside and told me how well I was doing. They weren't words that came naturally to him, and it made for an awkward conversation where we both avoided eye contact. Just when I thought we'd both made it through, Coach touched my arm. His touch made me look at his face. He was wearing a very serious expression.

'You need to stop with the disappearing act. This is game season. You need to show up for the team.'

On the day of the first mixed basketball game I felt vaguely sick. I couldn't tell if it was a catch coming or just nerves. I'd already played a game with the girls' team, but it hadn't felt like a big deal. It was just us against another school during the day with a few girls' parents watching. None of the boys came, they were all playing their own game. The mixed game was being played in the evening and loads of people kept telling me they'd be there to watch.

I spent the day at school counting the hours until the game. Most of my teachers seemed to alternate between ignoring me or being understanding that it was a big day for me. As if they could see how nervous I was and were a bit kinder because of it. Lin and Rohan tried hard to keep the conversation away from sport when we talked at lunch, but most of the other kids around me didn't. I got a few slaps on the back and wishes of *good luck*. I also got a *don't fuck up*, which was mostly what I was thinking. I wondered how many others were thinking it too.

At the end of the school day Coach scheduled a quick pep talk in the gym before we went home. He talked us through the game strategy and reminded us about the strengths and weaknesses of the team we were playing against. I was feeling so nervous that my imaginary wall was starting to break down. Waves of nausea were creeping through my body. I concentrated on building the wall back up instead of listening to Coach.

When Coach had finished talking, I watched Etienne gather his things. He wouldn't be feeling nervous like me. My guess was he was feeling excited, looking forward to being on the court and getting the ball in his hands.

Etienne stuck around to speak to Coach, so I was saved from an awkward walk home where we had to avoid each other while heading in the same direction. At home I tried to eat a little. I closed my eyes and focused on making sure the wall was solid and safe. I looked for cracks and sealed them with my mind and my breath.

Mum got home early from work and didn't hassle me about anything. I could see the effort she was making and was grateful. The sickness I'd been feeling had returned to just that same vague feeling I'd woken up with. I'd been drinking a lot of water to hydrate for the game, so I hoped it was just a little too much water that was making me feel like this and not someone who was about to need catching.

I went back to school well before the game to warm up. Mum, Dad and Meg stayed behind and planned to arrive at game time. On the walk to school I called Lin.

'Do you think it will be like this every game? I'm just trying to imagine a time when I might actually enjoy playing.'

I didn't say *like Etienne does*, but that's what I was thinking.

'Maybe it's going to be like catching is for you. Awful before and during, but good afterwards? At least losing a basketball game will never feel worse than losing a catch.'

It was a weird thing to say but it cheered me up a little.

At warm-up I tried to focus on what Coach wanted me to do. I kept my eyes on the ball. In my uniform, on the court, with the team around me calling out and passing balls back and forth, I started to feel a bit better.

When we gathered together as a team I was pushed up alongside Etienne. I wanted to turn to him and say something like *good luck* or *let's do this*, but I couldn't make the words come out, so I just looked at the ground, at my other teammates, anywhere but at him. Our shoulders touched, my hands smacked on top of his as everyone put their hands in for a final, rousing cheer. I wasn't feeling it. 'Go,' I mumbled under my breath as the others shouted.

Etienne shouted beside me. I felt his focus on the game, not on me. I wondered if he felt anything as our bodies were pushed together. Whether he was hating me, hating having to touch me, hating having me in the team with him. But I didn't feel hate from him. When we were pushed together, when our hands met with everyone else's, it wasn't hate. It wasn't anything, which was perhaps worse.

I looked up into the stands as we took our positions on the home team bench. Mum and Dad were sitting with Meg and Rik. Lin and Rohan were nearby. I saw other kids I recognised, and parents too. And then in another section, like there was an invisible line, I saw people I didn't recognise. The opposition's people. Some of them looking intently at the court, mouthing instructions to their kid, others on their phones or talking to the people next to them.

Coach put me on the bench to start. I was so grateful not to be thrown onto the court straight away that I thanked him, which turned out to be the wrong thing to do. He glared at me before moving on to instruct the players. I took my seat and watched our team move into their positions on the court. We made the first few points, but the other team quickly found their feet and the game scores stayed close.

Etienne was graceful on the court. From the bench I could watch him as much as I pleased – everyone else was, so it wasn't weird. I could see he was respected by the team on the court, the way he was in training. He had control of play a lot of the time and his focus was completely on the ball and the players around him.

Each time the whistle blew I would freeze, waiting for Coach to call me on to the court. I still felt a little sick and there was a vague feeling of wanting to run, but it had eased since I'd gotten here. I was starting to feel confident it wasn't a catch.

At the end of the quarter Coach looked at me.

'Get ready, I'm putting you on next.'

I thought about saying, *No, not me, we're doing so well*, but I didn't because I realised if I wanted to stay in the team I actually needed to get up and play. I nodded, and focused on what Coach was saying to the team.

Etienne took a seat on the bench for the start of the second quarter and I took my place on the court. I tried not to hope he was sitting there watching me the way I had been watching him. I also tried to block out the noise coming from my family, who were shouting my name and clapping. I focused on the ball.

The game was faster on the court than it looked from the side, and at first I felt like I was running without much idea of what was going on or where I needed to be. I fumbled the ball when it came my way, allowing the opposition to gain control and score. The visiting team were rough and strong. They weren't afraid to push their bodies against us, and to be fair most of my team weren't afraid to push back, but I felt a bit overwhelmed by the speed of the game.

I tried to breathe and focus. I tried to get involved, to get my hands on the ball. I tried to feel hungry for the ball the way everyone else around me seemed to, the way I sometimes felt in training.

In a dead-ball moment Tommy came up to me. He steadied me with his hands on my shoulders and looked into my eyes like he understood what was going on.

'You've got this.'

I waited for more, for some instruction, but that was all he had. When play started again I found it was enough.

I started to follow the game a little better. I got to the ball a few times and moved it to other team members. It was nothing spectacular, but it was a start.

Coach called me off before the end of the second quarter. I tried to apologise, to tell him I could do better, but he shook his head and told me to sit down and take a breath. He told me I'd get a chance to get out there again soon and this time I was going to show them what I could do. I nodded, grateful he wasn't angry with me.

Etienne stood as I moved to sit on the bench. He shook out his legs and made his way to Coach to let him know he was ready to get back on.

I played some of the third quarter and my game kept improving. I got possession of the ball more and felt like once I had it I knew what to do with it. I was sometimes able to keep control of the ball. I could see the plays Coach had talked us through. I knew where I was on the court and where I needed to be.

At one point in the third quarter Etienne and I were on the bench together. Both trying to catch our breath as we sat at opposite ends. Both intently watching the game in front of us. I had to deliberately force my focus onto the game rather than onto him, and once it was there I was mostly okay. I didn't think it was the same for Etienne. I told myself he'd probably focus on the game like that no matter who was sitting with him on the bench.

The other team got a little away from us in the third quarter and by the start of the fourth we were behind. Coach reminded us the game wasn't over. That it was still within our grasp. We needed to get out there and show them what we could do. A win in the first round would set us up well for the rest of the season.

I started the quarter on the bench, but this time I wasn't grateful for the rest. I stood near Coach and stretched and bounced and waited until it was my time to get back onto the court. The other team got the first points of the quarter and I saw the game moving further from us as our team failed to score at the first few chances we got.

Etienne played the entire quarter. I could see the determination on his face, and he finally got some points on the board. I stood closer to Coach, to remind him I was there. He didn't take his eyes off the game, though he put a hand on my arm to let me know he knew I was there. But he didn't get me back onto the court until there were only a few minutes left.

I raced into my position and waited for the umpire's whistle to start the play again. In that moment before the whistle, Etienne looked at me. He nodded his head a little.

At the time I didn't understand. I nodded back, unsure if it was a signal or just acknowledgement that I'd almost made it through my first game. When play started Etienne got the ball and nodded to me again, a quick nod that others in the game probably didn't even see. Then he made a hard, fast pass into empty space to my right.

I don't know how he knew I could get there, how he thought it would work, but it did. I knew what he was doing with the second nod. I knew where the ball was going, and I was there in time to take it from the air and move it to our end of the court. I had the ball back to Etienne before the other team realised what had happened. Etienne scored from the three-point line.

We were still behind and there wasn't much time left, but I wanted to celebrate those points like we'd won. I looked to Etienne, who was still in the game. For him it wasn't over. He nodded to me again and I knew he wanted to keep making that play as long as we could. That he wasn't ready to celebrate until we had really won.

The opposition failed to score, and when the ball landed back in Etienne's hands he looked for space near me and threw the ball into it. I was there again to take it and quickly return it to Etienne, who scored again. He almost smiled at me after that, but we still hadn't moved into the lead, so we kept our focus on the game.

We tried for the same play as soon as we could, but the other team were onto us and a player was ready to block me from making my pass back to Etienne. I panicked and didn't pass well. The ball ended up moving to the other end of the court. I ran back to try to fix my mistake. The ball passed high in the air. Higher than I thought I could jump.

All I wanted in that moment was to win the game. And not even for Etienne – I wanted to win for me. I ran, I leapt, I caught, and as I started to fall, I threw.

The ball made it safely to our end of the court, where it was picked up by Tommy and put through the hoop by Maye. The whistle blew and a hand appeared in front of me. I took the hand, looking up from where I'd hit the ground. It was Etienne, leaning down to help me up. He didn't say anything.

We shook hands with the opposition and the umpires, and then jumped around for a while as a group. Etienne wasn't part of the jumping. He stood to the side, watching, smiling, patting people on the back, high-fiving others. When it came to me, he didn't hesitate. He high-fived me like I was one of the team, not someone who'd let him down.

I caught his eye and smiled at him. I couldn't help it. It felt great to have won the game, to be part of that win. Etienne smiled back at me. He was going to say something. After all this time, he was actually going to talk to me. Then someone pulled him away and the moment was lost.

I looked around and saw my family standing up and moving towards me. They were all smiling and looking proud. It was a rare moment. I smiled back at them and then turned to listen to Coach one last time. Coach was pleased with our play, but didn't want us to get over-confident. He also didn't like how close the game was. He told us the season was long and he wanted a few more comfortable wins.

At home it was nice to feel my family were proud of me. Maybe on another night I would have stayed up to enjoy their praise for longer, but with the excitement of the game gone, exhaustion was taking over.

I fell asleep faster than I had in a long time. When I woke I could barely remember going to bed. At first I was confused. I remembered the game and how exhausted I'd felt. It took another moment to realise why I'd woken up. I leapt out of bed and rushed to wake up Meg. I pulled on clothes and urged her to do the same, but Meg shook her head. She'd drive me in her pyjamas.

We crept out of the house and once we were in the car Meg asked, 'What is it? Who is it?'

'I'm not sure. Something small.'

'If you've got me out of bed for a kitten I'm going to kill you.'

'It's not a kitten. It's something precious.'

The streets were empty and it didn't take us long to get to where we needed to be. The apartment building was maybe five or six storeys. I felt relieved that whatever was coming towards me was not coming from a great height. I took my spot and Meg got out of the car to watch. I would have preferred her in the car. She'd probably be safer there, but I didn't have time to argue. I focused on the building.

The wait felt long. Too long. Perhaps I'd made a mistake. Maybe this time I was just confused. We continued to wait. I risked a glance at Meg, who was starting to look restless. Then I felt it.

My first feeling was relief that I was right. That Meg wouldn't be mad at me for dragging her out of bed for nothing. Then I was filled with fear, because I realised what was coming and I'd never caught anything so small and so new before.

The baby fell towards us. Meg cried out when she realised what it was. The blanket the baby was wrapped in came loose and the baby fell first, the blanket trailing behind. I adjusted my stance a little and caught the baby in my arms. It was the smallest person I'd ever held.

As soon as it hit my arms it started to scream. It screamed and screamed. Not like Jake. This was a scream of confusion and loss.

Meg rushed to collect the fallen blanket. She took the baby from me, wrapping it loosely. She jiggled it up and down, patting its back. I turned to the entrance of the building and saw a woman come running. I nudged Meg, but she refused to return the baby. The mother stood looking at us like she couldn't believe anything she was seeing.

I nudged Meg again to hand the baby over, but Meg was staring at the mother, unwilling to part with the baby. I said, 'It was an accident.'

The mother nodded. 'I didn't know she could roll. I only left her for a minute. I thought I'd lost her.'

Meg opened her mouth. I knew what she wanted to say by the way she held the baby. I stood close to Meg and put my hand on her back. I spoke before she could.

'I know.'

I pushed Meg gently towards the mother and she reluctantly passed the baby over. The baby stopped screaming as soon as it was in its mother's arms.

The father arrived and stood behind the mother. She turned to weep into his chest. Meg and I walked back to the car, Meg still fuming at the lack of care she thought these parents had shown. As she drove, she moved on to speculating about whether it was lack of care or something more sinister. Nothing I said could convince her it was just an accident.

When we got home Meg and I raided the fridge.

'You know it's time to tell them.'

I was pouring us both glasses of milk.

'I'm always going to try to be here for you, but after the baby comes ... I can't just leave it at night.'

I knew she was right. I handed her a glass of milk, nodding my agreement.

A nod wasn't enough for Meg. 'Say you'll tell them.'

'I'll tell them tomorrow night at dinner.'

SEVENTEEN

AT school people I'd never spoken to before came up and congratulated me on the game. It was nice, but I was looking for Etienne. I watched out for him in the corridors, hoping for a sign he'd forgiven me. That the basketball game had made everything better.

At lunch I caught his eye. I was heading for our usual table with Rohan and Lin. He was at his with Meg, Maye, Tommy and the others. I was about to sit down when I was caught by his gaze. I waited to see what he would do, hoping he might get up and come to talk to me about the game. Or at least offer a smile, a wave, anything.

He started to smile and I started to sweat because it was as if what I'd been hoping for was actually coming true. Then Rohan knocked into me as he sat down and I dropped the lunch I was holding. When I straightened up after retrieving it, Etienne had turned around, drawn back into the conversation around him.

After school Lin and I worked a shift in the bike shop and I tried to work out with her what I would tell Mum and Dad.

'Just say it. Just open your mouth and say it.'

'Say what? What part of it should I say?'

Lin handed me a rag so I could wipe the grease from my hands. She grabbed another one and had a go at the smudge I'd made on my cheek when I was trying to keep my hair out of my eyes as I worked.

'All of it. Let it all come out, however it comes. Then wait for your mum to ask questions.'

We both knew Mum'd have a lot of questions.

At home I took the knife from Meg and started chopping vegetables for a salad so she could get back to her schoolwork. I set the table and tried to make sure everything was there so we wouldn't get sidetracked by people asking where the pepper was or getting up for a drink. If I was going to do this, I needed to do it without distractions.

Meg came down to see if I needed any help. She saw how nervous I was.

'You could tell Etienne instead. He finally got his licence. I mean, it's an option if you really don't want to tell Mum and Dad.'

I looked at her and saw she was joking, teasing me because she knew I wouldn't choose Etienne over our parents. I have to say I thought about it a bit more than the last time she suggested it. I wondered whether he'd agree. What he'd really think of me if I told him. Whether it would make things better or worse between us.

We heard Mum and Dad pull into the driveway. Meg patted me on the shoulder. 'It's the right thing to do.'

I nodded, mute with fear. I was afraid they wouldn't believe me, or that by telling them I'd somehow ruin that taste of their pride I got after the basketball game. Mostly I was afraid of Mum's reaction when she found out I'd been keeping this from her for so long.

We sat down and as usual Mum talked first, asking us about our day and then immediately telling us about hers. She complimented me on the food and the way I'd set the table and asked Meg how she was feeling.

Meg didn't answer her question. 'Beth has something to tell you.'

She turned to me and waited. Dad paused, a forkful of salad halfway to his mouth. My throat went dry. I looked back to Meg and opened my mouth a little, but no words came out. Meg nodded at me, smiling in what I assume she thought was an encouraging way. I shook my head. I couldn't find the words.

Meg looked back to our parents.

'Beth's been catching people.'

She picked up her fork and started eating again. Mum and Dad looked from one of us to the other, trying to understand what was happening, what Meg was saying and why I looked so terrified. I put my head in my hands. Meg paused from her chewing.

'She knows when people are falling and she goes out and catches them. Sometimes from really big heights. And she doesn't hurt herself and she doesn't miss.'

'Sometimes I miss,' I said almost under my breath.

Meg kept going. 'She's really good at it. It's like a superpower. But she needs help. I can't keep driving her around at night, not with the baby coming. You guys need to start helping her.'

I lifted my face from my hands. Mum was looking at Dad, who had abandoned the idea of finishing what was on his plate. Mum returned her gaze to Meg and me. I could see the questions swirling around in her mind. I could see her wanting to dismiss the whole conversation as some kind of joke, but still no words actually came out of her mouth. It was Dad who spoke first.

'What help does Beth need?'

He said it to Meg as if everyone had agreed I couldn't answer for myself, which was pretty much true, so I wasn't offended.

'She needs car rides to get where she has to go. Sometimes it's late or too far to run to.'

Dad turned back to me. 'Is this true? Have you been going out at night without telling us?'

He seemed angry.

'Yeah.' I looked back down to my plate.

Meg tried again. 'She's not sneaking out for parties, she's going out to help people. It's a calling. Something she needs to do. You can't be mad at her for that.'

'I can be mad at her for not telling us.' Mum had finally found her voice.

'I know it sounds weird, Mum, but you really just have to go see for yourself to understand it.'

'Okay.' Mum said it really slowly, like she was actually saying *not okay*.

'Can we go see now?' Dad asked.

'It doesn't work like that.' I tried not to sound annoyed.

Mum got a bit more of an edge to her voice. 'Well, how does it work?'

I started to find the words then to tell her how I felt before I caught someone, how I knew where to go.

Mum was beginning to connect the dots. 'Is this why you've been tired all the time? Why your eating has been all over the place?'

I nodded. She frowned, and I knew she was unhappy I'd been lying to her.

I got up to help Meg with the dishes while Mum and Dad disappeared into their room to talk through what they'd just heard. Meg seemed pleased.

'See? That wasn't so bad.'

I wondered whose table she had been at.

'It was bad. It was really bad. Did you see the way Mum was looking at me? And the way Dad couldn't look at me?'

Meg waved away my comments with her tea towel. 'They'll be fine. They just need to see you in action. Maybe you should show them sooner rather than later.'

She knew it didn't work that way as much as I did. Meg gave me a hug. 'Everything will be fine, Beth.'

I went to my room and sat at my desk, doodling in the margins of my business studies assignment sheet and watching the light in Etienne's room across the street.

Mum came in and sat on my bed. I turned to face her, but she didn't speak. She was waiting for me to talk. I tried again to tell her when it started. How I felt, who I'd caught.

'I promise next time I feel a catch coming I'll let you know so you can see it for yourself.'

'But you don't feel one now?'

I shook my head.

I could tell she wanted to ask me more questions. I yawned and stretched and told her I really needed to get some work done on my assignment before bed. She nodded and left the room, reminding me to let her know if I felt anything. I agreed in what I hoped was a normal voice.

I didn't feel normal at all. I felt really weird. Like I'd disappointed them both so much, and not just because of the lying. Also just because of me.

EIGHTEEN

AT the next basketball training session Coach praised Etienne and me for the play we managed to execute in the game before he split us into smaller groups to train. Etienne and I were put in the same group.

Etienne didn't talk to me and I didn't feel brave enough to say anything to him, but we were openly looking at each other as we passed the ball or ran in close proximity. He wasn't avoiding my gaze anymore, and while there was no smiling, there was something else. Something that felt like connection. Like working together.

Coach pulled me aside at the end of training and told me I was fast and good at getting the ball but my skills were letting me down. He wanted me to practise my dribbling and shooting. He showed me a few drills and told me I needed to keep them up every day.

It took three days before I felt the next catch. Three painful days of Mum asking me if I felt sick. Three days of Mum meeting me in the bathroom at night because she'd heard me up and thought I might be leaving to catch someone.

'Mum, I'll let you know. I want you to come with me.'

I was whispering in the hallway so we didn't wake Meg. When she looked doubtful I said, 'This is not something I do every day. That's a good thing, isn't it? That people aren't falling every day?'

I'd told her about Lin and the boundary she'd drawn. I could tell from the way Mum held herself, from the questions she asked, that she was offended I'd told Lin before I told her.

'Tell me again how the map works?'

It was too hard for me to explain. I didn't have any idea how it worked. It just did.

We were sitting at dinner when I felt it. It came on so fast I nearly threw up on my plate. I quickly stood up.

Meg smiled. 'You're up, Mum.'

Mum was a bit slower to catch on. When she did, she threw down her fork and stood up too. She glanced at the food left on the table, as if she was thinking she needed to put it all away.

'Go, you need to go.'

Meg pushed Mum towards the front door. I was already heading to the car. Mum told Dad to come and they rushed to the car with Meg waving to us from the door.

In the car I directed Dad as best I could over the top of Mum's questions. I tried to answer her in between directions, but eventually I had to tell her she needed to be quiet. Mum wasn't used to me talking to her like that, but this catch was feeling so urgent I had to focus on it.

The traffic was terrible. We were heading into the city and there were cars and people everywhere. Mum and Dad started to discuss the best ways to go, tossing up whether there was another road they could take, but I asked them to please just keep going the way I was directing.

We got to a point where I had to start running. I told them I was getting out of the car, that it would be faster. Mum wanted to come too, but then she fussed about whether or not to bring her bag until I had to shout, 'Mum!' because I couldn't wait any longer.

Me shouting didn't help – she was still trying to work it out, still trying to direct Dad so he could meet us. I took off down the street and heard her footsteps following behind me. I had to run four blocks with two turns. I didn't know if Mum would be able to follow me or if I'd lost her.

I made it to the apartment building and looked up. The child was already falling towards me. I barely had time to plant my feet before he dropped into my arms. He was a small boy, I guessed about four. He let me hold him and gazed up solemnly into my face. He didn't cry or squirm. I returned his stare and tried to hold him so he felt secure without feeling trapped. I watched the building entrance in case a parent came for him, but all I saw was Mum jogging towards us.

She was sweaty and panting from the run, with her hair all over the place. I smiled at her because she looked such a mess and because I felt so calm and happy holding that boy. When Mum joined us, the boy wriggled out of my arms. He ran to the building's entrance. We followed him. Someone was walking out as he arrived and he pushed his way past them and into the foyer.

By the time we got there the glass doors had closed. He stood on the inside looking back out at us with his big eyes. Then he waved and stood on tiptoe to push the lift button. We watched him as he got into the lift.

'Shouldn't we make sure he's okay, Beth? Tell someone? Find out who he is?'

'He's okay.'

Mum studied me. 'How do you know?'

I shrugged. 'I just know.'

Mum opened her mouth and then closed it. There was something she wanted to say but she had decided against it. Instead, she suggested we find Dad and the car.

When we got home, Mum told Meg how strong and calm I was, how I had saved the little boy's life. Dad stayed quiet. All he had done was sit in traffic, so he didn't have much to say, but he had been silent since we'd told him and it was starting to bug me. I went to find where Meg had put all our uneaten dinner.

As we finished eating Mum began to think out loud. She started to consider that catching might not be good for my back and maybe I needed to see an osteopath or chiropractor.

'My back is fine, Mum. Better than fine.'

'But how do you feel after you catch someone? Does it ever hurt? Or is it more emotional? Do you ever feel upset?'

I thought back to the miss. To the pain and sadness I'd felt.

'Never. I'm completely fine.'

Mum took me to one of her social work colleagues to talk about how to manage trauma. Despite what I'd said, she felt catching was too much for me to handle. That the problems I was seeing were too big for a teenager to manage. I didn't completely disagree, but what could I do? I couldn't not catch.

We didn't tell the therapist about my catching. We gave her a vague story about being exposed to multiple traumas.

Mum's colleague was confused by us. She asked a lot of questions that we struggled to answer before she gave up trying to understand and ran us through some general points about dealing with trauma. When Mum pushed her for more, she pointed out that I didn't seem particularly traumatised by whatever it was I'd experienced.

That night Mum sat me down for a bigger conversation.

'I worry about what happens next for these people. Who's looking after them, and if they need more help. I understand why you don't want to do anything other than catch. It's not your job to look after them. I get that. And you don't have the skills or training to help them.'

It was a relief to hear Mum say it. I had been hoping catching was enough. Her saying it took a burden from me I didn't realise I was carrying.

'However . . .' Mum paused to make sure I was still listening. 'We need to think about when you should call the police, or an ambulance or some other kind of authority to look after these people.'

I didn't think it was ever appropriate. I didn't want to draw attention to myself like that.

'How can I report people falling without it looking suspicious, Mum?'

'Maybe call them in before you catch them. Let someone else catch them or talk them down before they jump.'

'I can't do that. Most of the time I don't know what's going to fall towards me until I get there.'

Mum hugged me. We agreed that for now I would do nothing but catch. And that I would always tell her about them.

The next night there were supplements on the table with my name on them. Something random Mum had found that she said would help.

'Help what?' I asked her. 'Are you trying to stop me catching or make me stronger?'

Mum looked offended. 'I'm just trying to help.'

'I'm fine, Mum. I don't need any help. Not like that. I just need help to get to the catches.'

Mum nodded like she understood, but then she brought up seeing an osteopath her friend had told her about. I thought about the therapist again. Maybe it would be good to see a therapist. One I went to alone, who didn't know Mum. Someone I could tell all those big and little thoughts to. I could tell them what I felt when I caught people. I could explain what it was like to feel the weight of other people's problems in my arms, and the pleasure I got when I held them and offered them comfort.

I would never have said this to Mum, though. I didn't want to let her think I needed any help other than the occasional lift. I didn't like the way she was treating me now. She wanted to talk about it endlessly. It didn't matter how many times I told her I was fine.

And mostly I was fine. Sure, occasionally I woke up screaming into my pillow when I dreamt about the woman I'd missed, but mostly when I managed to sleep, I slept fine.

Lin and I were still discussing my catching most days. I didn't mind these conversations. She was still searching for a pattern, a reason people were falling. She wanted to know if it was normal for this many people to be falling or if there were more than usual for some reason.

As we locked the bike shop, Lin showed me the graphs and maps she'd made. Colourful charts and documents that showed all my catches according to location, age and gender. I couldn't see any particular pattern in them and I didn't really see the point of trying to find one. All the stories, all the people I caught, were so different. Accidents. Carelessness. Desperation. Violence. I couldn't see any kind of order behind it. It was just life. Modern city life. We'd built these big structures to take ourselves high off the ground, to fit us all in; we put pressure on ourselves and others to be more than we were. Falling was one of the prices we had to pay.

Lin didn't see it like that. She wanted to find a hidden message, a reason. I liked that Lin's mind worked the way it did. That she was always looking for something that would never occur to me. She saw me as only a part of a puzzle, and was searching beyond me for another piece.

NINETEEN

THE mixed basketball team won the next few games. Coach was pleased with the way I was playing, even though I missed a training session for what I thought was a catch that turned out to be a false alarm. Coach wasn't happy, but all I could do was apologise and accept he was going to be harder on me at our next training session.

I didn't think I was very good at lying, but I seemed to be getting better at it. I told Coach things were going on at home I just had to be there for. Coach, like the rest of the school, knew about Meg and accepted my excuses, even though he frowned. The truth was, I still hadn't got that imaginary wall up as well as it could be and sometimes a whole lot of nausea flooded in and confused me.

I left once in an all-girls game. It was a strange catch, right on Lin's boundary, about as far away from the school as it could get. I knew as soon as I felt the nausea that I wasn't going to make it there in time. Not on my own. I was on the court thinking, *Maybe they'll change their mind. Maybe they'll realise it's not worth the risk and I'll be able to just keep playing.* But I knew that wasn't how it was going to happen. I could tell by the way the intensity was increasing. The way my body wanted to run further and harder than the game required.

I signalled to Ms Tan, who coached the girls' team games, that I had to get off court. Instead of heading to the bench I ran out of the gym. Etienne was on an outside court playing with the boys' team. I saw him as I ran through the grounds. I saw him watch me leave. I saw him frown, just a little bit, at me running through the school gates.

I thought about all the progress we'd made lately. The high fives after games, the occasional, almost accidental smiles. The couple of words exchanged during practice. I wondered if I was throwing it all away by leaving for this catch.

I called Mum as soon as I got out of the school grounds. She was at work and didn't want to leave. She said, 'Shouldn't you be in class?'

I stopped for a moment to catch my breath. Mum only answered the phone if she was between clients. If a client was due or already with her, her phone was off. She'd picked up, so I knew she could come if she wanted to.

'Mum, can you help me or not?'

I think then she remembered I was trying to save someone's life, and she got in her car and came to meet me.

The catch was at a bridge. Someone on the bridge was climbing a railing to take a clever selfie. Mum and I parked below the bridge. I stood on the road as Mum directed the traffic to go around me. The person dropped their phone as they fell and as soon as I had them on the ground they wanted to retrieve it from between the cars driving past.

Mum stopped them. Language was a barrier, so she pointed at the phone on the road, the pieces scattered, the cars running over it. Then she pointed them to the footpath. There was a lot of pointing and shaking heads on both sides until Mum finally got the message across.

As we were driving back to school Mum said, 'I can't believe no one else stopped to help. I'm sorry I didn't agree to come straight away, Beth. I know I should. It just feels hard to leave work some days.'

She didn't say she got paid to do her job, but we both silently added that to the end of her statement. I knew she was right. That she would lose her job if she kept leaving every time I asked. But we had agreed I would ask her. Then when I did, she acted like I was asking for too much.

I stopped asking Meg to drive me to catches. Her belly wasn't that big, she could still easily fit behind the steering wheel, but she was tired and trying to do extra schoolwork to make up for the time after the baby arrived when she wouldn't be able to get much done.

I didn't like asking Dad to help either. He was so quiet about the whole thing. I knew he'd do it, but he never got out of the car. He never asked me anything about the catch. He would just say, 'Okay?' and I would nod. Then he'd drive us home. It felt weird. Like he thought I was doing something wrong.

One night I went down to their room and asked Mum to drive me. It was about two in the morning. I wasn't in a panic, but I knew I had to get there soon. Mum groaned and rolled over, pushing Dad out of bed. I still had to shake him a little and push the keys into his hand to get him out of the house and into the car.

We drove in silence. I gave Dad directions and we didn't say anything else. I knew we were going back to the woman who'd slapped me. I felt really sad about coming back to catch her. She wasn't being pushed anymore – she was jumping. I didn't know if she knew I'd be there to catch her, but I expected she would slap me again. She'd also cry and let me hold her for a while before she'd turn and go back into the building.

This time after I put her on her feet I said, 'Please don't go back. Please go somewhere else.'

She said she had nowhere else to go. If she chose not to go back it meant she chose to spend the night on the street. She was more scared of spending the night on the street than she was of him.

She looked away from me, towards the building she was about to go into, and she whispered, 'Please stop coming.'

I moved to stand in front of her. I wanted her to see me.

'I'll be here next time. Every time.'

She walked past me towards the entrance. 'Please don't.'

Dad had stayed in the car. He'd parked it where he was close enough to hear me if I screamed but far enough that he couldn't see anything. It was a very deliberate position. He didn't want to see. He didn't want to know. On the drive home we were both silent again. I was thinking about the woman, about how little I was actually doing for her. I was thinking about Dad, too. How I felt like I was failing him, without really understanding how or why.

We didn't speak until we reached the house. Dad turned off the car engine and opened the front door for us. As I walked past him he said, 'Okay?' and when I nodded he said, 'Goodnight then.'

I went to bed and dozed a little, turning from side to side. The next morning I heard Mum and Dad in their bedroom. Mum was saying, 'Just get out of the car, just once, and see what your daughter does.'

It was nice to hear but also a bit weird, because she'd never said anything like that to me. Any pride she had in my catching seemed to be hidden among her worry and the difficulty of getting me places.

I didn't hear Dad's answer to Mum. Maybe he didn't say anything. That seemed to be his chosen response when things were happening he didn't like or didn't agree with. I wished he would say something, though. To me or Mum. I wished he'd just say what he thought. Even if it was bad. Just so I knew.

TWENTY

I woke up in the middle of the night. I didn't feel any urgent need to run. I was just awake. I lay in bed and listened to the house to try to work out why. I heard the murmur of voices coming from Meg's room. Maybe Rik had stayed the night. He was staying over a bit more often now that Meg was nearly due. When I got up I could hear more than two voices in her room.

I quietly opened the door and saw Meg, Rik and Mum in there.

Mum and Rik were sitting on the bed. Meg was pacing the small space available to her and telling Mum she was ready to go to the hospital. Mum was telling her she wasn't. She was trying to convince Meg to lie down and rest, which was weird because with Rik and Mum on the bed there wasn't really room for Meg. Meg kept pacing, saying there was no way she could lie down, the baby was coming. Mum agreed the baby might be coming, but she doubted it would arrive before morning.

Rik was having trouble staying on the bed. He wanted to get up and be with Meg, but Meg was pacing erratically and there was no room for him to pace with her. They saw me standing at the door and looked at me as if they were all trying to work out who I was and what I was doing here.

'Is there anything I can do to help?' I said.

They kept staring at me like I was a foreign object until Mum jumped up. 'Yes, great. You stay here with Meg.' She told Rik to go get some sleep on the couch and announced she was going back to bed. She patted me on the shoulder as she walked past me. 'Try to get her to rest.'

I looked at Meg when the others had left the room. She clearly had no intention of resting. I asked her what she wanted to do and she suggested a walk around the block.

I refused to take her all the way around the block, but we walked back and forth on the street. Meg caught me looking up at Etienne's house. At the dark of his bedroom window.

'How's it going?'

We both knew it wasn't a general question. She was asking me about Etienne.

'It's getting better.'

I wondered what he'd told her, whether he talked about me to her.

'He doesn't talk to me about you, but I see him looking around for you sometimes.'

It was like she'd read my mind. I wanted to know more, but she clutched my arm then and did a silent scream into the footpath. We both decided no matter what Mum said, it was time to go to the hospital.

Mum and Rik were still wide awake when we walked into the house. Dad had also been lying awake, so we all piled into the car with the bag Meg had packed a few weeks ago. I wasn't really sure what role Dad and I had in the baby's arrival, but Mum said we were going, so we went.

In the car, Meg tucked herself into Rik's arms and did a few more of those silent screams as we drove to the hospital. I pushed myself into the corner of the back seat as much as I could to give Meg room. Mum was trying to be calm, but she kept checking her bag over and over again to make sure she had her keys and phone. Dad kept looking in the rear-vision mirror at the three of us in the back as he drove.

At the hospital they ushered Meg into a room and asked her who she wanted to have with her. She said, 'Everyone,' and Dad and I looked at each other because we had been expecting to wait outside. As Meg got settled and Mum and Rik lit candles and put on music, Dad and I stood around reading the signs and examining the hospital equipment.

The midwife was young and brisk. She checked Meg and then left. There was a TV in the room, but the sound of it annoyed Meg when Rik turned it on to distract her. The music they'd chosen annoyed her too, so we ended up sitting in silence. Mum suggested a walk around the hospital corridors, but Meg shook her head. She was certain the baby would turn up at any minute even though the midwife's actions suggested otherwise.

It was a weird hour. Every now and then someone started a conversation that would take off for a bit and then die down when no one could think of anything to say. The midwife popped in a couple of times. She didn't stay long.

Eventually Meg's silent screaming routine got a bit more frequent and stopped being so silent. The midwife came back and stayed. Mum and Rik kept close to Meg and the midwife. Dad and I tried to melt into the background.

Mum noticed us and suggested we go and get everyone some food and drink. We tried to work out what everyone wanted, but no one was making requests. Mum gave us a look that meant *just go and get something*, so we walked out of the room and around the corridors looking for vending machines or cafes that were open in the early hours of the morning.

We found a vending machine and bought juice and nuts and a packet of chips. By the time we made it back the room was all action, with Meg sweating and swearing and Mum and Rik on either side of her saying how great she was doing. Dad and I stood at the door holding our juice and nuts and chips.

As everything got more intense I forgot how weird it all felt and became sucked into the drama in front of me. Dad moved forward to stand near Mum, resting his hand on her shoulder.

We waited and watched as the midwife gave Meg instructions and encouragement. At one point Meg grabbed Mum, crying that she couldn't do it anymore and she'd decided she didn't want a baby after all. Mum told her it was too late now. Meg gritted her teeth and let out a groan followed by a scream that pushed a tiny red baby, squirming and wailing, into our world.

Mum and Rik were crying. Meg started laughing. Dad and I beamed at each other as the midwife pushed us all out of the way so she could move around and do her job.

She weighed and measured the baby, then bundled her up. Rik and Mum took turns holding her while Meg had a shower. When Meg got back into the bed she held out her arms for the baby, and we all stood around looking down at the new little face. Meg passed her to Dad to have a quick hold. He offered her to me, but I shook my head.

'I don't want to drop her.'

Meg looked at me in disbelief. 'For God's sake, Beth, I've seen you catch grown men, you're not going to drop a baby.'

Mum, Dad and I smiled, but then we all realised what she'd said and quickly looked to Rik. He hadn't been let in on my secret. We looked at the midwife too, because it was a weird thing to say. Neither of them seemed to have registered anything unusual.

I stepped back and shook my head, and because of her mistake, or maybe just because she was focused on her own baby, Meg didn't push it. She took the baby in her arms like it was something she'd always done while we all stood watching and wondering what would come next.

Meg and Rik decided to call their baby Aimee. Mum was thrilled with the name, but hated the spelling. She didn't say so outright. Instead, she asked a couple of times if they thought people would misspell Aimee's name for the rest of her life. Then she put the same question to any hospital staff who happened to walk into the room to see if they'd offer an opinion that might support hers. The staff were wise enough not to get involved.

Rik left the room to call his parents while we said goodbye to Meg and Aimee. Rik and Meg needed to stay at the hospital a bit longer, but Mum, Dad and I went home to get some sleep. I must have fallen asleep quickly, because the next thing I knew, I was being woken by the sound of a baby crying.

My first thought was a baby crying as it was falling. That I had to wake up to go and catch it. As I became more awake I realised the sound was coming from Meg's room. When I went to have a look Aimee was on the floor having her nappy changed, and she was furious. Her skinny little legs were kicking out at Rik's hands as he tried to clean her up. Meg and Mum were standing behind him watching.

When Meg saw me at the door she explained, 'Aimee doesn't like having her nappy changed.'

I nodded. I wouldn't like to have my nappy changed on the floor with a bunch of people watching me either.

TWENTY-ONE

WE had a quiet week after Aimee arrived. I went to school and Dad went to the bike shop, but Mum took the week off work so she could be around for Meg. Rik went to a few lectures he couldn't miss, but most of the time he was at our place. The three of them took turns sleeping and looking after Aimee. When we were home, Dad and I moved quietly around the house trying to get washing or cooking done without waking anyone up.

Rik's father came over to meet Aimee, but his mother didn't. I had expected that Meg would have talked his mum around by now. While Tad was there, holding the baby and smiling and cooing, no one mentioned Mari. Tad left after hugging and congratulating everyone and Mum telling him to visit anytime.

I heard Mum and Dad talking quietly about Mari not showing up when they thought Rik and Meg were asleep. They both knew Meg expected Mari to come to her, but Mum wanted to call her or get Meg to take the baby over. Dad wanted to leave Meg and Rik to manage it in their own way. He didn't think forcing the issue was the right thing to do.

On the weekend all Meg's friends came by to see her and to meet the baby. They bought flowers, little outfits and a lot of noise. Mum and I made drinks and filled up snack bowls while Meg showed off Aimee, who was gradually passed around the group.

It was my job to answer the door and deliver the drinks. When Tommy and Maye came I let them straight in. They greeted me like a friend, before heading through to Meg and Aimee. When I answered the door to let Etienne in I paused.

I knew he'd be coming. I'd been expecting him each time I opened the door. I'd thought he'd come earlier. Soon after Meg got home and when there weren't so many people. But he'd stayed away. Maybe it was because he was busy or wanted to give Meg some time, or maybe it was because of me. Because he didn't want to have to see me without a lot of other people around.

At the door, in my pause, I wondered if this was the right time to talk to him. If there was something I could say in this moment that would fix things between us. But he looked like he didn't want to talk to me, so I pointed towards the lounge room where everyone was gathered. Etienne frowned a little at the amount of noise coming from the room, but when he walked towards Meg I could see he was smiling. That despite everything, he was still pleased to see her. Meg insisted Etienne hold Aimee, and I watched as he gently cradled her in his arms.

I tried to act normal with Etienne there holding Aimee. I knew Mum would be watching me. I tried to stay busy in the kitchen or chatting to the others, but the whole time he was there I tracked where he was and who he was talking to.

As I walked in with a fresh round of drinks Tommy came to stand next to me. He joked about basketball, complimenting me in a roundabout kind of way on how well I'd been playing. He asked me what it was like being an aunt and whether my sleep was disturbed by the baby crying. No one had asked me that yet. Everyone else asked me how Meg was or how the baby was, but no one had asked me how I was finding it all. Not even Lin.

I laughed. 'If only you knew the things that wake me at night.'

Tommy laughed too at that. 'Tell me more.'

He said it in a joking, suggestive manner, and I glanced over to Etienne. A reaction I hadn't planned. A reaction to Tommy's question I didn't want to have.

Tommy followed my gaze. 'Don't worry about him. He's a grumpy bastard, but he'll come round eventually. Anyway, time for me to go. See you at training.' He touched my shoulder as he left.

I looked back across the room and saw Etienne had been watching the whole exchange.

When most people had left and I came into the kitchen with a stack of empty plates and half-finished drinks, Etienne was chatting to Mum. He helped take some glasses from me and there was an awkward silence.

'Have you had a chance to practise the drills Coach set for us this week?'

I couldn't believe he was speaking to me. Looking at me. I shook my head and mumbled things about the baby and not getting much time or sleep.

'Do you have time to train for a bit now?'

I looked at Mum, who nodded.

'Plenty of time before dinner. I'll finish up here, you go do your training.'

I raced upstairs to change and put sneakers on, thinking back to the day Etienne and I ran drills in the driveway before trials. The day we ended up with our legs tangled, laughing, nearly kissing.

Etienne was hard on me when we trained. There was no pushing or bumping or teasing like before. He was more like Coach, demanding I pass, dribble or shoot again if my first attempt wasn't good enough.

He was reserved, his face almost unhappy. I couldn't understand it. It didn't make sense for him to be here with me when he seemed so down about it.

I tried hard to do everything right. To do the drills the way he was asking me to do them. I wanted to do something that would make him smile, something foolish enough to bring back the old Etienne. But I couldn't think of anything, or perhaps I was too worried that I'd try something silly only to find the old Etienne wasn't there anymore.

I couldn't work out what he wanted. The best I could come up with was that it was all about the basketball. That what he wanted was to win in his last year of school and he needed me up to scratch to do it.

We ended the session with a shoot-out. He beat me like we both knew he would, but he also acknowledged I'd improved, which made me smile to myself. Etienne was still too serious for me to try smiling at him.

We stood for a bit, him bouncing the ball, looking at the ground or the street. Anywhere but me. I waited in the silence, hoping he was about to tell me what was going on with him and why he was looking so serious. When he did finally speak it was disappointing.

'I need to get going.'

'Okay. Thanks for the training session.'

He'd made no steps towards actually leaving.

'No problem.' He passed the ball back to me. 'Anytime.' But he didn't say it in a way that made me think I could just turn up at his door and ask for more training.

He went to walk away, but stopped and turned back to face me.

'Beth?'

I paused the dribbling I'd started to do. Here it was, the thing I'd been waiting for that could take us back to where we were, to where I wanted to be. Or the thing that would tell me it was never going to happen.

'Be careful around Tommy.'

'Tommy?'

I was confused. It wasn't at all what I was hoping Etienne'd say.

'He's an okay guy, but just . . . just be careful.'

'Around Tommy?'

'Yeah.'

'Why?'

'Guys like Tommy . . .'

'What?'

'They—'

'Tommy's helped me in training. He's acted like he wants me to be there. He's being a friend.' I wanted to say, *Unlike you*. Instead I said, 'There's nothing between Tommy and me. It's not like that.'

Etienne looked back towards his house, like it was calling him. 'Okay, fine. Forget I said anything.'

I watched him walk away, then went back to dribbling the ball up and down the driveway. Rik turned up and we walked into the house together.

Inside, dinner was being put on the table. Meg had the baby but as soon as she saw me she strode over and shoved Aimee into my arms. I had so far managed to avoid holding her. There had been enough other people around that I hadn't needed to, and after the first time in the hospital Meg hadn't pushed. Now she just deposited her into my arms, and when she saw my body stiffen and the fear on my face, she told me to get over it. I looked to Mum, but she just shook her head a little and got on with bringing the last plates of food to the table. Then Meg took Rik outside and they had a full-blown argument we tried not to listen to but couldn't help hearing.

'You need to go home. You aren't meant to be here today.'

Rik's answer wasn't as loud or audible.

'We need some space.'

Rik didn't want be away from Meg and Aimee. He wasn't ready. We could all see that.

'Rik, we agreed we'd stick to the plan. This is the plan.'

Rik eventually agreed to leave, probably because there was no actual point in arguing with Meg at the best of times, and this certainly wasn't the best of times. She was exhausted from having her friends there on top of all the night-time feeds.

Mum quickly cleared his place at the table and moved everything around so it didn't look like anyone was missing. I was still standing there holding Aimee.

Meg came back in and sat at the table. She started hurriedly eating. Dad arrived home and we all sat down to join Meg, only I was still holding

Aimee. I was starting to feel a bit more comfortable about holding her, but I couldn't work out how to eat with her or how to put her down.

I looked to Mum to see if she'd help me, maybe take the baby from my arms and put her in her bassinet so I could eat. But she just started on her meal with the others. It was as if they'd all decided it was my evening to look after Aimee without anyone actually telling me.

I walked carefully to the bassinet and tried to put her in it. When I got her in there and extracted my arms she looked like she was still asleep. I held my breath for a moment, thinking I'd managed it, but as soon as Aimee realised she'd lost contact with a person she started crying.

Everyone kept eating, so I picked her up again. I walked back to the table and sat holding her while everyone else ate. I didn't realise how much Aimee objected to being put down, but it seemed like she hated it almost as much as she hated having her nappy changed.

'Now you've realised she's not so scary, Beth, can you mind her? I need to get some study done.'

Dad held Aimee while I quickly ate, and then I spent the rest of the evening holding her and watching her sleep. I sat in front of the TV so it looked like I was watching it, but I really only watched Aimee. Whenever she started to stir and seemed about to wake up, I stood up to walk around for a bit until she settled. Mum came in to check on us a few times, but she left me to it.

It was late when Meg came back downstairs to take Aimee from me. When she was out of my arms I missed having her there. I missed her warmth and her smell and that surprisingly solid feeling of her tiny body close to mine.

TWENTY-TWO

WHEN I saw Lin at school, I almost showed her the assignments that were due or overdue and my homework I hadn't done. I knew she'd look at it all and see a way for me to start getting it done. But I didn't show her. Maybe because I was embarrassed to admit how far behind I was. Or maybe because school was feeling even more irrelevant than usual. I told her about Etienne instead. About our training session and the weird Tommy conversation.

'I think things might be getting better. I think there's a chance we can at least start to be friends again.'

We had just walked into the lunch area at school and were heading to our usual seats. Lin pointed across the schoolyard.

'Maybe that's why he's ready to be friends again.'

I looked over to see Maye sitting next to Etienne. Her arm was draped over his shoulders. They weren't alone. There were others, their usual crowd talking and laughing. Maye seemed to be doing a lot of the talking and laughing. I couldn't see Etienne's face. I turned away. It was too hard to watch.

I could feel tears forming.

'Yeah, I guess that's it then. I mean, it's a good thing really if we can go back to being friends.'

'Yeah.' Lin was nodding, but she said this in a way that sounded like she disagreed with me.

She turned me away from our regular seat and towards the library instead, where we spent the rest of the break. I tried to use the time to do some schoolwork, telling myself that not having to think about Etienne would free up some mental space.

I rewrote my list of things that needed to be done in all my subjects. Meg would tell me to pick something easy from the list and do it, just so I could have the satisfaction of crossing something off. None of them looked easy. None of them looked like things I could get done in a lunchbreak.

I looked over at Lin, who was working through her maths book with a focus I could only dream of. I looked back at my list, telling myself to just pick one thing, but all I saw was Maye's arm, casually flung over Etienne like a statement of ownership.

I spent the rest of the day dragging myself through classes and occasionally wondering where Rohan was. He'd been missing for a few days and I worried something had happened.

At dinner Mum and Dad were looking uptight, but we'd all been a bit on edge lately with the demands that Aimee put on us all. So I just thought it was the disturbed night's sleep. They hadn't recovered from me occasionally waking them up, and now they had Aimee crying above their heads too.

When we finished eating Mum pulled out a letter addressed to them from the school. There it was. In black and white. The missed classes, the half-days, the unexplained absences, the lack of assignments and the drop in my grades which, the principal quite rudely pointed out, weren't that high to begin with.

Meg looked at me sympathetically. Mum and Dad tried to be reasonable. I tried not to be angry.

'I have a lot more to deal with than the average sixteen-year-old.' I looked at Meg. 'No offence.' I didn't want her to think I was blaming her or Aimee.

She smiled at me. 'None taken.'

'Maybe I need to leave school.'

It wasn't what I wanted at all, but it felt like a way to get out of the conversation and situation.

Mum shook her head. 'That's not an option here.'

I was relieved. I couldn't imagine not seeing Lin every day. Not playing on the basketball team with Etienne, even if he did now have a girlfriend.

I looked at Meg and wondered if she knew about Maye and Etienne. If she was going to tell me. She was probably in the loop even though she hadn't been to school since Aimee was born. I couldn't ask her. I didn't want to have it confirmed.

'We're going to have to go to the school and talk to the principal. I'm not going to lie for you, Beth.'

'You can't tell them!'

I didn't want the principal, the teachers, knowing about me catching.

'No, I guess we can't. We'll just have to be vague. In the meantime, you need to get on top of your schoolwork.'

I nodded, thinking of the list I'd written at lunch. 'I'm already working on it.'

'I can help.'

I looked at Meg, her arms full of her new baby, with her own study to do.

'I'm fine. It's under control. I let things slip a bit with the catching and the excitement of Aimee coming. I'll just put my head down now and catch up.'

It sounded believable to me when I formed the words and said them out loud, but when I looked around the table I realised no one was buying it.

With my parents' meeting with the school principal looming, I tried to keep focused in class and get some of the overdue assignments finished. I figured if I handed a few things in there might be something positive to say at the meeting.

The day before my parents' appointment I left school to catch. I told Mum when I got home so she was ready for hearing about it the next day. I could see the words written on her face, the ones she wanted to say but knew she couldn't. The *could you not have just let this one go?* face.

I told Mum about the catch. About how I'd felt a little bit sick all morning, but nothing I needed to act on. When it got stronger I knew I was going to have to go. I wanted to leave school at a time when it might not be noticed, so I left at lunchtime. It was a different kind of catch.

It wasn't one where I felt like I needed to hurry, and the position was weird. I couldn't sense any buildings, any trees, any ladders. I hoped I'd get back to school before the end of lunch.

When I got to the catch it turned out to be a train station. I struggled to see who it was I needed to catch. I walked slowly up and down the platform, watching people waiting for trains, trying to spot who wasn't getting on and working out how I was going to manage this catch.

By the time my first afternoon class would have started I saw him. He was leaning on a post towards the back of the platform, picking furiously at his fingernails. Just from the look of him, I wasn't sure it was safe for me to approach. I stood as close as I dared and watched him as another train entered and left the station.

I didn't know what I would do if he jumped. I wasn't going to get down onto the tracks to catch him. I waited, watched and hoped when the time came I'd know what to do.

It took him another hour to make his move. I studied him throughout that hour. He was thin, really thin, and he looked upset, lost and a little scary. He didn't see me. He wasn't looking around the platform. He barely lifted his head.

When he made his move my body reacted before I knew I was ready. He'd walked to the edge of the platform and was looking down the tracks at the train coming in. He didn't jump. He leant forward, like his mind was dragging his feet.

I ran behind him and grabbed his shirt. I pulled him back hard away from the edge.

The train pulled in and people started getting on and off. I didn't think anyone had seen us. I stayed holding his shirt as the train moved away, though I knew he wasn't going to try again. I could feel the defeat in him, and something else too. Something like hope.

He turned to look at me, then shrugged off the hold I had on his shirt. He walked slowly along the platform towards the steps. At the halfway mark he stopped to turn and look back at me. He didn't look so upset now, or scary, but he still looked lost.

There wasn't any point in going back to school. By the time I'd get there it would be finishing. I went straight home. I called Lin as soon as I thought she'd be out of the school grounds and told her about the catch. She suggested again that if I was going to catch people in busy places I should be hiding my face. This time I agreed, because really she was right. It was just something I never thought of at the time.

After we ended the call I did some schoolwork and tried not to look out the window too often for a glimpse of Etienne coming home.

I didn't tell Mum that bit, or the bit about Lin urging me to hide my face. Or a lot of the other details.

'This is too much, Beth. Too much for someone your age.' Mum reached up to stroke my head. 'I think the time has come to talk through what we need to do. How we hand this over to someone else. To an adult to deal with. You can go back to being a teenager.'

I ducked my head away from her hand. I didn't want her sympathy or her reminding me I wasn't a normal teenager.

'Hand what over, Mum? This isn't something you can just hand over. No one would believe me anyway, and then people like that guy today would be dead.'

I stormed off to my room, leaving Mum sighing.

TWENTY-THREE

THE next morning Mum and Dad drove me to school. Meg was still at home with Aimee. She was starting to miss school now. She missed her friends and that daily interaction with teachers. And she was tired. More tired than she had expected, so she was worried that she wasn't going to manage her classes.

The meeting at the school was with the principal, Mrs Hanrahan, who smiled and shook all our hands when we walked into her office. She indicated the chairs we were to sit in.

The first few minutes of conversation were about Meg and Aimee.

'How is Meg managing? Is there anything more we can do to support her before the trial exams start?'

'Meg's great, and the baby is too.'

I could see Mum was on the verge of pulling out her phone to show Mrs Hanrahan the latest hundred photos of Aimee when Dad gave her a nudge and she remembered why they were here.

Mrs Hanrahan had been the principal of our school since before Meg started. She was old now, but still holding the school together. She wasn't unkind. She had been good to Meg, and I was hoping she was going to be good to me too, even though we'd all agreed not to tell her about catching.

'Things have been a little different in our house this year. There's been a lot going on for Beth. A lot of new things for her to manage.'

Mrs Hanrahan sighed like she was used to having to deal with people lying to her, and showed Mum and Dad a list of my current marks and rankings in my classes. I was at the bottom of almost every class.

Mum and Dad nodded seriously at what they'd been shown.

'Well, now that we're aware we'll make sure Beth does better.'

It was unusual for Dad to speak in these situations, but it was good to hear him try.

Mrs Hanrahan had more to say.

'All children are different, aren't they? Different needs, different strengths. Even if they're from the same family.'

She was saying I wasn't smart like Meg.

'But school is essential for everyone. Beth needs to attend every day, for the whole day. If she doesn't, the school needs to know why.'

We all nodded again as she ran through the support the school could offer me. Things like the homework club and the counsellor. Mum had never rated the school counsellor, so I was confident she wasn't going to send me there. And I couldn't get to homework club most days because of basketball training or my work schedule at the bike shop. But we didn't say any of that. We kept nodding as if it was all new information that we would consider.

After we walked out of the office, Mum and Dad were looking at each other to see who was going to speak first. I took it out of their hands.

'I'm really going to try from now on. I'll get on top of it all. We can talk about it more tonight, but I should get to class now.'

There was visible relief in Dad's eyes. He was always better when he'd had time to think about what he wanted to say.

I really did try after that meeting. I showed Lin my list of overdue assignments, and with her help I managed to finish a few. We spent our lunchtimes together in the library working to help me catch up. Rohan was still absent from school.

I only had to leave school once in the days after the meeting, when Jake fell from his tree again. I wrote the date and time I left in the notebook Mum had bought for me, and Mum called it in to the school as a family emergency. After the event, but still an explained absence like Mrs Hanrahan asked for. I hoped with the explanation and the couple of assignments I'd managed to hand in, I'd escape another lecture or the threat of suspension.

On Sunday night Mum and Dad went out. It was the first time they'd had a night out together since Aimee had turned up. I was in my room trying to get more schoolwork done, and Meg and Aimee were asleep. Understanding there was a catch came on quickly. There was no warning. No slow creep of nausea. Just a sudden urge to vomit.

I rushed to Meg's door, but stopped. I couldn't wake her. I thought about calling Mum and Dad, but they'd been so happy to be spending time together away from the house I couldn't bring myself to call them either. I would have run, but I wouldn't have made it in time.

I looked across the road to Etienne's house. Etienne had been almost friendly at basketball training that week. I could only assume that it was because he was happy with Maye.

I rushed to his door and knocked loudly. Etienne answered quickly and looked worried when he saw me.

'Everything's fine. I mean with Meg and Aimee.' I was sure that's what he'd be most worried about. 'It's just I need a lift. It's really important, and it won't take long. Meg is asleep and Mum and Dad are out.'

I thought about explaining more or making up a story, but I didn't have time.

'Can you drive me or not? Because I've really got to go now.'

Etienne nodded and reached for his keys.

In his car we sat silently. I gave him directions, but aside from that we didn't speak. I think Etienne wanted to ask me questions, but he needed to concentrate on his driving. He wasn't a natural driver, which was funny because he seemed so coordinated everywhere else. I tried to focus on where I needed to go. On how to get there. On whether I was too late. I tried not to look like I was gripping the car door to stop myself lurching every time he changed gear.

The catch was taking us to an edge of my boundary that I hadn't been to before. It was a block of apartments surrounded by houses. There was a big park across the street and the area was quiet. I asked Etienne to stop the car.

'It's really important you stay in the car.'

'You're not robbing someone, are you?' He said this with a nervous smile.

I shook my head. 'Please just stay in the car.'

Then I ran.

The building had about nine levels. I looked up and saw her on the roof. She was looking towards the sky, and I thought she might have changed her mind – she was just hovering there. I hoped she'd changed her mind, because there was always a chance I was going to miss.

Then I felt her give up. I felt her give in to the desperation and sorrow she was feeling, and I watched her fall towards me.

I moved into position as she fell through the air. I saw the fear and regret on her face, in her flailing arms. I worried those arms were going to ruin the catch. That they would knock me off balance. She was young, but she was also large. I widened my stance a little. I let her fall into my arms where I could hold her tight.

She let her body go slack and put her head on my shoulder. I stood looking at her and at where she had come from. When I looked to the side I saw Etienne standing at the corner of the street. Our eyes met and he gave me a half smile, uncertain about what he'd seen. Weirdly I didn't feel worried now that I knew he'd seen me catch. I felt relief. I held the girl until I felt she was ready.

When I put her feet back on the ground, she hugged me and I hugged her back. I took my time with her because she needed it and because I could see Etienne was happy to wait. She let me go, then pulled me in for another hug before she turned and walked back into the building.

I went to where Etienne was standing.

'Thanks for driving me. We can go now.'

He nodded and we got back into his car.

On the way home Etienne focused on the roads. He still needed me to give him directions. I didn't talk any more than I had to so he could concentrate on getting us safely home.

When we were back in his driveway Etienne turned off the car engine. We both stayed sitting, neither one of us ready to move.

'I asked you to stay in the car.'

'I'm glad I didn't. That was amazing.'

I tried to shrug it off, but I did feel amazing after that catch – and now sitting in Etienne's car with Etienne smiling at me. I looked him straight in the eyes.

'It's something I started doing this year. I don't know why or how.' I took a breath. 'It's why I left the movie, why sometimes I leave basketball or school.'

It took Etienne a moment. He kept his hands on the steering wheel and stared straight ahead while he processed the information. I saw him start to put things in place. He turned to me.

'Why didn't you tell me?'

'I didn't really tell anyone. I mean, I told Lin, and later my family, but only because I had to. And you weren't really talking to me.'

He nodded. 'Sorry about that, I was . . .'

He reached out to hold my hands in his. He turned them over, inspecting them like they held the secret to my catching.

'Maybe we should try that movie again.'

He looked at me and smiled. I smiled back, but then remembered Maye.

'What about Maye?'

He looked confused.

'Won't she be annoyed if you're going to the movies with other people?'

'Why would Maye care what I do?'

I had to tell him how I'd seen them together. How she'd had her arm around him. How I'd assumed they were seeing each other.

Etienne shrugged. 'Maye and I are just friends. Tell me again how you know where to go. How do you know people are falling?'

I explained it to him as best I could, telling him about the map and boundary, about how I felt sick. I could have stayed in that car with him all night just talking, but it was late and no one in my house knew where I was. I looked over the street to our driveway. Mum and Dad weren't home yet.

'I better go.'

'But the movie?'

'Sure. Anytime. Thanks again for driving me tonight.'

'Thanks for asking me. It was amazing. You're amazing.'

I was finding it hard to leave him, especially as he was still holding my hands.

Etienne drew me to him, pulling my hands towards his chest and our faces close. He kissed me then. A small, sweet kiss, on my lips. I drew back to look at his face and we smiled at each other.

I whispered, 'Goodnight,' and got out of his car. I walked towards home before I could say something that would mess the whole thing up, because right now it felt too perfect to be true.

TWENTY-FOUR

THE next morning I hoped to find Etienne waiting for me outside the house. I'd spent the night imagining us walking to school together. Holding hands as we went through the gates. Confirming for myself last night was real and not something I made up.

When I opened the front door there was no Etienne. Instead of my imagined hand-in-hand walk with him, I got Meg. She was going for the Year Twelve trial exams, which meant she only had to be at school if there was an exam. She had two today, so she needed to be at school for most of the day.

She'd been busy pumping milk out of her boobs and giving Rik instructions. Rik had Aimee settled into a pouch on his chest and was jiggling her up and down to keep her asleep. He wanted Meg out of the house before Aimee woke up and realised she was gone, but Meg was still fussing with instructions and making sure she had everything she needed for the exams.

When we finally walked out onto the street I looked over to Etienne's house. Meg watched me. I hadn't told her anything about last night other than he'd driven me to the catch, but I felt sure she'd read between the lines. That kiss was probably still showing on my face.

'He went to school early today.'

I nodded like I knew that or didn't care. I desperately tried to think of something else to talk about so I didn't dwell on the idea he regretted the kiss and was avoiding me.

'What does it feel like to be leaving Aimee?'

'It's fine. It's good for Rik. And Aimee.'

She said it quickly and with force. Like she absolutely believed what she was saying. But when she finished speaking she looked towards our house as if she'd prefer to be walking back inside.

'Do you think Mum will actually go to work, or call in sick so she can keep an eye on Rik?'

I thought it might be a light-hearted distraction, but Meg wasn't easy to distract, and she didn't want to contemplate anyone straying from her plan.

'She'd better go to work.'

Meg had been insistent that Rik needed to learn to look after Aimee on his own but only at our house. It was part of the plan she was so rigidly sticking to. She'd also been saying how much she was looking forward to being at school and getting these exams done.

As we walked she started to look less sure of herself. She checked her phone a couple of times. At the school gates she gave up the internal battle she was having and called Rik to double-check when he'd bring Aimee in for a feed.

I spent my school day looking around corners for Etienne. When I didn't see him at lunchtime I started to become certain he was avoiding me. That he'd woken up regretting the whole thing, taking me to the catch, our conversation and the kiss.

Lin and I sat briefly outside to eat lunch before our usual library session. I was desperate to tell her about Etienne. I had been avoiding telling her over text because I wanted to see her face when I said the words.

As Lin ate her lunch I told her about the catch and how I'd had to ask Etienne to drive me. Lin raised her eyebrows a little at the mention of Etienne, but she was more interested in the catch. I told her what I knew of the woman I caught. Lin asked me how I felt after a catch like that. I thought back to the kiss with Etienne. 'Great. I felt great.'

As we got up to go to the library, I looked over the schoolyard and saw Meg surrounded by friends. Rik was standing nearby looking out of place. He was still wearing the pouch, but it was empty. Aimee was nestled into Meg's arms and Meg's friends were crowded around her. I noticed it was mainly girls, that the boys Meg was friends with, including Etienne, had stayed away.

I wanted to go over and hold Aimee too. I wanted to claim some sort of ownership over her – she'd become so much a part of my life. I wanted to protect her from all those other hands. It was hard now to imagine our house without her in it. I felt jealous watching other kids crowd around like they were trying to get a piece of her.

Later when the bell had rung and Lin and I were heading back to class I saw them again. It was just Meg, Rik and Aimee. Rik was sitting beside Meg, and Meg was feeding Aimee. They had their heads close to one another as they talked and watched her feed.

Despite searching all day, I didn't see Etienne until basketball practice after school. He was there when I walked in, like he was waiting for me. When he saw me, he took my arm and gently pulled me into the storage room at the side of the gym. I searched his face to see if I was about to get bad news about how last night had been a mistake.

He pulled me in close to him and I dropped my gaze for a moment. It wasn't bad news.

Etienne put a hand under my chin and gently lifted my face until our eyes locked. He said, 'Hello,' as if I was something new and wonderful he'd just discovered. I smiled back at him and echoed, 'Hello,' because to me, right then and there, he was something new and wonderful. All the fear and worry I'd been feeling about last night vanished. I could tell he wanted to kiss me, that he would if only we weren't in a gym storage room so close to all the other members of our team.

We were interrupted by Coach calling us in to start training. Coach tried to hurry us up as we walked over together, our bodies close.

'Next week is the first of the finals for the year. I want to see you all train today like you're playing that final. It's going to be a tough game, but I expect us to win.'

This training session was the most fun I'd had for a long time. The pressure Coach put on us couldn't make a dent in the pleasure I felt being on the court with Etienne and knowing he wanted to kiss me.

My world had suddenly grown lighter. I forgot to worry about whether I was going to have to rush out to catch. I forgot to worry about anything. I almost forgot to catch the ball like a normal person, and took some pretty wild passes I saw Coach raise his eyebrows at. The rest of the team were too busy running and competing with each other to notice, but Coach had seen. I made a point to miss a few after that and to tone it down when I did get the ball.

Etienne had also seen my catches, but he had smiled in delight. I had spent months assuming people would be disgusted or angry somehow if they found out what I could do. That they would single me out or avoid me. Label me as weird. But there was nothing except joy in Etienne's face. I wondered if that was just Etienne, or if others would be the same. If I would be labelled a hero instead. I wondered what would happen if Coach knew the truth. If he would be still let me play.

At the end of practice Etienne came to me, lightly holding my arm again. He whispered in my ear, 'Wait for me.' I nodded and watched him jog off to speak to Coach.

I got my things together slowly in the hope the other girls would leave before I did so I didn't have to explain why I was hanging around. I saw Maye glance my way, a question on her face. I turned away and started worrying about how bad I smelt and whether I should change my clothes. I had nothing with me but my school uniform. I couldn't imagine that would make me smell any better. When the change room was empty, I spent some time at the sink, splashing water under my arms and over my face.

I stood outside the gym as the last of the kids left, wondering what was taking Etienne so long and whether I had missed him. I was getting ready to give up and leave when Etienne came out. His face broke into a smile when he saw me. I wanted to ask what took him so long, but he was thanking me for waiting and taking my hand like it was normal for us to walk home hand in hand after practice. After so long of him ignoring me or looking solemn, I couldn't believe this was happening. It left me speechless.

We walked in silence until Etienne broke it by bringing up our training session and the next game. He wanted to win as much as Coach did. I could feel it in him, that desire to leave school with a final victory.

I didn't want to talk about basketball. I wanted to talk about him.

'Where were you all day? I was looking for you, but it was like you vanished.'

Etienne stopped walking and pulled me towards a large tree. He leant back against the trunk and pulled me closer so that I was standing millimetres from him, our bodies not quite touching. As he spoke he touched my hair, moving a stray piece back behind my ear, running his fingers down the side of my face.

'I have exams, remember? And I was in the Year Twelve study area the rest of the day – I didn't want to have to rush home after practice tonight to study.'

He looked at me with something close to nervous embarrassment to see what my reaction would be.

I couldn't think of anything to say, so I just leant forward. I put my lips to his and kissed him. I tried to make the kiss a little stronger than last night's, a little longer too, and when I pulled away from him he smiled and grabbed me, holding me so that our bodies were close. We kissed and we kissed and we kissed, and I forgot to worry about how I smelt.

I don't know how much time had passed when I had to pull my body away from Etienne's and let myself be still for a moment. Etienne watched me.

'Is everything okay?'

'Yes . . . I thought for a minute . . . I think it's okay.'

I knew I wasn't making a lot of sense, and even though I wanted to get back to where we were before, the mood was broken and we agreed it was time to head home.

We started to walk, hand in hand again, until I had to stop. This time I was sure. Etienne didn't need me to explain.

'Do you want me to drive you?'

'That's okay. It's not far. I think it will be faster for me to run.'

'It's getting dark.'

'I'll be fine.'

Etienne took my bag. 'I'll leave it at your door and let Meg know.'

I looked at him standing there with both of our bags, just for a moment. Just to enjoy knowing he was here helping me. Liking me. Then I turned and ran.

I started to feel annoyed as I ran. I wondered where our time together would have gone if I hadn't had to leave. I also felt annoyed about the catch. I didn't know who I was about to catch. I just knew it was annoying.

As I got closer everything started to feel familiar. I still couldn't work out why until I was in position and looking up. When I saw the shape of the person I was there to catch, everything, including my annoyance, fell into place.

Rohan apologised as he landed in my arms. I didn't hold him as long as I usually held catches. As soon as I was sure he was okay, I put him on his feet. I wanted to turn and walk away. To not even speak to him.

I'd realised he just wanted to see me. He had jumped to get my attention. Just so we could talk. I was furious. I yelled at him.

'What if I couldn't get here in time? What if I'd missed?' I pushed him a little, not hard enough to knock him to the ground but enough for him to know I was angry. Rohan hung his head.

'I'm sorry. I knew you'd come. I wasn't scared. In retrospect I realise it was a stupid thing to do.'

'Yes.' I knew I was being harsh, but I couldn't have people purposely falling to get my attention. 'Where have you been, anyway? Why haven't you been in school?'

'I wanted to say goodbye. Mum and I are leaving tomorrow.'

'Rohan, there's other ways to say goodbye.'

There was more I wanted to say, but Rohan looked so miserable I started to feel bad. A little bad. I was still mad. I also felt his pain and fear, his worry for his mum and himself. I softened a little and let him lead me upstairs.

In his apartment Rohan searched through the fridge and cupboard. He chopped and cooked and presented me with little plates of garlicky vegetables to go with crackers and cheese, telling me they needed to empty the cupboards anyway. I ate while he talked about leaving again.

'Where will you go?'

'I'm not sure. We're just leaving. And then we'll see where we land. I hate it, but I think Mum needs it. It makes her feel safe.'

Rohan walked me out as I told him to never do that again.

'I know it's a weird thing I can do, but I don't actually get it right every time. Sometimes I miss. You're probably going to be too far away for me to get to you again, anyway.'

It was a hard thing to say. Knowing people were falling outside of my boundary was difficult to admit to out loud even though I thought about it all the time.

I got home to find my bag at the front door and my family in various stages of getting ready for bed. Meg and Aimee had disappeared into their nightly routines of studying and sleeping and feeding. Mum was watching TV and Dad was in the kitchen wiping the benches down.

'Do you need any dinner?'

'I just ate, thanks, Dad.'

Dad wanted to know where I'd eaten.

'I ate with the person I caught.'

'Is that safe? Going to a random person's house for food? Just because you caught them doesn't mean they're good people.'

'It wasn't a random person. I wouldn't do that. I only went in because it was someone I knew. A friend from school.'

'Oh.'

I figured that was the end of the conversation, because Dad's limits on my catching were even shorter than on other conversations.

I walked upstairs and dropped my bag at my bedroom door before creeping into Meg's room. She and Aimee were crashed out on her bed, Aimee tucked in under Meg's arm like they were still one body.

I walked quietly over and lifted Aimee away from Meg. She opened her eyes a little and smiled, stretching her arms up above her head. I wrapped her in a blanket and put her in her bassinet. I stroked her eyebrows the way I'd seen Meg do and she closed her eyes again, breathing deeply and evenly.

I could have stood there watching her all night, but I'd told myself I was going to get some schoolwork done before bed. I went back to my room to unpack my bag and found a small piece of paper tucked inside.

Movie? Saturday night? E.

I smiled and carefully folded the note into one of my drawers. I looked out my window at Etienne's house and the light coming from his room.

I wrote a couple of sentences on my business assignment that had been due last week, and did a few maths problems. I watched Etienne's light turn off and then went to bed, telling myself I would get up early to finish the assignment.

TWENTY-FIVE

I slept late the next morning and woke up wondering how I'd missed hearing Aimee cry or Meg pounding on the stairs. I had just enough time to get my books in my bag and get out the door to make it to school before the bell went.

It wasn't a great day. My teachers were loading us up again with assessments and talking about study for exams that were coming up. My lack of focus, my inability to hand anything in on time, on top of that stress, was bugging them. I told Lin about Rohan moving and how he wouldn't be at school anymore. I still felt a bit worried about him, but he was leaving my boundary, so there wasn't much I could do.

I also told Lin about Etienne, about how he'd waited for me at the start of training, about walking home hand in hand and kissing up against the tree. Lin was kind about Etienne and patiently heard me out, but she wanted to talk about catching.

'I've been looking at the data. I think I've found a pattern, or at least a few hot spots.'

'Okay.' I wondered how she managed to sift through all of that data she'd gathered and keep up with schoolwork.

'I'm thinking that if we know the danger signs or the danger spots, we can do something to help.'

'What, like a sign? Or a fence?'

I didn't want to talk about catching, I wanted to talk about Etienne. About what I should wear for the movie date.

'No, not like a sign or a fence. More like . . . I don't know yet. Something that will help people.'

Lin couldn't understand why I wasn't as interested in talking about catching as she was.

'I help people now.'

I didn't know how to tell Lin that the catching was all I was meant to do. I wasn't meant to stop people falling or make anything better. I was just meant to catch them when they fell.

Lin wouldn't understand that. She wanted to know more. She wanted to fully understand what was going on for each person before I caught them and what happened to them afterwards. I believed that fully understanding it would make it so much worse. What I did understand was bad enough.

'But don't you want to understand why? Why you? Why now?'

I shook my head. 'Not anymore. Not now.'

'Because of Etienne?'

'Because it's enough. What I do is enough.'

It didn't seem to be enough for Lin.

At the end of the day I was pulled out of PDHPE and into the principal's office. Ms Tan wasn't pleased to have me taken from her class, but there was nothing she or I could do about it.

While I was waiting for Mrs Hanrahan to see me I started thinking something had gone wrong at home, or with Mum or Dad. Or that they had discovered my catching. I started to imagine them sending me for tests or to a different school. When Mrs Hanrahan finally called me in, I found out it was just because of my failure to hand in schoolwork again.

Mrs Hanrahan seemed tired when she spoke to me. She didn't sound angry or disappointed, just tired. I wondered if she felt like she'd been doing her job too long. If she'd moved past any satisfaction or pleasure. The teachers, the students, everyone expected her to retire at the end of every year, but somehow she stayed on. When I looked at her sitting there, a frustrated expression on her face, I couldn't understand why she bothered to keep working.

She was still talking and I hadn't been listening. I tried to catch up with what she was saying. The point seemed to be that even though I was at school more and my absences were explained, I wasn't keeping up with the work. I needed to think about whether I was going to be able to make it through to the end of Year Eleven. Whether it was worth going on to Year Twelve.

'School might not seem important right now, but you never know what's going to happen later in life. You're here, Beth. You might as well make the most of it.'

She started a story about another student back when she was a teacher, but I didn't really follow. I was looking out the window and wondering how long she was planning to keep me here. If listening to her was my punishment.

At some point I tried to speak, to say I'd been trying. I tried to tell her I knew I'd slipped behind again, but I really would catch up. She wasn't interested in hearing what I had to say, though – she was only interested in talking.

She had moved on to me giving up extracurricular activities, and I was thinking that wasn't much of a punishment given I didn't do any. I thought maybe she meant upcoming excursions I wouldn't be allowed to go on, but then she started to talk about basketball and I realised she was talking about taking me off the team.

I don't know how Coach knew I was in there, but it was around then, when I was starting to understand what was going on, when I was protesting this form of punishment, that he knocked on the door. Mrs Hanrahan tried to tell him she was busy, but Coach came in anyway. He sat next to me and started arguing with her like he'd been there for the whole conversation.

I could tell by the way they were talking they'd known each other a long time.

'Margaret, I understand where you're coming from, but Beth is an important part of the team. I can't lose her now. Not when we are about to start finals. I think we have a shot this year.'

He looked at me then.

'I'll make sure Beth gets the helps she needs. She'll be on track with her work for the rest of the year, and she'll stay on track.'

I nodded, to him and to Mrs Hanrahan, confirming that I would stay on track.

Mrs Hanrahan did not look convinced. Coach asked me to let them talk alone. Mrs Hanrahan gave me a slight nod, so I went to sit in the waiting area outside the office.

Etienne came to find me and I was pleased to see him, but still felt a bit worried. I asked him how he knew I was there, and he said Coach had got a message to him. Coach knew a lot more about us kids in his team than he let on. Etienne asked me in a whisper about my catch last night, and I told him it was fine but didn't give him any details. I told him they were talking about stopping me from playing in the mixed team and felt embarrassed to have to admit how behind I was on schoolwork.

Etienne took my hand and gave it a squeeze. We sat like that until the door opened. I quickly dropped Etienne's hand and we both stood up. Coach glanced at us and walked out of the office and into the school grounds. We followed him, waiting to hear what he had to say.

'Well, I've managed to convince her to let you stay on the team. You can play the next scheduled games.' He turned to Etienne. 'Give us a minute, would you?'

Etienne told me he'd wait for me at the gate and walked away.

'You need to catch up on any work you're behind in. And then you need to keep up. She's pretty upset about me going in and arguing like that, so this is your last chance.' He patted me awkwardly on the shoulder. 'I know you have a lot going on, but we need you in the team. You're one of the best players we've got, and the team wouldn't do nearly so well if you weren't there.'

Coach looked towards where Etienne was standing.

'Don't hold back when you're playing. I know you can do more than you're doing on court. I want to see that, Beth. Etienne isn't the kind of guy to worry about a girl being better than him. He wants to win as much as I do.'

I thought about what a game would look like if I caught every ball I could, if I ran as fast as I could.

'I'll try, Coach.'

It was better to let him keep thinking it was because of Etienne that I sometimes held back or fumbled balls.

'If you need anything, I want you to come to me. Get your work done, get enough sleep before games.'

I nodded my agreement. 'Thanks for sticking up for me, Coach.'

He patted me on the shoulder again and walked off towards the gym.

Etienne was leaning against the school gates when I got there, a physics book in his hands. I touched him lightly on the shoulder. He closed the book and looked at me carefully.

'Everything okay?'

I nodded. 'Coach thinks I'm holding back because I don't want to outshine you on the court.'

Etienne laughed. 'I think you'd be quite happy to outshine me on the court.'

I smiled. 'Yeah, but I can't make impossible catches. I have to try to play like everyone else.'

Etienne agreed. Perhaps too quickly.

I tested the water. 'Do you think it would be that bad if people knew about me?'

Etienne reached for my hand as we started to walk home. 'They wouldn't let you play.'

As we walked, I thought about what he had said. I thought about who 'they' were and what else they'd do to me or exclude me from if they knew. At my house I headed for my front door.

'I need to go in and get working.'

'Yeah, I have a pile of work to do too.'

Etienne had followed me to the door. I could see that he wanted to kiss me, but I was nervous wondering who was home and if anyone would see us.

Etienne saw my anxious look. He laughed a little and kissed me quickly before turning towards his own house. As he walked away he called, 'What are you going to tell them on Saturday?'

I laughed.

'I'll tell them I'm going to a movie with you.'

TWENTY-SIX

GETTING through the schoolwork wasn't as easy for me as I imagined it was for Etienne, for everyone else really. I tried meditation. I tried having a snack. I tried making a list. Eventually I gave up and called Lin.

Lin came over and we sat down together in the kitchen to tackle my assignments. Her job was to keep me focused and put dinner together. My job was to keep my eyes on the page and my hand writing.

It wasn't long before I started to become aware I needed to leave. I told Lin I had to go. I think she would have questioned me on whether I really did need to leave, but I'd already raced out the door.

I arrived at the now-familiar garden with the big tree and Jake just as it was getting dark. Just as he was about to fall. When I caught him there was a blinding flash. I closed my eyes and put him on the ground, covering my face as I felt his arms strike out at me.

I was blinking and trying to work out what was going on. I could hear someone moving around me. There was shuffling of feet and the sound of the gate closing. When I was able to see properly again, there was only Jake hitting me and Jake's mum trying to calm him down. No one else was there.

I felt unsure of what had just happened. Jake's mum looked upset. She apologised, a soft 'Sorry' escaping from her lips. I wasn't sure if it was about me having to come to catch Jake or for the blinding flash.

'It wasn't my idea.'

She was talking about the flash.

'It's just that I mentioned it to a friend and . . . you'll still come, won't you? If he needs you?'

I reassured her that I'd always come if I could, but that I'd prefer not to – I hoped she might find ways of keeping Jake out of the tree. I'd left Lin in the kitchen on her own, so I jogged back home without saying anything more.

When I got back everyone was sitting around the table. Aimee was snuggled on Meg's lap. Rik was over and sitting next to them. An extra place had been set for Lin next to me.

No one blinked an eye when I came in late and sat down.

Meg was the only one who checked in with me. 'Everything okay?'

'Yes, fine.'

I didn't want to think about what the blinding flash and Jake's mum's apology meant for me. No one else asked me anything. They were all busy congratulating Lin on the delicious pasta she'd made.

After dinner I tried to clear the table. Mum stopped me. 'Lin has explained all about your schoolwork. You need to go focus on that. I'll clean up.'

Lin offered to help her. Mum protested that the cook shouldn't do the washing up and that she and Dad would do it.

I walked Lin to the door and thanked her for helping out. She asked me about the catch and I told her about Jake's mum and the blinding flash. Lin got it straight away. She stood on her tiptoes and hugged me tight. She left without saying anything more about it.

When I walked back in Meg was handing Aimee to Rik and telling him to give her a bath and get her ready for bed. Then she followed me into my room.

'Why didn't you tell me you were behind again on your schoolwork? Why didn't you ask me for help?'

'I'm sick of asking everyone for help. And you have Aimee to look after now . . .'

'You still should've asked me.'

We sat together at my desk and Meg pushed me through some of the work I needed to do. I loved having Aimee in our lives, but this time with Meg, the two of us at my desk was like nothing had changed.

Meg started to look tired and stretched out on my bed so she was still there if I needed her. I kept my head down and my focus mostly intact. When I turned to ask Meg a question I saw she had fallen asleep. I went to take Aimee from Rik and cuddled her while Rik carried Meg to her own bed.

Aimee was still a bit damp from her bath, and smelt sweet and clean. I sat her on my lap at my desk and she tried to grab my hair and pen.

I gave up working and just played with her until Rik came back to take her to bed.

⸺

By the end of the week, with Lin and Meg's help, I had most of my schoolwork up to date and my teachers were starting to be less grumpy with me. Every time Coach saw me in the hall he'd check in to see how I was doing and whether I needed any help. I'd tell him I was fine. That I was catching up. He'd look at me with something close to suspicion before slapping me on the back and telling me to keep it up.

I didn't see much of Etienne that week. Occasionally we passed in the hall and stopped for a brief chat, a moment of touch between us, hands on arms or backs. Small moments that carried me through the rest of the day. I counted the hours until our movie date while I sat in class.

On Friday night I reminded Mum about my basketball game on Saturday and she said she'd try to make it. Meg had bowed out due to the pressure she was under with study and Aimee, and Dad was away riding that weekend. Just before I went to bed, when Mum was engrossed in one of her TV shows, I said as casually as I could, 'After the game Etienne and I are going to go see a movie.' Then I raced upstairs to bed before she could ask me any questions.

⸺

On Saturday my usual fears about having to leave mid-game to catch came back. I spent the morning at the bike shop feeling sick and trying to work out whether it was a catch or just worry. I went to the lane behind the shop with a basketball, trying to bounce out the nerves while Lin took care of the front counter.

In a quiet moment Lin came out to talk to me. She showed me some pictures she had on her phone. Pictures of me catching. Blurred images mostly, with one in sharp focus of me catching Jake.

'I've been collecting them for a while and waiting all week for the Jake one to appear.'

'Where from?'

'Different places. People usually post them on news sites.'

I flicked through the photos again. The one with Jake was really clear. It was the only one where you could tell it was me.

'I keep telling you to hide your face.'

I nodded and tried to think of a way I could remember to do that.

We closed the shop early to get ready for the game. As I quickly moved through the house to change, Mum tried to have a conversation with me about Etienne and the movie plan.

Her questions went like this.

'What movie are you going to see?'

'When do you think you'll be home?'

'Who else is going?'

I answered all the questions the same.

'I'm not sure.'

'Is this a date, Beth? Is there something going on between you and Etienne? I don't want any more secrets in this house.'

I rolled my eyes and put my head in my hands. 'Mum, I don't have time for this. It's just a movie.'

I had only confused her more. I could see it on her face. In the way she moved her fingers through her hair. She stopped asking questions, though, and let me leave for the game.

The rest of the team were there when I arrived at the gym. All I had time for was a quick smile at Etienne before Coach had us moving through the pregame warm-ups.

I saw Lin up in the stands. She was reading a book with one eye on what was happening on court. Just as the game was about to start, Mum walked in and took a seat next to Lin. They started talking.

Lin saw me looking up and mouthed, 'Okay?'

I nodded. The sickness I'd felt all morning had gone away.

As we stretched and jogged and listened to Coach's final instructions, I let my eyes wander towards Etienne. I watched his body, the strength of his muscles and the graceful way he moved. Etienne took the opportunity to stand next to me as Coach dismissed us. He leaned in a little to gently nudge my shoulder. When we moved to take our positions for the start of play he touched my lower back, just briefly, to say *good luck*.

I took my position on the court near Maye. As we waited for the other team, she asked me what was going on between Etienne and me.

I didn't know how to respond. I couldn't say he was my boyfriend, because I didn't know if he was. He felt like he could be. He acted like he wanted to be. But I didn't know if he was.

I wondered how you got to that point. If it was something you discussed and decided together, if one person asked the other, or if it just happened. I tried to think back to Meg and the boyfriends she'd had before Rik. There'd always seemed to be something formal that was announced or decided, but when she met Rik it just was. They didn't put any kind of name to it. They were just together.

I looked up to see Maye looking at me weirdly – I'd been lost in thought and hadn't responded to her question. The whistle blew to start play, so I was able to just shrug and smile and start moving. I figured she'd come to her own conclusion anyway.

Coach started shouting at us as soon as play began. He was so excited by finals he couldn't contain himself. I found his instructions confusing. I couldn't work out what he wanted me to do. I tried to focus on the ball, on the play in front of me. I tried to block out everything but our players, their players, the ball and the hoop. It kind of worked, but maybe not like Coach would have wanted.

We moved the ball up and down the court, pretty much matching each other point for point until we started missing and they kept scoring. Their defence was hard to break through and the game was getting away from us. They were edging further into the lead and I wasn't sure we'd be able to catch them.

When I was off the court I focused on the play in front of me. I watched for opportunities, for weaknesses in their side. I watched our team, too. I watched to see where we were strong, where we needed to be to win.

As soon as I felt ready I signalled to Coach to let me back on. He did this for Etienne and Tommy as well. I could feel disapproval from Maye. She thought as a senior girl she should be on the court more than me, but I didn't care at that point. I had seen cracks in the opposition's defence and I wanted to get back on to see if I could turn those cracks into points for our team.

On the court Etienne was not Etienne the boy next door, or Etienne under the tree kissing me. On the court Etienne was a teammate. We were separate parts of a whole, working together. There was no romance once the whistle blew. It was all about the game.

By the fourth quarter the cracks in the other team's defence had widened and we moved into a comfortable lead. Coach did not relax. He kept pacing on the sidelines and pushing us to do more with the ball. It wasn't until the final whistle blew and we knew we had won that he started to calm down.

When we came off court I started to think about the game and how I had played. I wasn't sure how much I had kept my skills in check. I would need to ask Lin later to make sure I didn't do anything too weird or out of the realm of normal.

The rest of the team were jumping up and down, hugging and slapping each other. I joined in as people started coming down from the stands to congratulate us. Coach stood to the side to watch. He was already starting to think about the next game, the next challenge.

In the middle of all the congratulating and jumping up and down Etienne found me to give me a hug and whisper in my ear, 'Meet you out front of your house at six?'

I nodded quickly before we were grabbed by other people and pulled in different directions.

Lin told me she'd call me later, and I wondered if it was to check on the movie date but suspected it was more likely she wanted to reprimand me about some of my more noticeable catches on the court.

As Mum and I walked home she questioned me again on the timing of the movie.

'We're leaving at six.'

'And it's just the two of you? For a movie? I didn't know you two liked the same movies.'

I didn't know how to answer her question without going into the kissing that Etienne and I had been up to.

'I guess we've never really celebrated our basketball wins, and Etienne is the one who got me to join the team.'

Mum said, 'Yes,' slowly, like what I'd said still didn't make sense to her, which was fair enough because in no way had I answered her question.

'Beth, are you sure . . .'

'What?'

'Well, I just wonder if Etienne is missing Meg and . . .'

I knew what she was saying. What she was thinking. Like Meg at the start of the year, she didn't want me to get my hopes up. I wondered why it was so hard for her to imagine Etienne wanting to spend time with me.

We'd arrived home, so I didn't feel the need to answer her. I left her downstairs and went up to find something to wear.

I had decided on jeans with a nice top. I thought about borrowing a top from Meg, but worried Etienne might recognise it, which would be weird. I knew when people found out about us, like Mum, they would assume Etienne was substituting me for Meg. I didn't think it was true, not really, not when I was with him, but I knew others would.

When I went downstairs to wait for Etienne, Mum suggested he come in rather than us meeting outside. That there was no reason to sneak off together.

'We aren't sneaking off.'

'Is he going to drive?'

I nodded *yes*.

'I'm not happy about you being in cars with teenage boys.'

I sighed. 'Mum, it's Etienne.'

I didn't mention his driving skills. Mum nodded a little, and I knew she'd given up.

'What time will you be home?'

I shrugged. 'Not late.'

As soon as I saw Etienne walk out of his house I went over the road to meet him. He went to kiss me, but I was worried Mum would be watching from the window. I quickly moved to the other side of the car and got in. Etienne looked a little puzzled, but when he saw me glance back towards my house he laughed and got in to start the car.

'Sorry. You have no idea how weird my mum is being about . . . this.'

Etienne laughed again. 'I thought she liked me.'

He reached for my hand, which was nice even though I wanted both of his hands on the steering wheel.

At the cinema we grabbed popcorn before heading to our seats. I asked Etienne where he'd like to sit and he chose the back of the cinema. I raised my eyebrows at him.

'Tall people sit at the back, Beth. It's only polite.'

I looked around the cinema – there weren't many people to annoy with our height, but I didn't object.

We sat close together, our legs touching, our fingers meeting as we reached into the popcorn bucket. We talked a little about the game, and Etienne asked me if I thought I would have to leave during the movie.

I shook my head. I was feeling good. Better than I'd felt in a long time. There was no sickness. Just a pleasant exhaustion from the game and a warm glow from having Etienne so close.

Etienne said, 'Good,' and leant across to kiss me. He tasted like salt and popcorn. I felt that nothing could be better than sitting here with him.

We talked a bit more about school and exams, about Aimee. Etienne wanted more details about Mum's reaction to us going to the movie, but I didn't know what to say. I didn't want to tell him she thought I was a substitute for Meg.

So I talked about how she didn't want me to grow up, but what I really wanted to say was, *I don't know what this is, so I can't tell Mum what this is.* I wanted to ask, *Do other people ask you about me the way they ask me about you?* I didn't, though. I didn't say or ask any of it.

I'd never been good at watching movies. Movies for me were like books. As soon as they started I would drift off into thinking about other things and forget there was even a movie in front of me. This movie was all action. Etienne seemed to enjoy it, and I enjoyed watching him watch it. When he noticed me looking at him, he would kiss me until a noise caught his attention and he would turn back to the screen. It was a pretty good way to watch a movie.

When the movie finished we left the cinema hand in hand and talked about where to go for food. I felt a tap on my shoulder and turned to see a guy smiling at me. He hugged me like he was an old friend.

'I thought that was you. How are you? You never called me.'

It was the guy in the suit I'd caught the day Meg drove me for the first time. The one who gave me money and his business card.

'Why didn't you call?'

I didn't have an answer.

He pushed another card at me. 'Call me this time. I can help you. I'll make you rich. Really.'

Etienne and I walked away, Etienne glancing behind us at the guy, who was now surrounded by his group of friends. I didn't read his card. I just shoved it into my back pocket. It was something I needed to talk to Lin about.

We went for ice-cream after the movie. Etienne wanted to know about the guy in the suit. I told him about the catch. About how Meg had been with me for the first time. About the guy insisting on giving me money.

Etienne was worried about the money. He seemed worried about the whole interaction. I told him every catch was different. That I'd tried to give the money back, but the man had rushed away.

Etienne had more questions. He had opinions and concerns, but I didn't want to talk about it anymore. I asked him what his plans were after he finished school.

'Mum wants me to take a year off and see the world, but I don't know . . .'

I thought about what this would be like. Etienne finished with school while I was still there. Etienne at the airport, getting on a plane, while I was working at the bike shop and trying to study for Year Twelve.

Etienne shrugged and took my hand. 'It's just an idea. I haven't made any decisions yet.'

On the drive home we were quiet, but when we parked at Etienne's place neither of us was ready to say goodnight. The conversation had become stilted. It wasn't that we had run out of things to say, it was that there were too many things we didn't want to say. We kept talking about basketball and the movie we'd just seen. About nothing, really, until the light went on at the front of my house telling me Mum knew I was there and was waiting for me to come home.

Ettienne kissed me quickly. 'How about I come over tomorrow?'

We worked out a time between my work at the shop and his study. Even though the evening had not been easy and all I could think about was the idea of him not being around next year, I was happy I had him to look forward to the next day.

TWENTY-SEVEN

IN the morning, Lin arrived at the bike shop soon after me. I wanted to tell her about Etienne, about our night and how it had all gone sour after seeing that guy, but she had the local paper in her hand and wasn't listening to anything I had to say.

She spread the paper in front of me, pointing to an article with a bunch of blurry photos next to it. There was a big bold title that read *MYSTERY CATCHER*. The article talked about someone going around catching people, like the catcher was doing something wrong. Like people were in danger. There were no comments from anyone who had been caught, just vague statements from people who'd seen it happen, who seemed worried about everyone's safety. I noticed it skipped over the bit about me saving actual lives.

I looked up at Lin. 'Shit.'

'I'm sure it'll be fine.'

'What should I do?'

'Nothing.' Lin went to change the *Closed* sign on the door to *Open*.

'Nothing? That's your answer?'

'Well, I told you to wear a hoodie or a hat, but you won't. You could at least wear a mask or glasses.'

'I never remember. And I need to be able to see.'

'So, nothing. You should show this to your parents, though.' Lin folded up the paper and passed it to me.

'How bad do you really think it would be if people knew?'

I was starting to wonder what it would be like if everyone knew. Etienne's reaction made me think it wouldn't be good. Even though he thought my catching was great, he hadn't seemed to think others would feel the same.

'I don't know. Maybe they'd make you do tests and experiments. Work out why you can catch and how it works, and the extent of what you can do. It could be interesting. Or maybe they'll try to make you stop. Declare it's illegal and not something you're allowed to do.'

I tried to imagine the tests and experiments. Maybe I could manage them if I had to. But I couldn't stop catching. I couldn't sit back and do nothing while I felt people falling.

'Let's just wait and see what happens next. If anything.'

I tried to put it out of my mind by focusing on the bike Dad had been working on. He'd left instructions for me, and I started to connect the gears he'd bought to the frame he'd prepared. In quiet moments Lin came in to watch me.

I started discussing the bike with her. Dad was usually so meticulous. The branding, the dates – he liked bikes to be true to the time they were made. This bike was a mash-up of different eras and styles. It didn't make sense.

'Hasn't he told you?'

'Told me what?'

'This bike is for you. He's trying to build something strong and fast. Something you can use to get to catches.'

I looked at the bike again. It still didn't make sense, but Dad didn't have all the parts yet. Maybe it would when he'd finished with it.

I felt pleased, though. Dad had been thinking of me. He'd found a way to show he was with me on the catching, even if he wouldn't get out of the car to see it for himself.

When I got home from the bike shop all I could hear was Rik and Meg arguing upstairs. Mum was in the kitchen with Aimee. She handed the baby to me and said she had to head out for a while. I took Aimee and we sat in the lounge room. Me with my maths book, Aimee with some jangly spoons she liked to suck.

The arguing stopped and Rik came downstairs to see Aimee. He looked sad, and I wanted to say something that would make things better, but I didn't know what I could say. His mother was still refusing to come and see Aimee and Meg, but that wasn't a conversation I was going to bring up with him.

We chatted about Aimee instead. About how cute she was when she smiled or played. Rik talked about the sounds she made when she was sleeping and how she loved to make eye contact with strangers. Then he left, looking even more miserable than when he'd come downstairs.

I carried Aimee and my maths book upstairs and wrapped her up for sleep, but Aimee made it clear she wasn't interested in sleep until she'd been fed. I took her to Meg, who barely looked up from her textbook. She took Aimee and shoved her onto her breast.

'He asked me to marry him.'

'Oh.'

'I think his mum really got in his head. I'd already told him not to. He'd agreed not to.'

Meg was still looking at her book. I went back to my room and to my maths problems. Meg brought Aimee back to me when I was only halfway through the first problem.

'You okay, Meg?'

'Yeah, he'll get over it.'

She went back to her studying. I settled Aimee to sleep in Meg's room and started to tidy my room. I put a load of washing on and made Meg a plate of fruit and nuts and cheese. By the time I sat back down at my desk Aimee had woken up. Meg took her into the front yard to lie on the grass.

I sat and watched through the window as Etienne came out of his house and crossed the road. I heard him stop and talk to Meg and Aimee. They talked for a long time. I tried not to be impatient or jealous. I told myself he and Meg were friends, and Meg needed to talk to a friend at that moment.

I was starting to think about going downstairs to interrupt them when I heard footsteps coming up the stairs. Etienne knocked and then pushed open my door. He looked so gorgeous I wanted to climb into him. I forgot all about the awkwardness of last night and the idea of him leaving. He stood in my doorway for a moment like he wasn't sure whether he was allowed to come in, and then his eyes met mine. He smiled that new smile that was just for me. He stepped into the room and shut the door.

'Hello.' I moved to be close to him.

We hugged and kissed briefly before he broke away and began to examine my room. I cringed as he looked around and asked me questions about pictures I'd displayed of Meg and me as babies, or books I had been given. Watching Etienne in my room made me wonder why I didn't think to hide my old stuffed toys, or all those books I hadn't got around to reading.

Etienne looked back at me and saw my embarrassment. He came to stand near me and I saw again that here was a new Etienne. My Etienne. Here was an opportunity for me to be a new Beth.

I pulled Etienne down to sit with me on the end of my bed, wanting to stop the examination of my room. The examination of me as a young girl. A girl he'd known, but a girl he didn't seem to have much interest in. I wanted him to see me as I was now. We sat with our hands entwined and talked about our mornings. We avoided any mention of our conversation last night.

There was a moment of silence, a quietness, a shyness about being together on my bed. Then we started kissing. I pushed him on his back and we giggled as we moved further up so that our whole bodies could lie the length of the mattress.

I was amazed by how comfortable I felt. How right it all seemed. How much I wanted his hands on my body and how little I was thinking about whether my breasts were the right size or my legs too bony. I was amazed at how brave my hands were. How good it was to touch his skin and to feel his hands touching mine. I loved how little I thought and how much I just acted. How I let my body do what it wanted to do.

We tussled a little, laughing as he rolled to be on top of me and I rolled him back to be on top of him. We didn't hear Mum walking up the stairs. We only realised she was there when the door opened. She stood in the doorway looking at us, me astride Etienne, my legs hugging his hips.

I slowly got off him and sat on the edge of the bed. Etienne sat up next to me, but not too close.

Mum tried to have a normal conversation. She asked Etienne how he was, and whether anyone was hungry. We shook our heads, but she suggested we come downstairs anyway and say hello to Dad who'd just returned from his weekend away.

I nodded and looked her directly in the eye. 'We'll be down in a minute, Mum.'

She turned to head downstairs, but she left the door wide open.

Etienne and I looked at each other and laughed quietly. I moved to kiss him again and he responded, but he stopped my hands reaching for his body.

'We should go downstairs.'

He was right. I knew he was right, but I was reluctant. I didn't want to leave this space where it was just the two of us. Etienne saw my reluctance.

'It's going to be fine. We have plenty of time.'

I nodded into his shoulder, thinking if he left to travel next year that really wasn't true.

Dad was in the lounge room with Aimee on his knee. Etienne took the armchair next to him and they started talking. I listened to Dad telling Etienne about his latest bike ride and I saw in Dad what I felt on the basketball court. This freedom in action where his mind stopped, where his focus returned. I wondered why I'd never seen it before. Why I'd never thought about his constant need to be on his bike.

Etienne told Dad about the basketball game and how good I was. He told him that he needed to come and see me play in the semifinals.

I left for the kitchen to get everyone water and found Mum there.

'You know there's an open-door policy in this house, Beth.'

'That's the first I've ever heard of it, Mum. Is this something that you made up for my benefit? Meg closes her door all the time.'

'Well, Meg's in a slightly different position.'

'You're treating me like a child, while Meg, who's only a year older than me, can do whatever she wants?'

Mum sighed and didn't say anything else. I took the water back to Dad and Etienne, and Etienne suggested we go out to shoot a few baskets before he had to go home. Mum came into the lounge room to invite him to dinner, but Etienne said he had plans with his parents. Mum smiled at me like she was trying to prove she was okay with us being together.

Outside we passed the ball back and forth, conscious that Mum, if she wasn't watching, was definitely listening. After a few minutes of play where we pushed and grabbed and fought over the ball to get it into the hoop, Etienne said he needed to go home and get some more study done. I asked if he really had plans with his parents, or if he'd just said that to get out of having dinner with us.

'We go out to dinner together every Sunday night. It's like the only thing we do as a family. I was going to ask you, but I wasn't sure you'd want to come.'

He sounded cross that I'd basically accused him of lying.

'I'd like to come.'

I spoke before I had time to really think about it. I wanted to make up for saying the wrong thing. I still had the ball in my hand, and I bounced it up and down on the drive.

'Okay. Great.' He didn't sound happy I'd agreed to come. 'Come over at seven.'

'Okay.'

I'd obviously made a mistake. Etienne turned and left. All the kissing and closeness and fun from our time in my room seemed to have vanished.

Etienne was almost at his door before he turned and jogged back to me. He pulled me to the side of our house away from any windows and doors, and he kissed me like he'd kissed me in my room. It felt so good I wouldn't have cared if Mum came out of the house to stand there and watch us.

'See you soon.'

I nodded, so happy he'd come back and made everything right again.

Back in the house Mum was acting like she was mad at me again, and I could only think it was because of what I'd said about her treating me like a child, or maybe just because of Etienne. I told her I would be out for dinner.

'Where?'

'I'm going out with Etienne and his parents.'

'Isn't it a little . . .'

'What?'

Mum shook her head. She'd decided not to finish her sentence, but I knew what she was thinking. I was thinking it too. It was too soon to be having dinner with his parents. I wasn't ready.

I walked over to Etienne's house just before seven. I didn't really know Etienne's parents. Neither did Meg. We'd met them, of course, and probably waved or smiled to them over the years, but I'd never had a proper conversation with them.

His parents were ready and waiting in the hallway, like I was late. Etienne introduced us and we all shook hands before his mother quickly moved us into the car. Etienne opened one of the back passenger doors for me and closed it after I got in. His father did the same for his mother. It was so formal, so proper. I worried my dinner table manners weren't going to be good enough.

In the back seat Etienne reached across to hold my hand. He squeezed it like he knew I was worried.

The restaurant was fancier than anywhere I'd been to before. I felt awkward – too tall next to his mother, and like there was too much of me as the waiter tried to tuck my chair into the table.

I was reading the menu when I first felt sick. I looked towards Etienne. Everyone was talking about what was good, what the specials were, what they had last time. I tried to get Etienne's attention.

When I finally made eye contact with him I shook my head a little to let him know I wouldn't be staying. Etienne took my hand. He was asking me to stay. Trying to hold me there.

I took my hand from his, apologised to his parents, and started running.

TWENTY-EIGHT

THE catch was a few blocks from the restaurant. I had time. I could have stayed a minute or two more and thought of an excuse, a reason to run out. But I didn't. I chose to run as fast as I could, and I got to the building with time to spare.

Someone else arrived soon after me. They stood beside me, a hoodie pulled over their head, hiding their face. They were bent over, trying to catch their breath. I tore my attention from the top of the building where I'd been trying to work out what was about to come towards me and exactly where I needed to be.

I tried to make my voice strong. I tried not to show the fear I was feeling. 'You need to move. You can't stand there.'

'You can't do this one on your own. I know you've been managing fine so far in your little patch, but you need me here this time. Trust me.'

I would have argued or maybe tried to push him away, but I didn't have time. I looked back up at the building and again tried to figure out what was coming. When I did, I realised he was right. I couldn't do this one on my own.

I looked at the guy next to me. I wasn't sure we'd be able to do it together either. I wasn't sure if he knew what he was getting into.

I widened my legs and rolled my shoulders. The guy next to me pushed the hood back from his face. He copied my stance.

'Rock.'

I looked from the top of the building to him and back, still wondering how this was going to work.

'What?'

'Rock. My name is Rock.'

'Oh. I'm Beth.'

'Hi, Beth.'

'I'm not sure we're in the right place. I've never tried to catch anyone like this.'

I had my eyes on the huge dark shape that was starting to fall towards us. He nodded beside me, his focus also on the falling object.

'Me neither.'

We both watched and waited as the largest man I'd ever seen fell from the sky and into our arms.

I ended up holding his legs while Rock had him under his arms. I'm still not quite sure how we did it. I put his feet on the ground and Rock pushed his top half forwards so that he was standing. The man we'd caught hugged us both at the same time, pulling us towards him so the three of us were jammed together, and I was forced to smell his sweat and fear.

Rock slipped out from under his grasp. He fixed his hood into place over his head and started to walk off. I gave the big guy a pat and slipped away too.

'Hey! Wait!'

Rock stopped. When I caught up to him I didn't know what to say. I had a million questions, but I couldn't form any of them into actual words. All I really knew was that I didn't want him to walk away.

'Don't leave.'

'I have to. Don't worry. We'll talk.'

'When?'

'Soon.'

He smiled at me, and I didn't get why. I was desperate to understand how suddenly I wasn't the only one. Rock took off, running at a pace that suggested he had somewhere else to be.

I turned back to the guy we had just caught. He was shaking now, his whole body racked with some kind of pain. I led him to a bench nearby and sat him down. We sat quietly as I waited for him to become calm. I asked him if he wanted to go to the hospital or to call someone, but he said there was no one. No one to take him to, nowhere to go.

We sat for a long time until he sighed and told me he'd be fine. I got up to leave. I felt like he would be okay. At least for now, he would be okay.

I walked home from the catch thinking about Rock and the man we caught, and then all the ways I could have left the restaurant better. All the things I should have said. I should never have gone to dinner in the first place. It was too soon to sit down with his parents, but I'd wanted to be that girlfriend who would go to dinner on a Sunday night with her boyfriend's parents. I didn't even know if I was his girlfriend.

Etienne came out of his house as I walked into the street, as if he had been waiting for me. Watching for me. I apologised for leaving the restaurant. I apologised for going in the first place.

Etienne pulled me into his arms. 'It's fine. I explained to them. I don't think they really understand, but—'

'You told them?'

'I couldn't think of any other way to explain you running out like that. I mean, I don't think they believed me anyway. There'll probably be a drug test on my bed in the morning or something.'

I stayed in Etienne's arms, my head on his shoulder. There was a moment of wanting to push him away. Of wanting to say that it wasn't his secret to tell. But I wasn't sure. I had put him in a situation where he'd had to come up with an explanation. Anyway, with the article in the local paper, with Rock showing up, maybe it was no longer my secret to keep. Maybe this was the time to let people know.

'I get it, but I still wish you hadn't told them.'

'I wish you hadn't run off like that.'

'Sorry.'

'Me too. I really like you, Beth.'

'I really like you, Etienne.'

We kissed quickly and hugged longer.

'Your parents are never going to talk to me again.'

'Well, you didn't really talk to each other to begin with.'

I pushed him a little.

'I mean, they barely talk to me. Don't worry. They'll get over it.'

'You think so?'

'They'll probably forget it even happened by the end of the week.'

―――

In the morning I showed Mum, Dad and Meg the article in the local paper. I told them about the other stories online that Lin had gathered. I had decided not to tell them about Rock, just like I hadn't told Etienne. I didn't want to over-complicate the conversation.

They all stood quietly and read the article. It wasn't a long article, but it took them a long time to read it. Mum and Meg finished first and exchanged a look like they'd had a discussion about this before. Like they knew this was going to happen.

Dad finished reading last. He cleared this throat. 'Well, then.'

He picked up his keys and left the room. We heard the front door close behind him.

I looked to Mum.

'He'll be fine. He's just worried about you.'

Meg announced that the article meant nothing. That you could barely tell it was me in the picture.

'Hardly anyone reads this thing anyway. I'm surprised Lin even found it.'

They were the words I wanted to hear, but the expressions on Mum and Meg's face, that look they'd exchanged as soon as they'd finished reading, was the complete opposite of those words.

TWENTY-NINE

ON the weekend we played our semifinal in front of a large crowd. It was an away game, which meant Etienne and I travelled separately. My whole family, including Rik and Aimee, came to watch. Meg was right. Rik did get over her refusal of his proposal, but he still found it hard to leave our house when Meg told him it was time for him to go home.

The team we were playing had won the final last year, so I didn't think we would be walking away from the game as winners. I didn't tell anyone that. When Etienne and Coach talked about how we had a good chance I nodded in agreement like everyone else.

We got lucky. Etienne and I made a few good plays. He would give me the nod. I would start running towards our end while he retrieved the ball from the opponents before throwing it the length of the court to where

I was waiting. Those plays were terrifying for me. I knew I had to sink the ball. That I had to do it quickly before anyone else caught up to me. I managed it a couple of times, until the opposition realised they needed to put a fast player on me.

Coach would take me off court then. He was possibly hoping they'd forget which one I was. Sometimes they did, but as soon as we'd make that same play again, they would be back on me.

In one of my breaks I looked up into the stands and saw Rock sitting there. He was watching me. Smiling. I spent the rest of the game distracted, constantly checking he was still there.

I'd told Lin about Rock, even though I hadn't told anyone else. She was desperate to meet him. To question him and compare notes. There was no way for me to tell her during the game that he was sitting there, only a few rows away.

We managed to win. Looking back, it never seemed to be in doubt. We led from the start, and we kept that lead all the way through the game. Coach was beside himself. Our school hadn't made it to a final for years. We'd made his life complete.

When I looked back into the stands after that final whistle blew, Rock was gone.

My family made their way down to congratulate us. Mum looked around for Etienne's parents, but Etienne told her they never came to his games. I wondered whether they'd really forgotten me running out on dinner. Etienne looked over my mum's head, met my eyes and smiled. I forgot about his parents and smiled back.

As we gathered our things to leave, Etienne asked me to drive home with him. I told Mum, who frowned but agreed. Everyone went their separate ways, Mum and Dad into their car, Rik, Meg and Aimee into Rik's car. Our lives were changing and splitting in different directions, and for a moment I had a sense of sadness. Then Etienne was next to me, asking me if I was ready to go. In the car I told Etienne Mum and Dad were going out soon after they got home.

'Maybe you'd like to come over?'

⌒

I texted Etienne as soon as Mum and Dad were out of the house and he came bounding up the stairs for another make-out session on my bed. I laughed to see him coming so eagerly into my room, and I groaned with frustration when, after what felt like two minutes but was probably closer to fifteen, he got up off the bed. I tried to pull him back down, I wasn't ready for him to leave, for us to stop, but instead he pulled me up. We went downstairs to sit on the couch with Rik, Meg and Aimee, who were watching a movie together.

It was nice to sit with them. Not as nice as being alone with Etienne in my room, but still nice. I felt like part of a couple, and it was easy and natural to be with Etienne in front of Meg and Rik. I didn't pay attention to the movie. I was focused on my hand in Etienne's. On Aimee's soft head in Meg's arms.

When my phone rang it took me a while to realise what it was. I took my hand from Etienne's and answered it without looking. I assumed it'd be Lin.

'Beth?'

The voice on the other end was immediately familiar. I checked my screen, but there was no caller ID.

I moved into the kitchen so the others couldn't hear the conversation.

'Rock! How did you get this number?'

'You're pretty easy to find. You might want to think about that.'

'Where are you?'

'I'm around. I'll see you soon. I just wanted to say hi and nice game today.'

Rock hung up before I could say anything else. When I walked back into the lounge room Etienne and Meg were watching me.

I shook my head. 'It was nothing. No one. Wrong number.'

Meg turned her attention back to the movie, but Etienne's attention stayed on me.

'It's fine. Really.'

I took his hand again and he squeezed it, watching me, his eyes searching mine. I turned my gaze back to the movie. I didn't know what to think about Rock or why I was keeping him a secret. I thought about what he'd said, about me being too easy to find. He'd found me at the basketball game and now he'd found my number. It was something I needed to talk through with Lin.

At the end of the movie Meg and Rik went upstairs to put Aimee to bed and Etienne stood up to leave. I wanted him to stay, and tried to keep him on the couch with me. I thought he would keep my mind from returning to Rock's call. I was winning until we heard Mum and Dad pull up in the car. I walked him to the door just as Mum and Dad came in.

Everyone was nice and polite as we said hello to them and goodnight to Etienne. Once it was just Mum and I in the kitchen she started grilling me on where we spent the evening and what we'd done.

'We were downstairs with Meg and Rik all night, Mum. We watched a movie. Ask Meg. I wish you'd trust me.'

Mum sighed and agreed she probably should trust me, but she was finding it hard to adjust to so many changes so quickly.

I had no sympathy for her and went to bed annoyed.

In bed I got a text from Etienne saying he'd forgotten to mention a party next weekend. A party he wanted to take me to. I felt reluctant about large social events. Lin and I had not been included in many of the ones held by kids in our year. Even if we were, we mostly preferred to stay home. Still, I was pleased Etienne was asking me. That we would be turning up as a couple. So I agreed to go.

I called Lin before I went to sleep and told her about the phone call I'd had with Rock. We talked through how he might have got my number and whether I needed to change it. I was reluctant to do that; I wanted Rock to contact me. Lin agreed.

'He seems to be able to find you anyway.'

'How, Lin? How can he find me but I don't have a clue where to go to find him?'

For Lin the answer was obvious. She'd been telling me and telling me to hide my identity, and I hadn't done it. I'd caught people in my school uniform, left my face exposed. I couldn't even remember to wear a hat.

'What do you expect, Beth?'

The party was going to be at Gabe's house. He was on the boys' basketball team, and I only knew him from training. When Etienne and I walked home from school together on Monday I pointed out that the party was to celebrate the end of the Year Twelves' trial exams. Only Year Twelves would be there.

Etienne shrugged this off, saying girlfriends were welcome and that I knew most of the Year Twelves anyway. We'd never said *boyfriend* or *girlfriend* to each other. When Etienne said it he looked at me to gauge my reaction, so I felt sure he was conscious of it too. That he was trying to make things more formal between us but probably didn't know how.

We had a good make-out session at our tree that afternoon and I walked to my house feeling flustered.

When I walked in the door I found Mum in the lounge room with Rik's mother. I knew Meg had kept up her refusal to take Aimee over to Rik's, so Mari sitting in our house with Aimee on her lap was a win for Meg.

I watched as Mari stared in wonder at sleeping Aimee, murmuring and laughing each time she squirmed or sneezed. I raised my eyebrows at Mum, but she shook her head just slightly so I left the room to go see what Meg thought of the whole thing.

Meg was victorious. It had taken her longer than she expected, but she'd won and made the woman come to her. I wondered if that was the point, if Meg even remembered the point, but for her it was a definite win.

I changed the topic of conversation to ask her about Gabe's party. 'Are you going?'

'I wasn't planning to, but if you and Etienne are going maybe I will. We'll need to go get some new clothes though. You don't have anything to wear to a party, and most of my stuff doesn't fit me properly now.'

I convinced Dad to give me Saturday morning off work so that Meg and I could head out with Aimee in the pram for us both to find something to wear that evening. I hadn't been out with Meg and Aimee before, and soon became conscious of how many people either looked disapprovingly at Meg or stopped us to coo at the baby.

Meg saw the surprise on my face, and laughed. 'You get used to it. I actually prefer the disapproval to the stopping and cooing. It takes up less time.'

I'd never been particularly interested in clothes shopping and Aimee didn't seem to be either, because she started screaming pretty much as soon as we entered any clothes shop. We ended up having to juggle her between us in the pouch. Me having her while Meg found something, and then Meg holding her while she made me try on dress after dress. Meg liked them all, but I settled on a simple blue spaghetti-strap dress with enough movement in the skirt for running if it turned out I needed to. Meg laughed at me. She asked if I would be running to catch someone or running away from the party, and I agreed that it could be either.

Rik came over after dinner, and Meg gave him instructions for the evening. I watched Rik to see if he was annoyed at being given babysitting duties rather than being invited to the party, but he seemed happy enough to settle down in front of the TV with Dad and Aimee.

Etienne had offered to drive, so we walked over to his place just as he was coming out of his front door. Meg quickly climbed into the back of his car, leaving me in the front passenger seat. Etienne was careful to compliment both of us on how we looked, and Meg returned his compliments. I felt too nervous about the whole night to think of anything nice to say.

In the car Etienne turned to smile at me and we just ended up both smiling at each other. It felt like an unspoken acknowledgement that this was our first official outing as boyfriend and girlfriend. We were about to kiss when Meg told Etienne to get on with it. She didn't mean the kissing.

'You know, I haven't had a night out since Aimee was born. I'd prefer not to spend it in a car watching you two.'

We laughed and Etienne started up the car. I tried to tell myself the night was going to be fun.

At the party the music was loud and the Year Twelves were louder. There were crowds around the front door and then a crowd that stretched down the hall. As soon as we walked in we lost Meg to a bunch of people who grabbed her and stuck a drink in her hand, demanding photos of Aimee. Etienne and I made our way into the kitchen and found some of the others from the basketball team.

Etienne kept hold of my hand until we were in the kitchen. I saw Maye and a couple of the other Year Twelve girls look at our joined hands and then look me up and down. I wondered what they thought and felt wrong in my dress, with my hair down and the lipstick Meg had made me wear.

Etienne dropped my hand and circled the kitchen bench to shake hands with the guys and kiss some of the girls hello. When he was offered a drink he asked for water because he was driving. One of the guys offered me a drink as well, but I wasn't feeling ready to drink anything, even water. Tommy arrived and told me I 'scrubbed up all right' before starting a conversation about our final game and who we'd be playing.

Etienne kept looking across the room to check if I was okay or ready for a drink, but I just shook my head and tried to smile. I was watching him with Maye. Or rather I was watching Maye with him.

I could see Meg across the living room with a different group of people, talking and laughing. I felt so envious of how comfortable she seemed to be in any situation. I wondered if I'd be able to mimic her. If I could just pretend to be her for the night.

I looked over at Etienne talking with his friends, at his ease and his enjoyment in their company. Maye leant towards him like she needed to be close to hear what he was saying, finding any excuse to touch him. I looked back to Tommy. I must have faded out of our conversation for too long, because he'd given up on me and was talking to the people on the other side of him.

I found myself standing alone, with conversations flowing around me but none I could be involved in. I left the kitchen to see if I could find somewhere quieter. I didn't want to watch Maye touching Etienne anymore.

Etienne found me as I was searching for Meg and asked if I was okay. I didn't tell him I wasn't. That I had felt the start of something like nausea and was fighting an urge to run. I told him I was fine and was looking for the bathroom. Etienne pointed me towards a door at the end of the hall.

When I walked into the relative quiet of the bathroom, I knew I was going to have to leave the party. Without all the noise and people to distract me from what I was feeling, I could tell the catch was there and that it was becoming urgent.

I went to find Etienne, Maye was no longer by his side. He was now with a group of people I didn't know well, Meg was part of this group too. Etienne looked pleased to see me and reached out to pull me to him.

It felt so good to be wanted by him, I tried to pretend there wasn't a catch. I tried to stay for him. I tried to involve myself in the conversation and the jokes about some of the teachers at school or the way Coach shouted at us when we were on the court.

At some point everything became blurred. I found it difficult to talk, hard to hear. It became impossible to stand there. I tried for as long as I could. I held on to Etienne's hand and I tried to talk and be part of what was going on around me, but in the end I had to turn to Etienne and apologise.

I think I saw surprise in his face. Maybe disappointment. I didn't try to explain or ask him to drive me. I didn't try to pull Meg aside to tell her what was going on. I just left the house, and once I was out on the street I kicked off my shoes and ran.

I realised as I ran that I'd made a mistake. I should have left as soon as I felt the catch, or I should have made someone drive me. I tried to cut corners. I didn't stop for traffic lights. I dodged between cars. At one point I felt something cut into my foot, but I still didn't stop. I ran until my lungs and legs were burning, and I still wasn't close enough.

I felt him fall. I felt his age and his weariness. His hopelessness and desperation. I felt his insanity. His delusion. I felt him wake as he fell. I felt his realisation, his regret, and then I felt his acceptance.

I stopped running. I could hear the ambulance. Someone else had already called it. I wondered if I'd arrive to find Rock. If he too had been caught up in something that had made him late.

I walked the rest of the way to the building I should have been standing next to ten minutes ago just as the ambulance arrived. There was no one else around. I didn't watch them work, but I sat in the gutter nearby and I apologised silently to the man who'd fallen.

My foot was starting to hurt. I looked down to see blood dripping from a cut in the sole of my foot. I'd left the party without my phone or keys.

Etienne had them in his jacket pocket. I considered limping over to the ambulance crew to show them my foot, but I didn't want to get too close to the man I'd failed. I didn't want to see what I had already felt.

My only option was to walk home. I looked around to get my bearings and start the long walk. My foot throbbed, and my legs were exhausted. I welcomed both the pain and the exhaustion. It was better than the gut-wrenching ache of missing.

A car pulled up next to me and I looked at it with a flash of fear and then with a flood of relief. Etienne ran out of the car to get me.

'I missed, Etienne. I was too late.'

Etienne held me and then tried to walk me to the car, but I refused to get in.

'My foot's bleeding. I don't want to mess up your car.'

'Who cares about the car? I don't. Just get in, Beth.'

I still refused. In that moment getting blood on his car felt like the worst thing I could possibly do. Etienne's car was nicer than our family car, and I couldn't be the one to ruin it. I was sure it would give his mother another reason not to like me.

Etienne realised I was serious, and he searched through the boot of the car until he found a T-shirt to wrap around my foot.

In the car Etienne decided my foot needed to be seen by someone. I was too exhausted, too numb, to argue. He took me to the hospital and messaged Meg, so she'd know what had happened. Then he held my hand and told me he'd tried to leave with me. He'd only stopped to tell Meg and make sure she'd be able to get home. He said he would have driven me. He would have been happy to leave the party.

My name was called before I had time to answer or explain anything. Etienne came with me while a doctor cleaned my foot and put a couple of stitches in to hold the wound together. When Etienne asked the doctor about me playing basketball, she said it depended on how well the cut healed and how much I managed to stay off it. She couldn't promise it would be okay for the final, but that if I rested until then I might be fine to play.

I'd forgotten all about the basketball final.

We drove home silently. At red lights Etienne reached over to touch my leg or to look at me with concern on his face. In his driveway we stayed in the car. I told Etienne it wouldn't have made any difference. Running or driving, I still would have missed. It was my fault I hadn't left sooner. That I didn't act in time.

Then I told Etienne about the man who'd fallen. I told him what I felt as he fell. I told him about his acceptance at the end. Etienne didn't ask me how I knew those things, he just listened.

I started to cry. I cried so much I wasn't sure I'd ever be able to stop. Etienne got out of the car and came to the passenger side. He looked at the bandage on my foot and announced he would have to carry me so that the bandage didn't get dirty. He lifted me out of the car and I cried into his shoulder. He held me close and when I lifted my face to look at him, he kissed the tears on my cheeks.

At the door I fumbled with my keys until I managed to open it. I whispered to Etienne to take me to my room. And then we were kissing. We were kissing like starving animals. I stopped crying and just wanted him. Etienne tried to carry me quietly up the stairs as I clung to him.

As soon as we were in my room he put me carefully on my feet and I closed the door behind us. Etienne moved towards me.

'I'm going to go and let you get some rest.'

I blocked his exit. 'Stay. Please. Stay with me.'

I kissed him and then moved a little away to take off my dress. In the morning I wondered how I'd had the courage to do that, but at the time it felt like the only thing to do. The only thing I wanted to do.

Etienne was unsure. I could feel he wanted to be with me, but also that he thought the right thing to do was to go.

'Please, I want this.'

I helped him take off his shirt. We lay down on my bed. For a moment we were still. We held each other. We felt our hearts beating together. I started to wonder if this would be it. If this was as far as Etienne was willing to go. But then I kissed him. I touched him. We started removing the last of our clothes.

Etienne kept checking if what he was doing was okay and I wanted to say, *More, do more*. I wanted to feel alive with him. I wanted to forget death and fear and pain. I didn't say that, though. I said everything he was doing, everything we were doing, was what I wanted and I would tell him if something wasn't right. If there was anything I didn't like.

I was nervous, though. I knew from Meg it was going to hurt. That it wasn't what I'd seen in movies. But I still wanted it. I wanted to feel Etienne as close to me as I could, and I could tell by the way he was looking into my eyes he wanted that too.

Etienne pulled away from me and searched his jeans for his wallet. He took a condom out and looked at me with embarrassment. He told me his mother gave them to him. Made him promise to carry them. I lay back on the bed and put a pillow over my face, trying not to picture that scene. I asked him through the pillow, 'When?' I wanted to know if she had given them to him a long time ago, or just when he started seeing me.

Etienne took the pillow away from my face. 'She started giving them to me when I turned fourteen. And she buys me new ones all the time. I started to notice she'll take the old ones out of my wallet and slip in new ones. Now I just leave my wallet around so she doesn't have to search for it. The last thing my mother wants is a child in the house.'

Then he kissed my fingers, my neck, my breasts and my belly. I pulled him back up so his face was close to mine, my mouth on his, my hands on his back. I wrapped my legs around him and held him to me.

Perhaps I should have thought more about Etienne and his life in that house across the street, but all I was thinking about was Etienne in my house – his mouth, his hands, the warmth of his skin against mine, the weight of his body on mine.

It wasn't the worst pain I'd ever felt. Etienne stopped and looked at me with worry in his eyes and I told him, 'It's okay, don't stop.' I watched him watch me until the intensity of what I was feeling forced me to close my eyes and arch my body towards his.

The plan was for Etienne to leave afterwards. He would creep out of the house and back into his own. But we ended up curled together. Still enjoying, wanting, that closeness of each other's bodies. I wondered at how I got to be here with Etienne in my bed and how happy I was that he was here. And then we fell asleep.

THIRTY

WE woke to sunlight streaming through the window and the sounds of Aimee crying and Meg singing to her.

It would have been nice to wake up relaxed with Etienne that first morning together. It would have been nice to stretch out my naked body alongside his and see if he had any more condoms in his wallet, but when Etienne woke up he sprang out of bed in a panic, which caused me to do the same.

Etienne pulled on his clothes as quickly as he could while I threw on my pyjamas. He whispered, 'How am I going to get out of here?'

I looked around the room and considered the layout of our house. I wondered whether I could get everyone to leave and how long that would take me.

I looked out my window and told him he was going to have to jump. That I'd go down and catch him. Etienne shook his head and told me there had to be another way.

'Not unless you want to go down the stairs and say good morning to my parents.'

Etienne looked out the window to the grass below in our front yard. 'Are you sure you can catch me?'

I nodded. I was as sure as I could be.

We took a moment to kiss goodbye. Etienne tugged at my pyjamas and told me he liked them. I looked down to see how childish they were and gave him a small push. I told him not to jump until he saw me there in position and he nodded seriously. I could see he was worried. So was I. I took his jacket to use as an excuse for needing to go outside, and Etienne pointed out I would never walk over to his place in my pyjamas. He was right, but that meant I had to get changed in front of him.

I tried to do it as quickly as possible. I wasn't sure why it felt different now. We'd been naked together on the bed a few minutes ago, but there was something embarrassing about him being dressed, watching me get undressed and re-dressed. Etienne watched with a smile, enjoying my embarrassment.

When I was finished, with a big sock over my bandaged foot, he came over to kiss me, running his hands up inside my top and then down over my bottom. I groaned and pulled myself away from him.

As I walked down the stairs I thought about how the conversation would go if I told Mum I needed more grown-up pyjamas. Not well, was my best guess. Followed by a load of questions and a subtly placed magazine article about the risks of teenage sex. Like I didn't know from Meg's example what the risks were.

I moved quickly through the house and out the front door without anyone stopping to question me. Then I threw Etienne's jacket to the ground and stood under my window. I motioned for him to come quickly.

It was tight for Etienne to fit through the window, but he squeezed himself out and, with only a small amount of hesitation, dropped into my arms.

I was impressed he did it. That he trusted me. I was relieved I managed to catch him, and surprised by the pain in my foot that caused me to stumble a little. I put him quickly on the ground. He grabbed his jacket before kissing me and heading to his house.

Etienne had told me his parents didn't pay much attention to his comings and goings. I wondered if that was true. If they'd notice him walking in or if they would even worry about him being out all night without letting them know.

I walked back into the house to find Dad waiting for me, his eyebrows raised in a question. I pointed behind me.

'Etienne lent me his jacket last night. I was just returning it.'

Dad didn't look convinced by my lie. I had thought the story was a good one. He wanted to question me more. Maybe call my bluff, but instead he asked about my foot.

'Stitches, and I have to rest it. I don't know if I'll be able to play in the final.'

He started to look uncomfortable. I think he had something else he wanted to say, but he was having trouble working out what it was. Maybe he was just thinking about the bike ride he was about to do.

'Do you feel well enough to open the shop?'

I nodded.

'I won't be long. I'll come and take over so you can rest your foot.'

I thanked him and gave him a kiss on the cheek. I wondered if I smelt like Etienne and hoped, if I did, Dad'd think it was because I'd been wearing his jacket.

As I walked through the kitchen to grab some breakfast Mum stopped me. All I wanted was food, a shower and to lie on my bed so I could properly think about the night that had just passed. But Mum had questions, and I had to sit down in the kitchen to answer them.

I told her about the party, about how I'd had to leave to catch. She knew this much from Meg. I told her about cutting my foot and how Etienne had found me and taken me to the hospital. I showed her the bandage and told her I had a script for antibiotics just in case I needed it. Mum wanted to know more. She asked me questions about what time I got to the catch and how long it all took at the hospital, and I told her I wasn't sure, that I was too upset about missing the catch.

'I'm still really upset, Mum.'

It was true. Just thinking about it, having to talk about it, brought tears to my eyes. Mum stopped her questions when she saw the tears. She gave me a hug.

'Do you want to talk some more?'

I shook my head, went upstairs and had a long shower. I cried a little more in the shower and soaped myself down, touched my raw tingling skin. I let the shower and the memories of my night with Etienne take away some of the pain of the missed catch.

As I dressed and got myself ready for work, I found the business card from the guy in the suit. I'd shoved it under a pile of books on my desk, but it must have dislodged when Etienne had crawled through my window. I read it properly for the first time.

DAN MICHAELS

Property, People, PR

I told Lin about my missed catch when I saw her at the bike shop. I tried to give her just the basics. I didn't want to go into details. She took notes without comment. I expected her to tell me it was stupid to go to the party, to stay with Etienne rather than leave as soon as I knew, but she didn't. I wished she had. I wanted the argument to distract me from the pain. But Lin just nodded and wrote it all down.

I remembered the business card in my pocket and pulled it out for Lin to see. I told her about running into him at the movies.

'He said he'd make me rich.' I didn't tell her about Etienne's reaction to him. 'What do you think?'

Lin asked me for more details about Dan Michaels, and I told her again about the time I caught him. About the smell of alcohol on his breath and the way he insisted I take his money. Lin started checking him out online while I talked.

'Let's call him.'

I was surprised, even though I'd been thinking the same thing.

'Why?'

I wanted to know why Lin wanted to call him, because I didn't know why I did. Not really.

'I want to know what he thinks he can do. We probably won't like it. But I'd like to know what he thinks your money-making potential is. And who knows, maybe he'd be interested in my data.'

We both understood that it was probably all about him making money, but neither of us could see how or why my catching would lead to that.

I called his number. He picked up on the third ring. I had my phone on speaker so Lin could hear. She had a notebook in front of her to write down what he was saying and to write questions for me to ask him.

It was a strange start to the conversation. I didn't know how to describe myself, and Lin had suggested I not tell him my name until we understood what he wanted. I explained I had caught him and later seen him at the cinema, and after a moment of silence everything fell into place for him. His voice took on a whole different level of enthusiasm.

'I've been waiting for you to call! Took your time, didn't you? Look, you know I think you're great, right? I mean, amazing. But you need me by your side. This thing of yours could blow up anytime. Do you know . . .'

He reeled off names I'd never heard of in a way that suggested everyone knew them. He told me what he'd done for them. How much he'd helped them. How most of them had sponsorship deals now. He expected me to be impressed. I didn't know how to respond. I'd never heard of any of them so I had no idea what they'd done. Lin wrote the names down to look them up later.

'So how many people have you caught?'

I didn't know. I mean, Lin had all the numbers, but I had no idea without her going to look it up.

'And what sort of people are they? Have you caught anyone famous? Any politicians?'

Lin shook her head when he asked for details.

'I'm not really sure.'

'What do you want out of this catching thing?'

'I want to help people.'

'Of course, of course.' He said this quickly, like helping people was a given. 'I can help you help others, you know. I can get you everything you need so you can help more people. But what do you want for you?'

I didn't know how to answer. I supposed a bit more money would make the worry of doing badly in school fade a little.

'Let's meet for coffee. We can talk more.'

I looked to Lin. She shrugged.

'I have to go now. I'll think about it.'

I ended the call.

While I was talking to Dan, Etienne had texted telling me everything was fine when he got home. He wanted to know how things were for me. I texted back that Dad was suspicious but also sympathetic about my foot, and that I'd only be working a few hours.

Etienne was too distracted to study. He suggested I come to his place after work. He told me he had a lock on his bedroom door.

I spent the rest of my time at the shop trying to find small things to do while sitting down. I tidied parts in the workshop area and looked for the bike we'd been building. I couldn't see it anywhere and Lin didn't know anything about it either. Then I sat, with my foot on a chair, talking with Lin about Dan, trying not to think about the miss last night, and waiting for Dad to show up.

When I got home, I gathered some books together and told Mum I was going to Etienne's to study. I had considered lying, but decided sticking to the truth might make things easier in the long run. I tried to rush out the door before Mum could ask questions.

She came out after me, calling to me as I walked as quickly as I could on my bandaged foot. 'What time will you be home?'

Her voice was angry. Angrier than I would have expected.

'Four? Five? Before dinner.'

Mum nodded. I could tell she still wasn't pleased.

I knocked on Etienne's door and Etienne's dad answered. I wasn't sure he remembered who I was, so I introduced myself and told him I was here to see Etienne. He smiled and nodded at me, saying he remembered. I wondered whether I needed to apologise for running out on our dinner, but he just pointed up the stairs towards Etienne's room.

As I walked up, I heard music playing and headed for an open door. Every other door upstairs was firmly closed and everything around me was white, neat. There were a couple of paintings on the walls and no family photos. I stuck my head through the open door and saw Etienne at his desk.

He smiled when he saw me and stood up to pull me into his room. He wanted to kiss me, but it was my turn now to inspect his room. I looked through his bookcase and at his basketball and other sporting trophies. There were no photos of Etienne with friends or family like I had. Nothing particularly embarrassing. Etienne told me his mother was keen on keeping things minimal. There was a double bed in his room with a stylish cover in muted colours. He had his own ensuite bathroom.

Etienne closed his door and turned the lock.

'I thought we were going to study, I brought my books.'

I said it with a smile. Etienne grabbed me and threw me onto the bed.

'Study, yes, we are definitely going to study.' He kissed me and started to unbutton my shirt.

'What about your parents? What will they think? Won't they hear?'

'They're heading out soon.'

'Maybe we should study until they leave?'

Etienne sighed, but agreed. He helped me up off the bed and did my buttons back up.

The desk was big enough for both of us. He cleared a space for me and pulled up an extra chair. We opened our books and I tried to concentrate on the page in front of me. After about ten minutes, Etienne's phone buzzed and he told me his parents were leaving now.

We sat quietly waiting until we heard the front door close and the car pull out of the driveway, and then we leapt back onto his bed to pick up where we'd left off.

We started kissing and slowly undressing each other, but we were still talking about our parents, about our morning. I don't know why I said it. He'd asked about the shop. It just came out.

'I called that guy today. The one from the cinema.'

Etienne's hands went still on my body. I remembered how awkward that run-in with Dan had made our second, more successful, movie date.

'Why?'

'Lin and I were curious. We wanted to know what he thought he could do.'

'And?'

I shrugged. 'He said he could help me help people.'

I watched Etienne hesitate, question himself about whether or not he should speak. I should have kissed him then. I should have put my mouth over his and taken the words from him. I should have said, *It doesn't matter. I'm not going to meet him or take it further. We were just curious.*

But maybe remembering that movie date also made me remember that he might not be around next year, that he could be travelling while I'm here, alone. So instead, I sat up. I looked at him. 'Say it, whatever it is you want to say. Say it.'

Perhaps there was a tone in my voice, a warning or a challenge.

'Are you going to meet with him?'

'I don't know, probably not, maybe . . . I don't know.'

I put my top back on like I knew where this conversation was going. Maybe I did know where it was going. Maybe I'd been waiting for it ever since that first awkward conversation. Like the man who chased me that night. Something I always expected, dreaded, but now here it was, actually happening.

'I don't think you should.'

'Why not?'

'Think about last night, Beth. How hard that was. Why would you want to do more of that?'

'I could have got there in time. I should have got there in time. And maybe he could help me get to more people. Maybe he has connections or an idea that will help.'

'I don't trust him. It's weird.'

'You mean I'm weird.'

I stood up and started to gather my books.

'What are you doing?'

Etienne still had his shirt off. I could barely look at him.

'I thought you liked me catching. You told me you thought it was amazing.'

'I did. I do. It is.'

'Then why is this a problem?'

'Because you're talking about getting involved with some guy you know nothing about. Someone who wants to expose you to the rest of the world.'

I started to walk for the door. 'I can take care of myself.'

'Really?'

Etienne pointed at my foot. He was up off the bed now, moving towards me. I thought, I hoped, he was going to try to stop me leaving. That what he would say next would make everything better.

We heard his parents open the front door downstairs and footsteps coming up the stairs. I was close enough to the door now to turn the lock just as Etienne's dad knocked. I opened the door. He looked from Etienne, in the middle of his room, shirtless, to me, standing near the door, with my books in my arms, then back to Etienne.

'I forgot some papers. They were on the printer. You didn't pick them up, did you?'

'No.'

'Your mother must have tidied them, then.' He looked again between the two of us. 'Everything okay here?'

I looked to Etienne and he nodded to his father. 'Yep, sure.'

'Okay. See you later.'

We waited, listening to his footsteps down the stairs, the front door closing again and the car driving away. We waited in the silence.

Etienne looked at me and then away. 'I don't think I can do this.'

I didn't wait to hear what it was he didn't think he could do. I tightened the books in my arms and left.

THIRTY-ONE

THE last weeks of term were full of assessment deadlines. I handed in what I could, finished assignments as much as possible, but sometimes I just had to hand them in half done. Lin took on a seriousness in everything she did over this time. A seriousness way beyond her usual seriousness. She had become my constant study partner at school where we tried to support each other. Her with advice and encouragement, me with snacks and moral support.

Meg was also completely focused on her schoolwork and Aimee. She stayed up late and she got up early. Rik was over as often as she would allow. When he suggested taking Aimee home with him for a night Meg cried, because even though it was all too much, she couldn't bear to let her go. Instead, Rik slept on the couch with Aimee beside him and we all tiptoed around the three of them as much as we could.

I had to tell Coach I couldn't train before the final match. I was still hoping to play, but I couldn't risk opening the wound on my foot again before the game. Coach wasn't happy. He saw me walking in school without a limp and looked like he wanted to take my shoe off and inspect the cut for himself. Instead, he stared at me and then nodded as if to say, *I call bullshit, but I don't have time to argue.*

Etienne and I avoided each other. It was easier now because I wasn't going to basketball training and Etienne didn't always have to be at school. There were no texts between us. I started them. I even finished a few. But I didn't press send.

I didn't see or hear from Rock. I was waiting, watching for him. I told Meg about him and she made me tell Mum and Dad. They took the news better than they had taken my catching. It was like we were all starting to get used to the weirdness that was our lives now.

Dan called. He called every day. I hadn't given him my name, but I also hadn't thought to block my number when I'd made that first call. I was still thinking about him. About whether meeting him would make anything different. Lin advised against it. Her view was that we knew where he was if we needed him and, at the moment, we didn't need him.

I answered a few of his calls and let him say his piece. I told him I was still thinking about it, and that school was keeping me busy. I left most of his calls unanswered.

I was at school studying with Lin. If I hadn't cut my foot I would have been with Etienne at basketball training. I wondered if that would have been better. If being there would force Etienne and me to talk. I had been feeling a catch coming all day. There was nothing I could act on – it was just a vague feeling of nausea that told me something was going to happen.

As I sat in the library with my books in front of me, the desire to vomit got stronger. Training had about ten minutes to go and I needed a lift to get to this one. I knew it would annoy Coach, but Etienne was the only option I could think of that would work.

When Etienne saw me standing at the entrance of the gym he came without question.

The catch was at some high cliffs on the coast. We needed to climb down over rocks to be ready at the base of the cliff. Etienne wasn't happy about either of us climbing down, but was also unwilling to let me go on my own. Once we got down, I found a place that felt right. Etienne stood to the side. His job was to keep an eye on the waves. If he thought the surf was getting too dangerous, he was to call out and we would scramble up to higher ground.

I started to feel a bit unsure as I stood with the waves crashing behind me. I wasn't concerned about the catch or whether I was in the wrong place. I was worried about my stability. My foot, the waves, the rocks, how it would all work. There was no sign of anyone at the top. Etienne had suggested we stay up there to see if we could talk to whoever came, but I felt the determination in him and knew I needed to be at the bottom.

I wondered again why Rock didn't show up to these catches. How he knew I'd be here. If he knew. How he'd known to come to the first one when we'd met. I'd thought with two of us I'd have more help, but it hadn't turned out that way.

Etienne and I didn't talk about anything that had happened between us as we waited. We talked only logistics. The waves. The right place to be. Etienne had more to say. More he wanted to tell me or ask me, but my focus was on the catch. Whenever it looked like he was about to talk about something other than the catch I moved him away from the subject. I kept my eyes on the top of the cliff. My focus had no room for anything but the catch about to take place.

The boy came at me quickly, with force and conviction. Like he'd run from his home with no intention of ever stopping. He ran over the cliff edge and started to fall towards me. I caught him, but stumbled. Etienne stood behind me to steady us both. I put him on his feet as quickly as I could and we scrambled up the rocks a little away from the waves.

We spent some time, the three of us, silently sitting looking out at the ocean. Etienne and I sat together, our bodies close but not touching. I had room for him now. For the comfort and warmth of his body next to mine. I thought again about what it would be like if he wasn't here next year.

The boy I'd caught sat a small distance away from us, staring down at the waves crashing on the rocks that he had intended to fall onto. He looked younger than me and more exhausted than even I felt. We sat with him until the sun was low in the sky and then we guided him back up to the road.

Etienne told him we'd take him home and he obediently got into the car, directing us to a large house nearby. A dog was waiting at the gate. A long-haired, white, smiling dog who got excited at the car pulling up. When he saw the dog, the boy started to cry. Large silent tears ran down his face.

He didn't leave the car. The dog was going crazy, whining and barking and scratching at the gate. The boy wiped his eyes but still didn't make any move to get out. I walked to the passenger door and opened it for him. He understood that it was time to go. That I was telling him to move. I didn't know if I was being harsh. If he needed more time. I hugged him. He didn't hug me back, but he accepted my hug. Then he walked to the gate and the dog, who jumped and licked at him as soon as he got near.

I got back in the car and Etienne drove us home in silence. As he pulled into our street, we saw his parents weren't home yet and neither were mine. We clasped hands and walked quickly up to his room where he locked the door. We stripped off our clothes. I felt so hungry for his body, to have him close to me, holding me. At one point I cried, maybe because of the pleasure of being back in his arms, but I think mostly because of the boy I'd just caught.

When we showered we still hadn't spoken about anything that had happened between us. I wondered if this was it. If we would be able to move past what had happened this easily. If I could forget the gnawing thoughts about him saying he couldn't do this anymore. I held him in the shower. I looked into his eyes and I told him that I had missed him. Etienne kissed me in response. He had missed me too.

As we dressed my phone rang. Etienne was closest to it. He reached for it and glanced at the screen as he handed it to me. I couldn't read his face. It could have been anger. It could have been fear. I switched off the phone.

'He calls me every day, but I don't usually answer.'

Etienne pulled on his T-shirt. 'I can't believe you gave him your number.'

'Yeah, well, that was a mistake.'

'Change it.'

I didn't understand what he meant.

'Change your number, Beth.'

'I'm not changing my number just because one person you don't like has it.'

Etienne put his hands on my shoulders.

'Beth, I know men like him. I know who they are and what they want. My parents deal with people like him all the time. He's not calling to help you. He wants to use you, and you've given him your phone number to help him do that. You need to change it.'

I shook off his hands and picked up the rest of my things that were strewn across his room.

'I'm not changing my number, Etienne.'

I couldn't believe we were back in this place. That we could move so quickly from the bed to being apart again. I shoved my phone into my bag and muttered, 'Thanks for the ride,' as I walked out his door.

THIRTY-TWO

MY next catch was during the Business Studies final term exam. I thought I'd do okay in that one. I felt prepared, but when I sat down to read through the paper I realised I wasn't. The exam was asking for information I couldn't remember or perhaps never knew.

I wasn't upset when I got a sudden, intense urge to throw up. I grabbed my things and rushed from the room, past Ms Brown who was supervising the test, and out of the school. I headed for the city at a jog and then a run. I knew running could open the wound on my foot and that I was damaging my chances of playing in the basketball final, but I also knew there was no time to call for a lift, no time for anything but to run.

My foot ached as I ran. I didn't have time to stop and check it. When I reached the construction site I shouted to the people on the street to stand clear. I threw my bag down, still shouting at everyone to move, and then looked up and realised I couldn't do it alone. It was more than one catch. I looked around at the people nearby. Searching through them for Rock. I didn't want to have to make a choice.

The scaffold started to collapse. I moved into position for the first guy and watched the second fall soon after him. The distance was small, but too great for me. I couldn't safely catch the first and then make it to the second. I caught the first guy and felt the hammer in his tool belt slam into my leg. The pain wasn't good, but I was bracing for the worse pain of hearing the second guy fall to the ground. I put the guy I'd caught quickly on the ground and turned to see Rock standing nearby, the second construction worker in his arms.

Ambulances and police cars started to arrive. I became aware of the crowd that had formed behind us. The construction workers we'd caught were standing separate from the crowd, trying to work out what had happened. Other workers from the site were coming out to look at the damage.

People from the crowd started approaching to shake my hand. Others wanted to take photos with me. I looked around and picked up my schoolbag. Rock came and grabbed my hand, pulling me away from the crowd. A few people tried to stop us, but we shook them off and started running. The pain in my leg from where the hammer had hit me made it hard to move quickly, and my foot was still aching from the run to get there, but we made it to a bus going vaguely in my direction and that seemed to halt anyone who might have been trying to follow us.

On the bus I asked Rock where he'd been. I was thinking of my recent missed catch, wondering why he hadn't been there. Or why he hadn't been at the cliff.

Rock shrugged. 'Out of town. People fall in other places too, you know.'

He told me his name was really Robert, but everyone had always called him Rock. He didn't tell me who 'everyone' was. He said he had been catching for a year; it had started when he was sixteen, just like me. For him it hadn't felt familiar, like something that had always been there. For him it was a shock. Something that came out of nowhere. Something he had no idea what to do with.

'I was ready to give up the first time we met. It all felt too hard. Too lonely. And I was so tired. My family thought I was faking the whole thing to get out of school. Then you pulled me away from the train tracks that day and everything changed for me.'

I thought back to the person I'd stopped from jumping onto the tracks at that station. That person had been thin, dirty, lost. The person in front of me was none of those things. But when I looked at his face, when I looked into his eyes, I could see Rock wasn't making it up. It had been him there on that day, feeling those feelings.

'Just knowing you were there, that there was someone else around like me – that was enough to keep me going.'

We got off the bus and walked to my house. I took Rock upstairs to my room and laid out the map Lin had made for me. I showed him the boundary and explained how I used it.

Rock tried the map. He sat in the middle of it like I showed him and closed his eyes. He shifted his position as if he couldn't get comfortable, shaking his head. 'No, it feels all wrong.'

Rock's body was lean and wiry. He reached for my hand to pull himself up off the map and his hand felt solid and strong in mine. I told him about when it all first started for me. About how it was all too much, how I had to work with Lin to build the boundary just so I could function. How the boundary felt too small now, and I knew I should be doing more, but I needed the boundary to make me functional.

Rock nodded like he understood. He told me he didn't have a Lin. That for him the noise, the knowing, was always there in the background. He'd slowly learnt to live with it his own way. He could now stand somewhere, anywhere, and search within that space for someone who needed him, like a moveable boundary. Like a radar.

He offered to teach me.

'When?'

The idea of being able to work within my limits but without a boundary felt like a freedom I wanted to try.

'Let's start now.'

He was still holding my hand. He pulled me back down the stairs.

We ran into Mum and Dad as we were leaving the house. I wanted to rush out the door but I knew that wouldn't work for Mum.

'Mum, Dad, this is Rock. Remember I told you about him? He's like me. I mean, he catches people too.'

Mum and Dad smiled and shook hands with Rock. I could see Mum's questions starting to brew.

'We're just heading out for a bit but I'll be back soon.' I turned to Rock. 'That's the plan, right? We won't be long?'

'Sure.'

Rock and I walked back to the bus stop.

'We need to get away from your boundary.'

'Where should we go?'

'We'll get on the first bus that comes along and see where it takes us.'

The bus came and as we sat together, watching the streets and buildings go by, Rock tried to explain how he found his catches. For him it was a sense of excitement. His heart beating faster and an urge, like mine, to run. We stayed on the bus until Rock turned to me.

'Do you feel it?'

I closed my eyes and tried. I shook my head. I couldn't feel one thing. Without a boundary I could feel everything. A big mass of feelings was coming at me from all sides.

Rock pulled at my hand and stepped off the bus, then he stopped. I stopped with him, trying to feel something that was clear. Anything that might need me.

'This way.'

We ran down into a train station and then onto a train.

'Where are we going?'

'I don't know.'

'Who are we catching?'

'I'm not sure yet.'

I shook my head. I was starting to feel something, but it was confused by the movement of the train. By me not knowing where I was.

'Still your mind. Focus ahead. The catch, it's in front of us.'

I looked out of the window at the darkening sky.

'Here.'

The train had pulled into a platform. Rock was up at the doors, ready to run again. I joined him. I could feel his excitement even if I couldn't feel any urgency of my own. I could also feel my leg and my foot, both still aching.

We ran from the station into the street. Rock ran in front of me, turning occasionally to check I was behind him. As we ran I started to feel the catch. I felt him standing on the edge, his mind wavering, his body resisting. I ran harder.

Rock made it to the building as the man was falling. I made it in time to see Rock catch him. Rock put him on his feet quickly. He spoke to him, their heads close together. I walked closer as the man gave Rock some money. Rock patted him on the back and the man walked past me. He didn't meet my eyes – I knew his head still had him falling through air. He didn't know where he was. Who he was.

Rock waved the money at me. 'Hungry?'

'I should get home. I don't even know where I am.'

'Let's eat, then I'll take you home. Promise.'

I nodded. I wanted to spend more time with him. I still didn't understand how he knew to get where he needed to be.

We went to a nearby noodle house and over steaming bowls we talked more about how Rock found his catches. I asked him if he ever missed.

'All the time. But you know, I catch a lot too. I try to focus on that.'

I nodded, sipping at the soup around my noodles.

'You think it's wrong I asked that guy for money.'

I shook my head. I didn't know how I felt about it.

'This is my work, Beth. I can't get a job. Even if I could, I can't keep it. I've tried. And I don't have a family like yours. My family didn't understand. Didn't believe me. They didn't even try. I deserve to be paid, to be fed, for helping people. So do you.'

THIRTY-THREE

MUM wasn't pleased I'd stayed out so late or that she had to write a note to excuse me from the exam. She was even less pleased by the bruise on my leg.

'What do you want me to do, Mum? You want me to sit through an exam knowing they're going to fall? You want me to let them die?'

She hugged me then. 'People die, Beth, all the time. You can't save everyone.'

I shook her off. I was tired from the late night. 'I saved these ones, though. Why can't you feel happy about that? I was never going to pass that exam anyway.'

I told her school was becoming a waste of time for me. Then we had an *I'm not Meg/we all have our own strengths* argument before I stormed off to report the catch to Lin. I told her about the people crowding us after the construction-site catch. About the handshakes and photos.

Lin told me all the attention was inevitable. That we'd known it was coming and it was time to think about what I wanted to do with it. It was time to put a plan in place.

'What? What plan can we put in place?'

Lin sighed. 'I don't know, Beth. What do you want? If you're going to keep catching, you're going to have to make a decision about how you want to do that.'

I told her about Rock. About the money he asked for from the people he caught.

'I don't want to do that.'

'Well, then . . .'

She was talking about Dan. She was telling me it was time to call Dan.

'I don't know . . .'

I could hear her mother shouting for her in the background. 'I've got to go, Beth. Mum's lost her glasses again.'

Dad came home with the bike he'd built for me, finished and ready to ride. He'd had it coated to strengthen the frame. He asked me if I felt up to testing it out, so I hopped on and rode up and down the street for a bit. Dad watched, and called me back to lift the seat a little and tighten the brakes. I told him the bike was good. He probably wanted to hear more, but it was all I had. I was too busy thinking about Rock and catching trains. About whether the bike would help or hinder if I decided to go outside my boundary.

I expected immediate repercussions from the photos that were taken at the construction-site catch, but I left the house and went to school and nothing had changed. I thought perhaps the photos didn't work out, or people went home and realised what they thought they saw must be impossible, so they just forgot about it.

The next few days were the same. Like some sort of calm before a storm. I didn't need to leave any other classes to catch, and Mum tried really hard to be nice. My foot had almost healed and the bruise on my leg was fading. Rock didn't contact me and I built my boundary wall back up so I could get through the days like a mostly normal person.

Something changed for Meg too. Some kind of shift or relaxation. Maybe she finally realised it was pointless to stick to her plan if it wasn't making anyone happy. She allowed Rik to take Aimee to his house for a night and even though she cried, she also slept and started to return to something a bit more like herself.

Etienne had gone back to avoiding me, but I was so confused by the last time we were together that, even though it hurt, it was better not seeing him for a few days.

I felt the fire catch just as I walked in the door after school. The fire was fast and she had been napping, completely unaware. I grabbed my new bike and rode over. The bike was easier and quicker than running, and I reminded myself to thank Dad again for it.

When I got to the house she was at her upstairs window, clutching her cat. A small group of neighbours were in her front yard and she was shouting to them that she couldn't get down the stairs. Someone had gone for a ladder, but the heat and the smoke were coming so fast I knew he wouldn't be able to get it up to her in time. I called to her to jump. I told her I would catch her.

She threw me the cat.

I'd never caught a cat before and I hope I never have to catch one again. The cat scratched at my face, hissing, as I got my hands around its torso. It sank its claws into my shoulders and then down my back before it leapt free and made its way to the relative safety of a parked car. Once there, it hid behind a wheel, its eyes wide.

I turned back to the woman and told her it was her turn. That she had to jump. She told me to stop being ridiculous. I told her again she had to jump. That she had no choice.

I looked to the side. The watching crowd had grown. Some of them had their phones out. I knew they were filming the whole thing and wished I wasn't wearing my school uniform. I watched to see what she would do, worrying the smoke would get her before she realised she needed to jump.

The woman looked behind her, into the room she was in. She shouted that the flames were at the door. I yelled at her again to jump and some of the crowd screamed it as well. They wanted to get a blanket to break her fall, but I told them it wasn't needed. That I could do it. Someone went to get a blanket anyway.

When the woman realised she had no other choice she closed her eyes and jumped. She fell feet first, and I caught her around her middle. She kept her eyes closed until I put her feet on the ground. Then she patted me on the shoulder in surprise and turned to find her cat, who refused to come out from under the car.

I heard the sirens coming and saw her neighbours crowd around her with blankets and water. I picked up my bike and watched her house for a moment as it was engulfed in flames. I tried to cycle away but a few of the neighbours stopped me to shake my hand. They wanted to take my picture. I turned my face away from the camera.

That night the story came out. Lin spotted it first and shared it with me. The video footage was clear. Anyone who knew me would be able to recognise it. And the school uniform was obvious too.

After that people started to share images of me catching the construction worker in the same school uniform. Me walking away from the catch with Rock. People shaking our hands. Rock's face was hidden by his hood in all the photos and there were none of him catching.

In the morning Lin texted to say there was an article in the newspaper. Not the local paper, the big mainstream paper. Her text said, *Get ready*. She didn't say for what and I didn't ask.

I walked to school wondering what would happen now. Maybe it was better people knew. Maybe people knowing would make my failure at school a little more understandable. I could stop pretending I was missing school because of family stuff. I could stop lying all the time.

THIRTY-FOUR

AT first there was only quiet attention. Kids I didn't know nervously saying hello or snapping a picture of me. The further I walked into school the more intense it became. A crowd formed. Kids surrounded me, asking questions. I tried to push through, to pretend it wasn't happening. Kids started raising their voices. Shouting questions to me over each other.

Most of the questions being shouted in my direction were about whether it was really me, whether I could do the stuff that was being said. They wanted me to tell them, show them.

I tried to walk towards a quieter part of the school, but the only escape turned out to be the school office. I sat in there waiting for Lin, trying to think of what to say to the office staff, who were studying me with curiosity and a small amount of annoyance that I had invaded their space.

Lin arrived and we stayed there until the first bell went. The worry on her face became more pronounced as we walked to rollcall. I told her I'd be fine, but she was thinking it might be better if I went home. If I lay low for a while. I shook my head. It was too late for that. I didn't want to hide anymore.

Ms Bhat welcomed me into rollcall and called me to the front of the class. 'I can see no one is going to be quiet and read this morning, so come on, let's get all the questions out.'

Standing in front of a class has never been my idea of fun, but I particularly didn't want to do it that day. I reminded myself that rollcall only lasted ten minutes as I stood not knowing where to look. Most of the questions were stupid. 'Can you read minds? Are you an alien? A superhero? Can you share your powers? Are you working for a government agency? Do you get paid?'

I stood shaking my head and trying to think of something to say. Some of the kids were uninterested or confused. Others, like Lin, were looking at me with sympathy. Some had genuine interest. Stupid questions, but genuine interest. The rest were just trying to be funny.

I looked at the class and reminded myself that they were the same kids I'd been to school with for the last four years. Those same kids trying to get a laugh at someone else's expense. Me, standing up here, as weird as I was, didn't make anything at school different. It was just like it always was.

I let their questions wash over me and decided it was no big deal. That I could handle it. I wasn't going to answer their stupid questions. I wasn't going to try to be funny back. I was just going to stand here quietly, like I had since Year Seven, knowing they would get bored soon.

As the bell went for the first class, I turned to look at Ms Bhat. I wanted to know if she'd realise how cruel she'd just been. It didn't seem to occur to her until she saw my look. I grabbed my things and pushed my way out of the room into the hallway. Lin followed close behind and squeezed my hand before we separated.

I was heading for my first class when I was stopped by Mrs Hanrahan. She asked me to come with her, and when we got to her office there were two police officers waiting for me. Mrs Hanrahan told me she'd called my parents. They were on their way.

'You don't have to speak to anyone until they get here.'

I sat outside the principal's office while she sat inside with the police. I heard their low voices and wondered whether I might be in big trouble and whether I cared. Kids who came through the office for late notes saw me sitting there. They stared, but they didn't ask me questions or take photos, and I was grateful for that.

Dad arrived first. He sat next to me quietly while we waited for Mum. The police checked with Dad to see if he would allow me to start talking to them. Dad said no, he wanted his wife there. They smiled and nodded at him like everything was fine. We sat and waited another twenty minutes for Mum to turn up.

When Mum arrived, slightly out of breath and straightening her clothes, we all took a seat in the principal's office. I was in the middle between Mum and Dad, with the officers to one side and Mrs Hanrahan at her desk. It was pretty crowded. Mum spoke first.

'Are you charging my daughter with anything?'

The police laughed a little, like that was a ridiculous idea.

'We're just here to have a conversation. To ask Beth a few questions.'

Mum continued to press them. 'Has she broken any laws?'

'Well, to be honest we don't really understand what's going on. We've heard some pretty wild stories and we just want to clarify a few points.'

'If there's no charge, there's nothing to talk about.' Mum stood up and started to gather her things together.

'We can make a charge if that's what it will take for you to talk to us.'

Mum was already heading for the door. 'Fine, come speak to us when you've got a charge. Until then, I'll ask you to leave my daughter alone.'

She walked out of the room. Dad and I got up and followed her.

I expected them to stop us. That it wouldn't be so easy just to walk off. But it was. The police stayed in Mrs Hanrahan's office and we walked quickly away from it and towards the school gates. Dad asked me if I wanted to leave with him, but I shook my head. I told him it was fine. I was fine.

Mum gave me a quick hug and turned to leave. Dad hugged me longer. He told me to call him if I needed to. Then he caught up to Mum and I was left to walk back to class.

I found the day hectic but manageable. Kids were still snapping pictures of me in the hallways even though I tried to keep my head down. No other teachers asked me to stand at the front of the class and answer questions. I didn't know if Mrs Hanrahan had spoken to them, or if they were just kinder than Ms Bhat. A couple of kids from the basketball team pulled me aside to check if I was okay.

At lunch, Lin sat with me and tried to stare down anyone who approached. By then kids were mostly leaving me alone. Some were still staring, still asking stupid questions, but a lot more had become distracted by their day or their phones or friends.

After school I joined the basketball team for practice. It was my first session back since I'd cut my foot. I looked nervously at Etienne when he arrived. I couldn't read his expression. I wondered whether he was worried I'd been exposed or angry I'd let myself be found out.

Coach tried to start practice like normal, but discussions kept breaking out about me and whether it was legal to let me play. I stayed quiet.

'Look, it's the last game. The final. We've all worked hard to get here, and we need to keep working just as we have all season. This is not the time to get distracted. Not by anything.'

After practice Coach pulled me aside and I told him about catching. I told him everything. Coach didn't say much. He listened, nodded, then told me I should have said something earlier, but it was too late now and I was not to worry about what the team or anyone else said. I just needed to keep playing like I'd been playing.

'Sometimes I purposely miss the ball. And I never run full speed.'

'I know. I mean, I didn't know why. But I knew. Just keep doing exactly what you've been doing, Beth, and we'll be fine.'

Etienne stayed behind to help Coach pack up. I walked out of the school grounds with a few others from the team. I didn't see the pack waiting for me. I thought it was over. I thought I'd made it through the hard part of the day.

As I stepped away from the school I was swamped by lights and cameras. By microphones in my face. I looked around and saw my teammates had been pushed away. They were replaced by strangers demanding answers to questions I could barely understand. I blinked through the lights and tried to think of something I could say to make it stop.

Dan arrived in a screech of tyres and foul language. He barged his way through the cameras and lights and shielded my face with a thick wad of papers. He put his arm around me and shouted the crowd down. He told them I had nothing to say and if they wanted a story they'd need to go through him.

He walked me to his car and opened the door. The car was a bright yellow sports car, low to the ground with tinted windows. I had to fold myself to fit in the back seat. I stared out at the people standing on the footpath. Their cameras were still taking photos, recording whatever they could make of me from behind the tinted glass of the car window. Dan shoved the papers he'd been holding at me and told me to hide my face, but I kept looking because I'd seen Etienne come out of the gates. I watched him as he took in the scene. Me in the car, Dan in the driver's seat, the cluster of cameras and microphones around the car.

I turned my face away from him, away from the lights. Dan started the engine with a warning roar and drove us through the crowd.

As we headed away from the school I asked Dan to take me home.

'Of course, yes, I'm just going to throw them off your trail and then I'll take you home.'

I looked behind the car. I couldn't see anyone following.

Dan drove around in circles for a while, talking about how amazing I was. How much good I was doing. How I could help people in a way he'd never thought was possible. How he wanted to help me help people. I listened with my eyes closed and my head resting back on the seat behind me. I couldn't take in much of what he was saying. I asked him again to drive me home.

When we got to my house I thanked Dan for coming to get me. I'd considered lying and directing him to a house near mine. Jake's, maybe. But when it came to it, mine was the only address I remembered. Maybe it didn't matter anymore.

'I'll be here for you, Beth. Tomorrow when you wake up, I can be right here. You see that paper you're holding?'

I looked at the thick wad of papers he'd used to shield my face.

'That's a contract. An exclusive contract between you and me. You sign that and no one will be able to get to you without going through me. You sign that and I'll look after you.'

'How?'

'However you need. Cars, security. Whatever it takes.'

'And me?'

'You'd need to do a few interviews. Maybe a photo shoot. That's all – unless you want to do more. Just read it, Beth. Show it to your parents. And call me if you have any questions.'

I put the contract on the kitchen bench and waited for everyone to come home. Rock arrived as we sat down to eat. The press and attention had brought him to me. He didn't say where he'd been or what he'd been up to. He just said he was there for me.

The contract had been passed from person to person before dinner. No one had said much about it yet. Rock's eyes widened at the amount of money on offer. Dan had put in some figures of what he thought he could get me for doing the interviews. Meg pointed out they weren't real. That there was nothing real in the contract apart from the percentage Dan would take from any earnings.

Still, there weren't many objections. Mum suggested we look for an outside opinion or another offer, but I didn't want that. I didn't want to spruik myself to other agents in the hope of finding a better offer than Dan's. I called Lin and we talked through whether doing an interview would stop the attention I was trying to avoid. Lin came over and read the contract too. She thought it might, particularly if Dan could get an exclusive contract for me. She thought that would make me less attractive to other news agencies. And she didn't think the money in my bank account would hurt either.

I rang Dan and told him I'd sign the contract if he drew up an identical one for Rock.

Dan couldn't believe his luck. 'There's two of you?'

He came with Rock's contract within the hour and we both signed them in front of him. Dan told me there would be a car to take me to school in the morning if I wanted. I looked to Mum to check if I was still expected to go to school. She nodded, and turned to Dan.

'How soon will all of this happen? These interviews?'

'As soon as I can make it happen. News like this doesn't stick around long, unless you plan to feed it. We need to take control of the narrative. Who knows where they'll take it if we don't give them some direction?'

He looked from me to Rock. Rock wasn't going to say anything. So I shook my head.

'I don't want to feed the media attention. I want to make it go away.'

'Okay then. Let's make it go away for as much money as we can.'

Dan took his signed contracts, told us he would take care of everything and that there was nothing to worry about. Then he drove off.

Mum offered to make up the couch for Rock, but he said he was fine and he'd come and see me again soon. I walked him to the door and watched him leave, wondering if he knew where he would sleep.

When I woke up in the morning a car was waiting in our driveway. Mum went out to speak to the driver while I got ready. Meg came in the car with me and directed the driver into the staff carpark, away from the small group of people with cameras who were waiting at the school gate.

School was a lot quieter for me than yesterday. Kids continued to take my picture in the corridors, and in class people fought to sit next to me so they could whisper questions. I found I didn't mind this kind of attention. The need of other kids to be near me. Their desire to know what was going on.

Sometimes I answered their questions. Wherever possible, I was as open and honest as I could be. Sometimes I just smiled and shook my head when they asked me things I couldn't answer. Or when I knew my answer to their question was going to disappoint.

I ignored them if their questions were rude or mean, if they were unfair or cruel. There weren't many of these, but it happened and when it did I turned my attention to the teacher or the window.

I breathed and counted time until the end of class.

At the end of the school day I walked out the gates to find Dan waiting for me. He had his car illegally parked, ready to whisk me away. Rock was sitting in the back seat. There were no reporters, but Etienne was standing near the gates, staring at Dan. Dan had his arms crossed and was leaning against his car, paying no attention to Etienne. He was telling me he'd taken care of the reporters and that we needed to go and do an interview now.

'I think you'll be very happy with the money I've negotiated.'

I stopped and looked at Etienne, who was coming towards us. I wasn't sure if he was heading for me or Dan. Dan seemed unaware of Etienne approaching.

'Let's go, Beth. They're waiting for us. Let's not make them wait any longer.'

Etienne placed himself between Dan and me. He was taller than Dan and blocked his view of me.

'Who's the guy in the car?'

I realised I'd never told Etienne about Rock. 'He catches people. Like me.'

Etienne nodded, but I wasn't sure if he'd really taken in the information.

'What are you doing, Beth?'

All I wanted to do was fall into his arms and have everything fade away. If I could. If he could. I wasn't sure we could.

'I signed an agreement with Dan.' I pointed to Dan, still standing behind Etienne.

'You don't need him.'

'He got rid of the reporters.'

Etienne shook his head. 'They would have moved on anyway.'

I could have agreed. I could have pulled him into my arms and walked home with him. But I'd signed a contract and I did think I needed Dan. I wanted Etienne, but I needed Dan to make all the attention go away, to control it. Etienne couldn't do that, for all I knew he'd be gone most of next year anyway.

'I have to go, Etienne.'

I walked around Etienne and into the car, shutting the door behind me. Dan rushed into the driver's seat. I knew Etienne was still standing there, watching me go. I turned to Rock and tried to smile.

Dan drove us to a television studio and introduced us to person after person. He acted as if everyone we came across was an old friend. Rock and I followed behind, obediently shaking hands and submitting to hair and make-up.

They brought us to a studio and the reporter introduced herself and tried to make us feel comfortable. I looked to Rock. He relaxed into his chair and smiled at me. I looked at the exit. I wanted to run. I wondered if we could. If the contract we'd signed allowed for that.

Rock reached over to squeeze my hand. 'Just give them a good story. Smile, take the money. Then it will be over and we'll get out of here.'

I nodded.

There were more cameras and lights than I expected. They had all sorts of ideas about wanting to film us catching someone. They thought they could stage a fall, or follow us to a real one. I realised I had made a huge mistake. I shook my head, and Dan quickly started talking about the agreement, an interview and a studio photo shoot only.

I stumbled through the interview questions, my head down a lot of the time to avoid the lights. Rock was better. He answered their questions and gave them stories. I know he made some of the stories up. I understood why, but I wasn't that quick. I couldn't think of anything to make up that they'd like, so I opted for saying as little as possible.

The photo shoot was fewer people and more lights. They put on some music and told us how good we looked. They took photo after photo of the two of us. Rock relaxed back in a chair, but I was rigid. They kept asking me to shake it out, to relax, to smile. To keep my eyes open. When they suggested we perform somehow, to show our strength, I refused.

After it was all over, everyone turned away from us and began to pack up their equipment. We were no longer the focus and for me that was nothing but relief. Dan put us back in his car and dropped me home first. When I turned to say goodbye to Rock, he again told me he'd see me soon. As I got out of the car Dan told me to watch out for the interview this evening, but I didn't pay attention to when it would be on. I didn't want to know and I didn't want to see it.

I don't know how many people saw the interview. Lin did, but didn't tell me much, other than I wasn't really in it much. They had focused more on Rock, which made sense given how little I managed to speak. I hoped Etienne didn't see it.

Dan transferred the money to me after taking his cut. When Mum and Dad refused to take any, Meg and I went to the bank and set up an account for Aimee. We split the money. Some for Aimee. Some for me.

Under the contract I'd signed there was the option of more interviews. Dan told me they didn't want to speak to me again, that I was considered 'bad talent'. He offered to train me and when I said, 'No, thank you,' he didn't push. My mumbling through the interview and my eyes closing in the photo shoot worked to my advantage in the end – the media world seemed ready to leave me alone and move on to the next thing.

THIRTY-FIVE

I woke up the morning of the basketball final feeling sick. I didn't even try to put it down to nerves. The game start time was mid-afternoon, so I could only hope I was going to get the catch out of the way before the game started.

At breakfast, I told my family, 'I'm going to have to catch someone today. I'm not sure when or where, but I can feel it coming.'

Mum wanted to know how, why, what was I feeling.

'I'm only telling you so you'll know where I am if I don't show up to the game or I leave partway through or I miss dinner. I'm not telling you so you can ask me a million pointless questions.'

Then I stormed off upstairs and called Lin. 'I can feel a catch coming. I don't know any of the details, and I don't know what to do.'

'You just have to keep going, Beth. Treat today like any other day. Warm up, play the game if you can. If you have to leave then you have to leave, and if people take pictures then people take pictures.'

It was reassuring to hear. I thanked her. I thanked her for everything she'd done and apologised that we hadn't spent more time thinking about what to do with all that data she'd spent so much time collecting.

'There's nothing to thank me for. And the data? I've been thinking maybe you're right. Maybe this is just about catching. Maybe that's all there is to it. I'll see you at the game.'

Nothing happened all morning. I stretched and shot baskets. I couldn't eat. The feeling that a catch was coming was still there, but it wasn't getting any worse. I walked to school with Etienne for warm-up. Our conversation was stilted. We didn't talk about Dan or any of our previous conversations. Instead, I told him how I was feeling. How I knew a catch was coming.

'Don't go, Beth.'

I couldn't believe he said those words. 'Do you understand what you're saying? What you're asking me to do? It's just a basketball game.'

'It's not the game. How can you think I'm worried about the game? I'm worried about you. Everyone knows you now. They'll all want a piece of you. It's not safe.'

'Asking me not to catch is like me asking you not to go away next year. Worse, really.'

'What are you talking about? Me going away is just an idea. My mum's idea. Nothing's been decided. I don't even know if I want to go travelling on my own.'

I shrugged and shook my head. 'You still can't ask me not to catch. You can never ask me not to catch.'

'I just did.'

Etienne strode towards the gym and left me standing alone.

I stayed outside and tried to calm down. It wasn't much use. By the time I walked into the gym Coach was instructing the team to start warming up. Etienne's attention was on the ball, on Coach, on the other people in our team. I tried to catch his gaze, but he refused to look at me through the entire warm-up. He didn't look angry, just focused. I decided to focus on the ball too, on Coach, the team, just like Etienne. I let my anger drive the ball from my hands into the basket or another player's hands.

As we slowed down and stretched our bodies, I wondered if Etienne was going to force me to choose between him and catching, knowing I couldn't not choose catching. Maybe this was his way of finally breaking things off with me.

I checked in with my nausea. It was still vague but constant. I started to hope I was going to make it through the game, really hope, as if somehow me being able to play the whole final would make everything right again between Etienne and me.

We sat next to each other on the bench as Coach gave his pregame speech for the last time this season. I tried to concentrate on what Coach was saying, but I'd heard it all before. I was more interested in the feeling of Etienne next to me. In trying to work out whether he was sitting there hating me, or whether he now regretted what he'd said.

When Coach finished speaking, we all stood up, shaking our legs out and patting each other on the back. Etienne's touch on my back was kind, lingering. It wasn't the pat of a teammate. I looked at him, hoping for something more, but he had already moved on to another player, his attention back on the game about to start.

Coach put me on court straight away. As we waited in position for the start of the game, something started happening with the other team. Their coach was talking to some players who were refusing to take their place on the court. We watched as they stood to the side with their arms folded, their eyes on their coach, who was now approaching the umpires.

The umpires motioned for our coach to join them, and my team started sharing looks. Etienne's eyes were on me now. Tommy's and Maye's and probably a few others' were too. We all knew what was going on. I almost went to leave my position, but Etienne shook his head a little and that kept me in my place.

I felt the catch intensify. Even if they let me play, I wasn't going to make it through the game. I looked up into the stands, to Lin and my family. We hadn't discussed who would drive me if I needed it, and I hadn't thought to bring my bike. Dad was watching me. The others were deep in conversation, their focus on the discussion between the coaches and umpires. Dad put his hand in his pocket. I watched him pull his car keys out.

I started walking off as soon as I saw Coach turn my way. I knew what had happened. The other team were refusing to play with me on the court. I collected my things. Coach quickly put another of our players in my place and the umpire blew the whistle for the game to begin.

I looked up into the stands again. Dad's seat was empty. I looked around and saw him standing by the door, waiting for me, his keys still in his hand.

We walked together out of the gym and towards the car. I didn't look back to see if Etienne or anyone else had noticed me leaving.

In the car I told Dad where to go and he drove quietly, confidently, quickly. He asked me if he needed to go faster, but I told him no, he was doing great.

'Dad, this time I want you to get out of the car. This time I want you to see what I do.'

Dad nodded. He didn't say anything, but at least he nodded.

When we got close I jumped out of the car, leaving Dad to park it, and ran to the apartment building. Rock was already there. He was wearing a jumper with the hood pulled up over his head, but when he saw me coming he pushed it back. I looked up at the building. I knew this building. It belonged to the woman who slapped me.

'What are you doing here?'

'Same thing as you, Beth.'

'This catch only needs one of us.'

'I wasn't sure you'd make it. With the basketball final and all.'

Rock was teasing me. Joking. He knew I'd leave anything to get to a catch. He looked better than I'd seen him before. He was wearing new clothes and looked more settled. Like he'd slept properly.

'They wouldn't let me play. They'll never let me play again.'

Rock looked up to the top of the building. 'There are worse things.'

I nodded. 'Yeah.'

Dad had arrived. He stood at the end of the street.

'You okay if I take this one? So my dad can see?'

Rock stepped back and made a grand, sweeping gesture with his arm. 'All yours.'

She fell slowly towards me. Her body was still, limp in the air. There was no struggle in her. I caught her easily. She had her eyes closed. I held her until she opened them. She looked at me sadly. I put her on her feet and waited for the slap. It didn't come. She turned and walked away.

Dad came to stand near me. He and Rock shook hands.

When she'd walked back into the building, I turned to Dad and Rock. Rock gave me a quick hug. 'See you next time.'

He started walking off, and I ran after him. 'Hey wait!'

Rock stopped, waiting for me to catch up to him.

'Don't worry, Beth. You'll see me again soon.'

'When?'

'Soon.'

He started to smile at me, but I didn't know why. I wondered what he saw in my face. Perhaps he saw some kind of desperation, because I was feeling desperate to understand how I was meant to contact him. How he always knew where I was, but I never knew where he was.

Rock didn't speak though. He didn't offer me a number to call, or an address, or day we'd meet. He just smiled and then took off, running at a pace that suggested he knew exactly where he needed to go next.

I turned back to Dad. He gave me a hug. 'It's going to be okay.'

'How do you know that?'

'I know you, Beth. You'll work it out.'

He hugged me again as we walked to the car.

Dad took me to a café where we ordered burgers and chips. We talked about normal things. The shop, Aimee. We didn't talk about the game I'd left, but I told him about the catch I'd just made. I told him about how she'd asked me to stop coming but how I couldn't let her go. I was wondering if that was fair. If I was actually helping her.

'If she really wanted to go she'd find another way. I think you are helping her, even if it doesn't always seem like it.'

When we pulled into our driveway I looked over at Etienne's house. The game would have been over for a while, and the light was on in his room. Dad sat next to me, watching my gaze.

'I need to go and see Etienne.'

Dad nodded like he already knew.

'I'll let the others know.'

I walked over and knocked on the door. Etienne's mother answered and barely looked up from the papers she was reading. When I asked for Etienne she pointed me vaguely up the stairs and then left me to walk up alone.

Etienne was sitting at his desk. He had showered and changed out of his basketball gear. Looking at him sitting there, all clean and fresh, I wished I had thought to do the same.

I sat on the end of Etienne's bed and he turned to face me. I wanted to tell him about the catch. About how the fight had gone out of her, and what Dad had said in the café, but instead I asked him about the game.

'We won.'

Etienne shrugged off the win. He didn't look happy about it.

'How was Coach?'

He smiled a little. 'Beside himself.'

'And you?'

Etienne shrugged again.

I stood up. 'What do you want me to do, Etienne? I don't know how to make this better.'

Etienne shook his head, as if he didn't know either. I wanted to move closer to him. I wanted him to pull me towards him, to draw me onto his lap and tell me, *Nothing, you don't need to do anything.* I wanted to wrap my arms around him and tell him he was all I wanted.

I stayed where I was.

'I can't not catch. This is who I am now. What I have to do.'

Etienne nodded. 'I know.'

We spent some time just being quiet. Both of us searching for words.

'Why me?'

Etienne picked up a pen from his desk. He looked at me and around his room and then back to me.

I asked it again. 'Why me? You could go out with any girl at our school, so why me?'

Etienne put the pen down. He half smiled. 'I don't know about any girl in the school. I just know you're the only girl I've ever wanted to be with. From the moment I saw you at the start of the year. Before that I didn't even know if I wanted anyone, but ever since then I've known I just want you.'

'Even when I have to leave to catch?'

'I don't know. I don't know if I can do it.'

I wanted to say, *Do what? I'm the one out there catching, I'm the one who's not allowed to play basketball, who has to leave exams. What is it you have to do?*

But I didn't say it. I didn't want to argue. I was too tired. I didn't want to have to fight him to be with him. I wanted him to accept the catching. To like the catching. To feel proud of me the way he did when he first found out.

I turned towards the door. 'You need to work that out.'

I walked out of Etienne's room and down the stairs. I didn't look back to see if he'd tried to follow. I knew he hadn't.

THIRTY-SIX

AT the start of the school holidays Dad and I made some adjustments to my bike, but I didn't have any reason to use it in that first week. Lin and I talked at work in the bike shop as usual, mostly about catching and how Dan was right, the interview really did seem to stop the media, or even people in general, having much interest in me and what I was doing. Lin kept tracking any mention of me – it wasn't nothing, but it wasn't a lot.

It was hard to believe the hectic attention and people trying to photograph me could be over just like that. I was still waiting for more. I started to notice police cars on my way to work, or saw them driving down the road the bike shop was on. Lin said I was being ridiculous. The police had plenty of other things to do and there was no way the police would be watching me. I thought she was probably right but I still jumped a little every time I saw one of those cars. I was still worried they'd want to try and stop me from catching people.

I didn't see Etienne. Not properly. I watched his light at night, watched for him as I came and went from the house. I was waiting. Waiting for him to come and apologise, or to come and finally, firmly, break everything off between us.

I hadn't seen Rock either. Lin had shown me images she'd found of me catching the woman, with Rock in the background watching on. The pictures were clear and good quality. Possibly professional. Other images of Rock had started to appear, as well as stories on social media and in online newspapers. Dan was quiet about it. He avoided my questions about whether he was the one organising it. He only asked if I wanted to do any more interviews or stories. I refused all his offers, and he didn't push. I guessed he was making enough from Rock that he didn't really need to invest in making me 'good talent' anymore.

I was watching basketball on TV with Dad after a long day at the shop. It wasn't easy. I thought I'd be fine, but the more I watched the more it sank in that basketball was over for me. I'd never be allowed onto a court again to play a proper game, and if I couldn't play an actual game, I wasn't sure I wanted to get on just for fun. It felt like catching was taking everything I liked away from me.

My mind moved from basketball to Etienne – I was sure he'd be the next loss. Then suddenly there was a catch.

I stood up quickly. Dad offered to drive, but his eyes were darting back to the screen. I knew he would come with me if I asked him, but the catch felt close and the bike was running really well. I told him I'd ride, and he didn't put up a fight about my decision.

The catch was at a raucous party about seven floors up in an apartment building. Teenagers. Older than me, but still teenagers. Mainly boys who'd had too much alcohol. I could feel it all as I rode there. The excitement, the fear, the anger in some of them. I didn't know which one was going to fall or jump. I just felt the mix of them all together. Of everything getting more and more intense.

As I stood below the balcony on the dark street, a figure walked in my direction. I assumed it was Rock. I hoped it was Rock. I didn't like the mood of the party, and I was worried there would be more than one body falling towards me. I stood, alternating between watching the figure approach and watching the balcony. I had my bike if I needed to get away quickly.

As I watched the person emerge from the darkness, the walk, their frame, all became familiar to me. Etienne came to stand beside me.

'I saw you leave your house alone.'

'I'm fine.'

'I know. I'm just here for the company.'

I would have smiled, but a fight had started on the balcony. There was pushing. Angry words. I still wasn't sure who was going to come my way, or how many, but I felt fear mixed in with the anger and I knew something would happen soon.

'Thanks for the company, but I'm going to have to get you to step back a little now.'

Etienne took a couple of steps away from me just as the guy fell. Was pushed, actually. We watched him fall and we heard the others on the balcony swearing and fighting over who did it and what they should do next. The music abruptly stopped. Everything went quiet.

I stepped forward and caught him in my arms. Etienne moved quickly to my side and suggested we move away from the area. I looked up at the balcony. It was emptying out as people rushed down the stairs to see what had happened. The guy in my arms was silent and breathing fast.

I carried him to Etienne's car and bundled him into the back seat. Etienne brought my bike to me and I hopped on and rode with Etienne following in the car.

When we'd gotten a fair distance from the party I stopped and Etienne pulled over. We helped the guy out of the back seat. He held on to our arms and pulled us towards some bushes that he leant into. He started vomiting. We smelt the fear and alcohol in his vomit and turned our faces away.

'Thanks for coming tonight.'

'I'm really sorry, Beth. I'm sorry I haven't been here more.'

The vomiting had finished now and the vomiter wanted to go back to the party. He wanted to finish the fight. We told him it was time to go home. The party was over. We asked him where he lived.

He started to look as if he was just working out what had happened to him. That dawning realisation was making him feel like he needed to vomit again. He grabbed at Etienne's jacket. 'They could have killed me.'

Etienne released the guy's hands. 'Let's get you home, buddy.'

'Are you sure you want him back in your car?'

Etienne nodded. 'I think the worst of it's out of him. I'll take him to his place and meet you back at home.'

The guy had pulled his licence out and was showing it to Etienne. 'Here. I live here.'

I rode home slowly and waited at our front door. Etienne pulled up in his driveway a little later and walked over the road to me.

'Hi,' he said, like we hadn't just seen each other.

'Hi. Everything go okay?'

'Yep. All fine. You okay?'

I nodded. 'So you saw me leaving from your window tonight?'

I loved the idea that Etienne had been watching for me the way I watched for him.

'I'm sorry, Beth.'

'What are you sorry for?'

'All of it. I should have known better. I should have been better.'

'I don't know what you want.'

Etienne moved a step closer to me. 'I want you.'

I looked up at him. 'Are you going to tell me I can't catch, or that it's not safe?'

'No.' He put his hands on my shoulders.

'What if you can't do it anymore again?'

'That was a stupid thing to say.'

'I felt like I was doing something wrong.'

'I don't think you're doing anything wrong.'

'Or that you think I'm weird.'

'No.'

His hands were on my face now, his eyes searching mine, waiting for me to let him back in. I started to kiss him. He trailed his hands from my face down to my hands, holding them close to him. Holding me close to him.

I thought about Etienne and his family. His parents, so formal and wrapped up in their own world, encouraging Etienne to travel on his own whether that was what he wanted or not. His house, so ordered and empty. He wanted me. He wasn't used to the chaos I brought, but still he wanted me. Out of everyone around him, it was me he'd let in. Me he wanted to watch for.

He wasn't promising never to say stupid things again. I knew he probably would. I probably would too. But we were going to try. All we could do was try.

ACKNOWLEDGEMENTS

MY first thanks goes to my friend and fellow writer, Joe Weatherstone, who encouraged me to return to this story and kept on encouraging me through the writing and rewriting.

Big thanks to all at Allen & Unwin. Particularly Jodie Webster who saw the absurd and liked it, and Hilary Reynolds for her tireless and meticulous work. Also to Jennifer Castles for initially keeping me in the loop, and Debra Billson for the cover design. Every interaction I've had with Allen & Unwin has been kind and thoughtful, and I really thank you all for that.

My thanks too to Susan Hawthorne, Renate Klein and Pauline Hopkins from Spinifex Press, who have continued to support me as a writer over many years now. This kind of support from such clever women is greatly appreciated.

Thank you to Erin Bennett White for her generous time and super helpful comments, and to Shane Mattiske, who unknowingly provided information and inspiration about all things bike. Thanks to Wendy Hawke for always being ready with medical advice and for putting up with us on writing weekends, and to Maddy Goto for the late-night conversation about Japanese mothers.

Thank you to my friends, old and new, who stamped their feet and clapped their hands when they heard this book was going to be published. I hope you all realise how important you are to me regardless of whether we see each other once a week or once a year.

Thanks always to the Perth Brills, Susan, Elliot, Jeffrey and Deborah, who have been long-time and unerring supporters of me and my writing. Particular thanks to Debs, who has been an early reader of this and other work.

Thank you to my three sons, Zeke, Henry and Milo. I could have done this without you but then it wouldn't have been any fun. Thanks for everything that you are and all that you add to our family.

This book, like my other writing, contains fragments of dialogue and stories I've collected over time. There are moments from my past or remembered news headlines in here. There is also a line of dialogue that was some of the last words a dying friend said to me. And even though that is a very sad thing, I'm glad to have found a small place in print to remember our friend Nat who is no longer around but often in our thoughts.

Finally, writing and motherhood have not always been a good match for me. To write this book I took time away from my family and sometimes didn't get to do all things we mothers feel we should be doing. Joe and I had weekends away to write our books where we talked about the emotional cost of leaving our children behind. We dreamed about getting to the end of the process and seeing all of our work complete and in print. And here we are. And the children seem fine.

Look, Joe, we did it!

ABOUT THE AUTHOR

SARAH BRILL grew up in Perth, Western Australia and began writing plays at the age of fifteen, mostly because she was annoyed with her drama teacher but also because it meant she got to come to Sydney for young playwright workshops. While initially focused on playwrighting, she also wrote for film and radio. Her first novel, *Glory*, was published in 2002. After having children, Sarah did a Masters in sustainability and almost took a right turn into academia. She was saved by the publication of her second book, *Symphony for the Man*, which was published in 2020. Sarah lives in Sydney with her three sons and two cats.